For my wife Vera,
and my daughter Michelle.

Translated and abridged by Reverend Basil Solounias from the Arabic of
Jurji Zaidan's 1897 historical novel *Fatat Ghassan*.

Printed with the blessings of the Jurji Zaidan Foundation.
http://www.zaidanfoundation.org

Printed in Canada by the McCallum Printing Group.

McCallum Printing Group, Inc.
Campus Office
B – 31 Cameron Library
University of Alberta
Edmonton, AB, T6G2J8
campus@mcprint.ca

First Printing, 2015

ISBN 978-0-9939634-0-7

Edited, compiled, and designed by One Cent Press

One Cent Press
6352 184 ST NW
Edmonton, AB, T5T2N8
ocp@onecentpress.com

1 3 5 7 9 8 6 4 2

JURJI ZAIDAN's

فتاة غسان

The Girl of
Ghassan

A Novel of History, Love, Sports,
Culture, and Conquest

Translated by Reverend Basil Solounias

From the Arabic of Jurji Zaidan's
1897 *Fatat Ghassan*

CONTENTS

CONTENTS

Characters

Jabalah ibn al-Aiyham	One of Ghassan's Kings
al-Harith ibn Abi Shimr	One of Ghassan's Kings
Abdullah	an Iraqi Emir
Hind	King Jabalah's Daughter
Tha'labah	King al-Harith's Son
Hammad	Emir Abdullah's Son
Saada	Hind's Mother
Salman	Hammad's Servant

Western Arabia

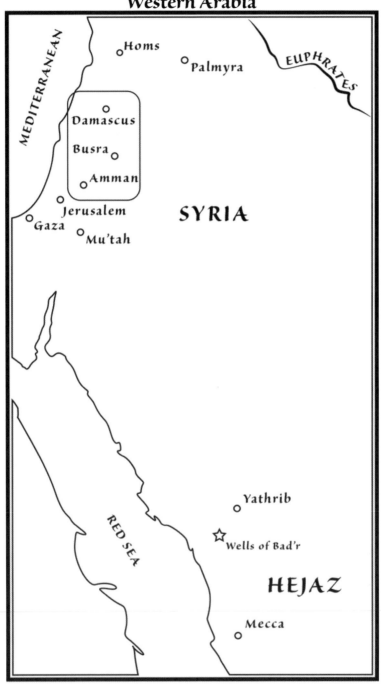

Roman Syria (Ghassan)

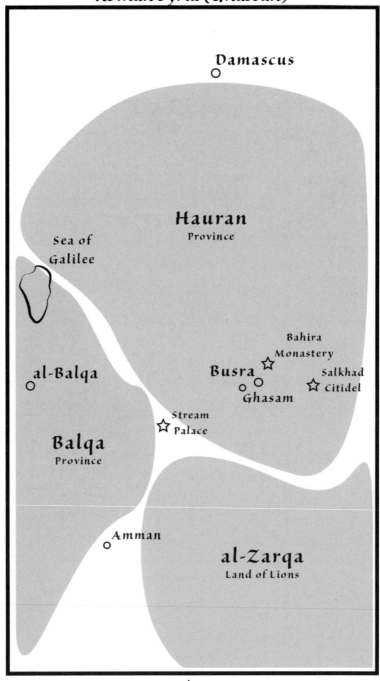

Damascus

Hauran
Province

Sea of
Galilee

Bahira
Monastery

al-Balqa

Busra

Salkhad
Citidel

Ghasam

Stream
Palace

Balqa
Province

Amman

al-Zarqa
Land of Lions

A Note from Father Basil,

Be courageous. Believe that you can conquer the unknown. Do not let fear overcome you and stop you from achieving your goals, whatever they may be.

When I decided to translate this novel from Arabic into English I knew it was going to be challenging and I faced many difficulties in capturing the spirit of Arabic writing. Translating this novel seemed something that I never thought I could do, it seemed impossible. And yet, what stands in our way is not fear but hard work. I knew I would have to be in this for the long haul. I set my mind to it and worked at it each and every day. I kept reaching for my goal and finally achieved it.

I am grateful and thankful to be where I am today and to have met so many amazing people in Canada and around the world. I am blessed to have friends and family who are my inspiration and support every day. They are the ones who have brought us together today.

May I earnestly hope, good reader, that this beautiful novel will be a valuable addition to your library and your home. It warms my heart to share this novel with you because it shows us how to make our choices with passion and conviction and to love every moment of our lives because they are all worth living to the fullest.

God bless, and good luck.

Esteemed Readers,

It is with great joy that we join you today to share with you a story of love, perseverance, and the ceaseless march of history.

It is our hope that this translation carries with it the heart and culture of the Arabic people who lived in Syria at the time of the birth of Islam, both Muslim and Christian alike.

English readers will find many delightful nuances with the telling of this tale as it is presented in an oral fashion, a story being told from one generation to another to impart truth and history through fiction.

The Ghassani people of Syria were among the last of the Christian Arab tribes, operating under the rule of the Roman Empire, and were a proud and powerful nation of devoted followers of God. As the light of Islam spread across the land, conflicts between Arab cultural traditions and Christian religious traditions rose between the many peoples as they struggled to reconcile ancient pagan traditions with new religious beliefs.

And, underneath it all were the people, human beings all alike, prone to love, hate, pride, jealousy, hope and the full range of human emotion.

This is a story of these people, of their lives and their culture, so please pull up a cushion, enjoy your favorite tea, and join us now for the story of …

فتاة غسان

The Girl of
Ghassan

629 AD

The Race

A long time ago, Syria was under the rule of the Romans and a puppet state of Constantinople, the Eastern throne of the Roman Empire. The Roman governor of Syria had made his capital at Damascus from where he commanded the two kings of Syria. The Syrian kings were native-born cousins. King al-Harith ibn Abi Shimr presided over Busra, capital of the Hauran province south of Damascus, and King Jabalah ibn al-Aiyham ruled from the province of Balqa to the north of Amman. The two kings were known as the Sons of Ghassan and they and all their people were Christian Arabs.

King Jabalah had a beautiful and intelligent daughter named Hind. From the time she was a very small child Hind had become very fond of horse races, so much so that before Hind's twentieth birthday she had become renowned as a rider equal to the greatest horsemen in racing. Hind spent most of her days at the Stream Palace on the border between Hauran and Balqa. The palace was made of massive stone slabs and surrounded by parks and orchards through which manicured streams flowed. Adjacent to the palace a wide plain stretched for more than two miles which was specially prepared for horse-racing at certain times of the year. People from far and wide would come take part in the festivities. Hind competed in many of the races herself, often claiming victory. That spring, King Jabalah held a race for which he declared the prize to be a masterwork breastplate that he himself would bestow upon the victor.

On the day of the race the most important men of the country made appearances, some mingling alone and others parading with their entourage dressed in the most striking and colorful attire, with fezzes, turbans, and head-cloths enclosed by hand-made ikals – there was even a show of hats imitating the latest Roman fashions. Tents had been pitched to provide the racers and on-lookers with shelter while the horses were gathered on the plain and made ready. At the front of the assembly was the large tent of King Jabalah. The king's tent was luxuriously lined with red silk and spread with rich, thick carpets, and the king's prized breastplate was proudly displayed upon the central pillar.

As the sun rose, the spectators waited with anticipation for the arrival of the king and his daughter. King Jabalah came first with his men following behind him, marching out into the park from the courtyard with the doors swung wide open to accommodate them. The king's light complexion was framed by a powerful moustache and beard, and he carried his great height with regal bearing. He wore a silk-embroidered garment and upon his head sat a crown set with precious stones that symbolized his sovereignty. Stopping at the tents, the men dismounted and the king's servants led the horses, whose manes and tails had been braided and decorated with gold pieces, to their specially prepared shelter. When the king reached his tent he sat himself on a throne made of mahogany and inlaid with gold. At the entrance of his tent a servant stood along with his attendants, some of whom were carrying his sword and arrows while others offered refreshments. As the preparations continued, the king entertained visitors while poets came to sing praise with complimentary verse.

Meanwhile, the princess had departed the palace with her maids. They made their way through the garden paths of the park while the eyes of all the horsemen turned in their direction. Hind's walk revealed her radiant health and serious nature. She was tall and full-bodied with a round face and black eyes. Her luxurious black hair was braided and hung down her back, plaited and intricately held together with gold ornaments. She wore a small crown set with diamonds, pearl earrings and a necklace of corals. One of her wrists was adorned with a heavy, twisted, gold and ruby bracelet, and on her fingers she wore rings set with emeralds and rubies. Her robe was made of striped silk that draped gracefully and reached the ground, showing only the tips of her satin shoes. Two of her attendants accompanied her to the king's tent while the rest remained in the park. She entered the tent and was warmly welcomed by her father who bade her to sit at his side. The smile that lit his face as she joined him betrayed a love that commanded his heart, his mind, and his actions.

The maidservants joined the rest of the attendants near the seats of King Jabalah and the princess so that they might have the most favorable view of the racers. Just then, a turmoil grabbed their attention which they soon learned was the arrival of Tha'labah, the son of King Jabalah's cousin al-Harith, the King of Busra. Tha'labah had come for a visit so he could watch the races, accompanied by his attendants. Hind disliked her cousin and became anxious as he made his way to the royal tent. King Jabalah stood up to meet Tha'labah, who was a short man of slight build with a thin face, large protruding eyes and ears, and a stiff moustache that bore the pride he took in his father's position. Tha'labah, however, lacked the solemn and distinguished manner befitting royalty and the only indication of his position was his attire. He wore a fine, laced silk robe reaching the ground in the Roman fashion with a sword set with precious stones that hung at his left side. There was much speculation whether the prince would ask for Hind's hand in marriage or not because of customs established long before, although it was known that she abhorred the idea of marriage to her cousin. King Jabalah showed courtesy to his cousin's son, however, and showing the manners of royalty, welcomed the boy warmly for the sake of his father. Hind saluted her cousin as usual then sat down, busily observing the sprawling plain and mountains, then concerning herself with the crowding horses. As Tha'labah addressed his uncle his eyes were on Hind. He wanted to win her admiration, but the more he sought it, the more she despised him.

Tha'labah turned to Hind and asked, "Are you going to participate in the race today, princess?"

"Not today, cousin. I have no intention of joining this race, although I might change my mind," Hind dismissively replied, turning her attention back to the horses.

As the morning sun continued to rise, the King's nobles arrived and finalized the preparations for the race. They stretched a rope for the starting line so that all the horsemen would be aligned properly. One of the men prepared a long reed at the end of the course. The objective was for whomever reached the reed first to retrieve it and return it to the starting line, and he would be proclaimed the winner. When all was ready, a man was appointed to announce the race who then called the gathering to order.

The horsemen rode their stallions to King Jabalah's tent and dismounted. Each man entered the king's pavilion to kiss his hand and the hand of his guest, Tha'labah. Hind was surveying the group as if she were looking for someone special. Her eyes fell on a young man who was more handsome than the others. She was certain in her mind that, given his features and dress, he was not of her tribe. His figure was square and muscular and he wore Bedouin attire, his black eyes were sharp and his head was covered with an elaborate square scarf encircled with an ikal, and he looked to be about twenty years of age. As their eyes met, Hind blushed and she quickly occupied herself to hide the color rising in her cheeks. The stranger proceeded to the king and kissed his hand and then left without noticing Tha'labah, who became vexed at being overlooked. Tha'labah looked at Hind with a feeling of pride then noticed her fascinated gaze at the stranger. Jealousy stirred within him. The horsemen then left the king's pavilion and lined up at the starting line while King Jabalah, Hind, and her cousin speculated on the outcomes.

"Who do you think will be the victor?" asked the king.

Tha'labah did not answer. Toying with his moustache, he thought of himself as the winner. He was accustomed to winning, not through worthiness, but because the horsemen often allowed him the chance to win since he was the son of a king.

"What do you think of that man riding the black horse?" asked King Jabalah. "He looks like he is flying, and he is the man who won the last race!"

Hind's heart skipped a beat at the mention of her mysterious horseman while Tha'labah shook his head with distain and said, "That stranger is ignorant. He claims a championship which he never truly earned, blind chance made him win the last race. If I were you, King Jabalah, I would not let him enter your tent while your daughter is present! He is a stranger and does not have respect for kings and their families."

With these words, Hind immediately understood the jealousy that was consuming Tha'labah. King Jabalah, however, interpreted these words with scorn.

"Why should we prevent a stranger from entering our dwelling?" the king asked. "Are we not the Ghassan tribe known for our generosity in welcoming strangers?" These harsh words of rebuke turned Tha'labah's face ashen and he lowered his head in shame. "Besides," King Jabalah continued, "I am curious about this young man who lives among us as a stranger. I have seen him quite often hunting with attendants as if he were a prince, and yet he hides his royal identity. No one knows a thing about him except that his name is Hammad."

Tha'labah listened intently to his uncle's observations, and using them as a pretext, replied, "That is what makes me dislike this stranger, Uncle! He might be a spy sent by King Zadijah of al-Hira, you know he has always been opposed to us, trying to bring evil upon us ever since we defeated his armies with the help of the Romans two years ago!"

King Jabalah frowned and said nothing. An attendant appeared and said, "All the horses are prepared. How would the King like to have the race conducted?"

"Divide the horsemen into groups of five, each group to race one at a time," the king ordered. "When all horsemen have raced, the winners of each set will compete against each other and the winner of that race will receive the prize."

And so, race by race, as each winner came back with the reed, a swift runner returned the reed to the finish line and the winner was moved off to one side of the plain until all the races were completed. Hind was eagerly watching the stranger called Hammad. When his turn came, her eyes were upon him until he was out of sight. She continued to watch until he returned victorious with the reed in his hand. Then King Jabalah said to Tha'labah, "I see the young man has outdistanced his opponents."

"This group was hardly a challenge," said Tha'labah with envy in his heart. "Let us wait until he races the other winners."

"How would those horsemen be any different?" asked Hind in a calm voice. "He rides as fast as the wind."

"There will be no winner except me!" said Tha'labah angrily. "I am going to teach him how to be a horseman! I will challenge the winner of the final group to a race!"

Fearing that her remarks might provoke her cousin against this man even more, Hind said nothing. The races of the preliminary sets came to an end by noon and twenty men were judged winners. The king ordered the men to rest and wait for dinner, and the attendants saw to the needs of the horses. The repast was laid out in the large banquet hall of the Stream Palace. The king invited the winners to join him for their meal. The cloth that served as a table was woven of gold and the plates and bowls were made of silver. They sat down on thick carpets set around the food, which had been served in both Arabian and Roman fashions. Among them was Hammad, as well as the weight of Tha'labah's jealousy. King Jabalah wanted to serve the men while they ate but they would not hear of it, so he sat and dined among them with Hind at his right side and Tha'labah at his left. Dinner was over by midday and the men were well rested. An attendant began to call the names of the winners to resume the race. Everyone was guessing as to who the winner would be. Hammad did very little talking but did a great deal of thinking, as if he had something on his mind.

Throughout the entire meal Hind was watching his face, a face in which she saw a handsome beauty, a delicacy of character and a humbleness in manner. Tha'labah watched her with disgust. He was praising his father and himself, boasting about how he fearlessly killed a lion while hunting. Hind and Hammad paid no attention to him. When the men were assembled, King Jabalah ordered the twenty men to be divided into four parties, each party to race separately. The four winners would then race each other to determine the victor. Tha'labah boastfully vowed to race the victor again, but silently prayed that it would not be the stranger Hammad. He had no heart for competing against a man who could very well beat him. After the next round of races was completed the winners were given a moment to rest while the horses were prepared for the final race, Hammad and his stallion among them.

The on-lookers lined both sides of the field waiting in excitement for the final round. King Jabalah, Hind, and Tha'labah were at the entrance of their tent also watching intently, each wondering about the outcome for different reasons. Hammad's horse was started behind the others, which caused Tha'labah to rejoice, but Hind knew that the best horse was always placed in the rear, often starting there herself. Soon after the four were out of sight Hammad returned victoriously with the reed which he then offered to Hind. All the people cheered as the winner was proclaimed, all except Tha'labah. Hammad dismounted and kissed the eyes of his horse. A man carrying a bottle of hunting blood came to dye the chest of Hammad's horse as a sign of victory to all.

Before he could do so Tha'labah objected shouting, "Wait, the race is not over!"

Hammad looked surprised, but King Jabalah said, "We have promised our cousin that he could race against the winner." Hammad bowed graciously and went back to his horse, mounting it while Tha'labah prepared himself. Tha'labah, who was vexed with the turn of events, sullenly mounted his horse, resplendent with a jeweled saddle and golden necklace, once his attendant had brought the magnificent animal around. Hind was very displeased with her cousin and wished him to lose, for she could see no reason for his fierce envy of Hammad. King Jabalah sent a servant to inform the people that a race would be held between Hammad and Prince Tha'labah. As the contest started, Hind feared for Hammad since his horse was already hot and tired while Tha'labah's was fresh and full of energy. Despite this disadvantage, Hammad returned a few minutes later with the reed and Tha'labah arrived behind him, complaining to all who would hear that it was not Hammad, but his horse, that defeated him.

"If I had his horse," said Tha'labah, "no one in this world could out-race me."

"Take my horse and I will ride yours," said Hammad, "and let us race again."

Hind grew apprehensive at this offer, fearing that Hammad might lose. Tha'labah could not believe that Hammad would exchange horses – had he known, he would never have used the excuse. Now he would have to see it through! The sun was setting as they rode off, and they had not returned by the time it had set and the night had begun to spread across the plains. The hour began to grow late and the crowd started murmuring that something might have happened. Hind was the most worried of all. At last, a huge cloud of dust filled the air as Hammad came into sight, with the prince following not far behind. Hind was overjoyed, but her father seemed rather displeased to see a stranger victorious over his nephew. Hammad felt he should make an excuse for the prince, and said, "By God, it must have been destiny, because Prince Tha'labah is a great rider. If he had been accustomed to riding my horse, he would have defeated me." Hammad then presented the reed to Hind who noticed with alarm that it was short and sharpened. She looked at him with questioning eyes and he returned a look that warned, "Do not ask."

By that time night had fallen and the time had come to declare the winner and bestow upon him the prize. The nobleman was called back to perform the ritual of painting the chest of Hammad's horse with the hunter's blood. King Jabalah then ordered the festivities to take place within the sanctity of the palace. Torches were lit and the crowd was led into the park, which was in full bloom, the perfumes of the flowers and trees permeating the evening air. They reached an area where an extra-large tent had been prepared. The floor of the tent was covered with lavish carpets and numerous candles shimmered on the walls. Jabalah sat upon a silk cushion in the head of the tent with his daughter on one side of him and Tha'labah on the other. The victor's seat was elevated to allow everyone a good view of the winner. A group of slave-maidens sat on the ground and sang songs of congratulations while the servants brought the breastplate.

Taking the breastplate, Hind rose from her seat and joyously approached Hammad. He stood up, his knees trembling as he saw her coming toward him with the prize. Taking the scarf and ikal from his head, his face was now in full view, a sight which made Hind more ecstatic. She and those around her were astonished to see that his hair was very long and smooth. Hind placed the gambeson over his head and began to buckle the breastplate into place. In the background the poets and the maidens performed, and Hammad was lost in a reverie of excitement. When Hind had finished, she whispered in his ear, "We will meet tomorrow at the Monastery of Bahira."

Already late, the people started to depart after they had taken their supper. Hind left for the palace after bidding good night to her father and cousin.

When they were alone, Tha'labah turned to his uncle and said, "I am angry because this stranger has attained the prize, not because he outraced me."

"He won the race. I am not displeased that this man secured the prize, but I am astonished by his secrecy," said King Jabalah. "I forgot to ask him about his family, but I will when the opportunity arises."

"Yes, we must find out about that," said Tha'labah, "for perhaps he is spying on us. I noticed that his accent resembles that from the land of al-Hira."

"We will see," said the king.

The Betrayal of Tha'labah

On her way to the palace Hind was met by her mother to whom she was very dear. Together they went to Hind's sleeping quarters on the upper floor. Her bed, laden with colorful, silk-covered pillows and a lovely, wide, sheer silk gown from Constantinople, had been prepared by her servants. The room was filled with the scent of amber from the numerous candles which were made from the best perfumes in the land. On the walls of the room, pictures were hung depicting the birth of Christ, his crucifixion, and his ascension, all in the Byzantine style, painted with natural colors and life-like expressions. Suspended on one wall there was a round plate of silver hung and polished in a special manner to serve as a looking glass.

After removing all of her jeweled ornaments, Hind put on her gown and stood before the looking glass while arranging her hair. Her mother sat quietly admiring the beauty of her daughter, patiently waiting for an opportune moment to speak of something that was on her mind. When she had finished, Hind lay down on her bed and went over the events of the day in her memory. The feelings she felt for Hammad were stirring inside her which led her thoughts to her defeated cousin who had been so vile to the young man. The more she thought about Tha'labah and his actions the more she despised him. Still, she was concerned about protecting her father's name, and fearing that Hammad might be of undesirable descent, she could not let her feelings for him overwhelm her. She would have to wait patiently until their rendezvous on the morrow at the Monastery of Bahira to learn all about him.

Hind's mother, Queen Saada, was forty-five years old and still very beautiful, truly the most beautiful among the daughters of Ghassan. She gave Hind a moment to relax in her bed and then asked, "Why did you not take part in the race, my dear?"

"I saw no reason for it," replied Hind, "there were many horsemen and an argument took so long to settle, there was no time left for me to participate. Besides, I have no use for a man's breastplate."

"What brought on the argument?" asked her mother, who smiled at the joke.

"After the end of the race," Hind explained, "Tha'labah demanded to race the winner. He then lost and his failure brought shame on us."

Queen Saada smiled, saying, "You said the horsemen were numerous, who among them was the victor?"

"A stranger named Hammad," said Hind, "which displeased my father and cousin. It is embarrassing to them for a stranger to win over all our men, so Tha'labah boastfully challenged the stranger and then lost."

"I saw them racing twice," the queen commented.

"The first time around, Hammad was victorious but my cousin complained and attributed the success to Hammad's horse," Hind explained. "Hammad then offered to switch horses, but it would have been better if Tha'labah had been satisfied with the first shame for he lost the second race as well. And more surprising to me was the reed that Hammad brought back, for it was sharpened and short. It looked as though it had been cut by a sword!"

The queen said with a smile, "Did he not tell you what sharpened it?"

"No," Hind replied, "As I was about to ask, Hammad prevented me from doing so."

"God bless him," said her mother, "he must be of noble birth and upbringing. It is a shame he hides his identity."

Hind cheered up when she heard her mother praising Hammad. "What do you mean, mother? Do you know about the sharpened reed?"

"Yes, I know," Queen Saada answered, lowering her voice. "That reed was cut by the sword of your cousin Tha'labah."

With surprise, Hind sat up squarely in bed eager to know how it happened, "What?!"

"Your cousin," said her mother gravely, "tried to kill Hammad, God forgive him. If he had succeeded, by God, he would have brought shame on us forever."

"How do you know this?" asked Hind with astonishment.

"I saw it happen with my own eyes," explained the queen.

"How could you have seen them, when we, who were nearer to them than you, could not?" asked Hind with disbelief.

"Calm yourself, child, I will tell you what happened," said her mother, moving to the door to close it. She sat down and cautiously began to relate the story.

"When you had all gone to the tents, I remained in the palace with the governess and some of the servants. We could see most of the racing field, but not the end of it, so we moved outside to get a better view of the finish line and of the winner racing past with the reed. It is an exciting scene, for there is nothing quite as exhilarating as victory. We went unseen through the gates of the park to the orchards bordering the river until we arrived at an area where we could observe the whole racing field. In the final race, I saw your cousin far behind Hammad, not because the horse was weak, but because your cousin does not know how to race and was fearful of falling. Hammad's stallion was straining for Tha'labah to let him loose and had he obeyed the horse he would have been the winner. Real racing belongs to the horses and has no place for inexperienced riders. Tha'labah's fear of falling was more shameful to him than running second to Hammad. However, Hammad, as unequalled a rider as I have ever seen, let your cousin's horse have free rein while he embraced the animal's neck and flew across the plains."

"From our vantage point," Queen Saada continued, "we could see Tha'labah with a sword in his hand, charging after Hammad who had already retrieved the reed. To protect himself, Hammad met the stroke of the sword with the reed, which sliced it through. After a struggle, Hammad pulled your cousin from the horse, threw him to the ground, and sat on his chest. We could hear the echoes of Tha'labah pleading with Hammad to spare his life. After a while,

Hammad released him and they both stood up, shook hands and returned. Hammad acted with honor, which is why I suspect his nobility."

Hind's heart trembled with admiration for Hammad's nobleness and charity, but her scorn for Tha'labah grew seven fold. Then she asked her mother, "Is this who Prince Tha'labah, the son of King al-Harith, truly is? Is it proper and fitting for Ghassan to have a king's son who is that vicious? Is it honorable for him to assault a man with no guilt except that of being a better horseman than he? Besides, Hammad is a guest in our country! Are we not responsible for the security of our guests and neighbors? Are we not renowned across the land for our hospitality?"

Queen Saada knew that her daughter spoke the truth but she did not wish hatred to fill her daughter's heart. She also knew that, since Tha'labah had the highest rank in Ghassan, he was the man most likely to marry Hind should King Jabalah and King al-Harith desire it. If Hind began to hate him now, it would be an unsavory situation for the whole family for generations.

"We will reproach and shame him for what he has done," said her mother, "until his behavior proves worthy of his family name."

Hind said nothing, not because she was convinced, but because she was anxiously waiting to learn more about Hammad on the morrow. She needed her mother's support in this matter but she could not confess her affection for the young man until after their first meeting or her mother may pass off her love as blind affection. Besides, a few questions remained. Where was he from? Who are his parents? Was he a Christian? Hind wanted to be sure that he was a Christian and not a heathen, or her parents would never allow them to marry. What did he have to hide that he was always so secretive? Indeed, Hind had invited Hammad to meet her in the monastery in order to get her answers.

To hide her intentions, Hind announced, "I vowed to go to Bahira Monastery some time ago, mother, and I have not yet made good my vow. After the evil we have seen today, I fear it is because I have delayed in acting upon that vow."

"Perhaps that is so," replied Queen Saada, "the monastery is worthy of generosity and respect. It would be wise to make haste, my daughter, and give the monastery the honor you have promised."

"I will go tomorrow," replied Hind, "and not waste any time."

"But I cannot go with you tomorrow," said her mother, "I am returning with your father to the city of al-Balqa. If you will put it off for a few days, we can go together."

"No, mother, I should not delay any longer. Besides, there is no need for you to go with me, I will go with some of the servants in disguise. I will pass the day there and return home."

"As you wish," said her mother, who took her leave for the night.

Hind spent the night sleepless, playing out the day's events over and over in her mind while she wrestled with the anticipation of her meeting with Hammad tomorrow at the monastery.

Hammad and His Father

Hammad returned from the Stream Palace, his mind reeling with the words, "we will meet tomorrow." When he left the palace, he was met near the tents by his servant, Salman, who was tending Hammad's horse. Hammad removed the breastplate and put it in his saddlebag, then mounted his horse and left with Salman for his home in Ghasam, a village six miles west of the city of Busra.

Hammad had come to Syria only a few months ago and had not been told why. He spent the better part of his days hunting, accompanied by his father Abdullah or by Salman. A few servants went with them on these trips and they would often return from the mountains of Balqa with gazelle and other game for their meals. Hammad had been taught to ride at an early age and now had one of the finest Arabian horses in the land. He had fallen in love with Hind even before he had seen her, enthralled by reading the stories of her racing glory and by hearing the poets who sang of her beauty and character. When his father requested that Hammad accompany him on a trip to Ghassan, Hammad was pleased to have the opportunity to meet her. After having arrived in Ghasam, he often set out in the direction of the Stream Palace on the pretense of hunting with the hope of catching a glimpse of Hind. When he finally saw her he was awestruck. Hammad would sit by the stream and watch her; she would see him looking but paid him little attention. In order to attract her attention, he tried to be wherever she was, at the bazaar, at church, or at the racing fields, and every time she saw him she gave him the same inquisitive glance. When the race was proclaimed, he rejoiced at the opportunity to race for her. He did not know but she too was curious about this stranger and pleased that he had joined the race. Before they were even aware of it they had fallen in love, as often happens with young hearts.

Hammad had been gone from Ghasam since early morning, so he rode his stallion hard, fearful of his father growing anxious. Despite his efforts, as Hammad approached the village he was greeted by the heavy drumbeat of hooves racing toward him and his father's voice calling, "Hammad! Hammad!"

"Yes, father, it is me. Why did you come looking for me? As you can see, I am on my way home," Hammad entreated his father.

"Why not? You have lingered in returning," said Abdullah with a rebuking tone. "Look, part of the night is gone and we are in a foreign land!"

Hammad sullenly said nothing and they both rode back in silence, passing the orchards of the village while the inhabitants slept peacefully in their homes. When they reached their own residence on the outskirts of the village, Hammad hurried to his room where the servants brought him fresh water and clean clothes. After bathing and changing he sat on a cushion with his father beside him. Abdullah was an Emir of Iraq and a wealthy man in his forty-fifth year. He had spent most of his life travelling extensively and commanding the wars throughout Syria, Egypt, Hejaz, Yemen, and Iraq. Experience and the passing of time had made him wise if not curt, and he had brought Hammad to Damascus to carry out an oath which he had sworn to uphold many years before.

"What made you so late, my son?" asked Abdullah as they sat and rested.

"Why, did I not tell you last night that I wished to go to the Stream Palace this morning for the race?"

"Yes, you did tell me, were there so many contestants that the race took till nightfall to conclude?" asked Abdullah.

"Yes there were," Hammad explained, "the race did not come to an end until the sun had set. Then they had a ceremony to award the breastplate to the winner. Among the racers were many of the princes of Ghassan, including the High Prince himself, Tha'labah, son of King al-Harith who rules from Busra."

"Who was the winner?" Abdullah asked.

"Your son Hammad won the breastplate," said the young man with a humble smile.

"God save your arm. Then you were victorious over them all, even though you are a stranger!" Abdullah was visibly pleased and asked, "Where is the breastplate? Did you wear it?"

"After a long argument with Tha'labah out of the sight of the others, I returned victorious with the reed and was proclaimed the winner and awarded the breastplate," Hammad replied. "I have seen the characteristic generosity and good manners of King Jabalah and of his men, too. The breastplate is here in my saddlebag."

"Did the daughter of Ghassan participate in the race this time?" asked Abdullah. "I have heard from others that she is a great rider, you yourself have mentioned her skill on a horse."

Hammad's heart beat faster at the mere mention of Hind and he became momentarily lost in thought. Abdullah saw Hammad's preoccupation and grinned, prodding the young man, "Why do you not reply, my son?"

Hammad's face colored. "I'm sorry, father, she did not race herself, but she watched the races and bestowed the breastplate on me," said Hammad, showing signs of pride in his face.

Noticing that Hammad was caught up in the tide of emotion, Abdullah asked, "How did you find the daughter of Ghassan? Is she as courteous and beautiful as the poets proclaim?"

Hammad's eyes brightened and in reply to his father, he started to describe her beauty and warmth but was at a loss for words that would do her justice. Though bemused, his father was suddenly struck with fear for he knew the difficulties that would stand in the way of a love such as this. Abdullah's concern took the shape of a frown on his face. Hammad looked with astonishment at the change in his father's countenance and said, "What is the matter, father? I see in your face that something is troubling you."

"God forbid, my son, no," Abdullah excused himself. "I was only thinking of that maiden which God has blessed with grace and beauty, as the daughters of kings ought to be."

Hammad was pleased with his father's approval of Hind but would not speak of his emotions any further for the fear that his father might forbid any hope of being with her. Abdullah wished to find out if Hind was aware of Hammad's feelings and so Abdullah asked him directly. The effect of the words on Hammad were so great and he was so moved that he felt compelled to tell all that his heart desired, but Hammad replied with some restraint, "I don't know what position I hold in her heart, but I know that she feels at ease whenever she sees me."

"I see that your heart has deceived you," his father said with caution. "You interpreted the courtesy which she has for all people as a special love for you."

"I do not think my heart deceives me," Hammad said defensively. "I have seen her enough to recognize her love for me."

"How can you tell she loves you when there has been no association between the two of you?" asked Abdullah, pressing his son on the matter.

"I do not know, all my feelings tell me that she loves me," said Hammad.

"I feel there is more to this, my son," Abdullah replied, "do not hide anything from me."

"I have told you that she cares for me," Hammad said wearily.

"Then you are pursuing her?" asked his father.

"I do not know, everything depends on destiny," was Hammad's response.

Abdullah was certain now that Hammad was strongly attracted to the maiden and began tugging at his beard while contemplating how serious a matter this was.

"Why do you not talk? Why do you frown so?" asked Hammad. "Are you displeased with what you have learned?"

"No, my child, it does not displease me," Abdullah answered with a sigh. "I was only considering how it effects our journey and our purpose in visiting these strange lands. Now I find you have something else on your mind."

"Tell me, what purpose have I forsaken?" asked Hammad, "for I do not understand."

"You do not understand? Where is your wisdom now, child? Did we not come from Iraq to Busra to perform the holy vow I swore twenty one years ago?" Abdullah retorted. "The time is growing short, a mere few days remain until we must perform our holy duty."

"No father," answered Hammad solemnly, "I have not forgotten about the vow."

"Then why did you have to complicate matters by falling in love?" his father said with vexation.

"Does what I have said to you mean that I am falling in love?" asked Hammad with a sheepish grin.

"Do you think me a dolt and unaware of the signs of love?" said Abdullah.

"Suppose I do love her and she returned my love," Hammad asked, "what has that to do with the vow?"

"We came for your haircutting ceremony at the monastery and your relationship with the princess could prevent us from accomplishing it," Abdullah sighed, and added with some encouragement, "There is a great correlation between the two which is difficult to explain until after the ceremony. When your hair is cut you will understand. So do not rebuke me now for my hesitation in consenting to your love for the daughter of Ghassan. It is a great honor to love her, especially if she returns that love, but I cannot explain more before that day, which is this Palm Sunday. We are in the middle of Easter fasting and only a few days remain before the sacred hour. You will reach your twenty-first birthday and then will be told everything, which might prevent any alliance with Hind."

Hammad was taken back. More eager for that day to arrive, he asked, "What might be the obstacle in the way of a union?"

"I told you I cannot explain now," said his father. "Be still, Hammad, do nothing in haste!"

Hammad had intended to tell his father about his appointment with Hind at the monastery, but now decided to keep his rendezvous a secret after he saw how serious his father was about the matter.

It was midnight and Hammad showed signs of fatigue. Abdullah took notice of it and suggested that they retire and get some well-earned rest. Sleep escaped Hammad, however, for his thoughts were of Hind and the forthcoming events of Palm Sunday.

The Monastery of Bahira

Early the next morning, Hammad rose from his bed, donned his clothes, and departed without telling his father. He mounted his horse and covered his head with a scarf, fastening it with his hand-twisted ikal before travelling east. Hammad's destination was the city of Busra. He took none of his servants with him, keeping his rendezvous a secret.

The road between Ghasam and Busra was straight and paved with large stones, an improvement brought by the Romans, and had thick walls three feet high that banked the wide street on each side. He arrived at Busra within an hour and his attention was immediately drawn to the western reservoir situated just outside the rampart. Hammad judged the reservoir to be more than six hundred feet wide and twice that in length. Busra, he could see, had cisterns in the east and to the north as well for the storage of clean water. They were a necessity for the survival of the inhabitants of the city who were too far away from the streams and rivers.

As Hammad approached the western reservoir he looked at its awesome size and thought to himself that it must be as large as a lake. He led his horse to a high terrace outside the city to have a full look at Busra. He had never visited the city before but read about it in the Persian and Kaldanian books and knew that it was situated in the south of the Hauran province and to the east of the Jordan River, approximately ninety kilometers southeast of Damascus and one hundred and thirty kilometers northeast of Jerusalem. This ancient city was built long before the time of the Jewish, Greek, or Roman rule. He looked down upon the city at sunrise and saw it as an almost perfect square that occupied an area of large, flat plain land which was encircled by a rampart over four miles in length. Outside the rampart Hammad saw masterfully planned orchards with varied species of trees, gracefully twisted vines, and to the north and east, across the horizon, the purple-hued mountain ranges of Hauran stood watch over the land.

For a time, Hammad found himself captivated by the glittering rays of the sun playing off the surface of the water in the cistern. Within the city he saw massive buildings made of Hauran's renowned brown stones. Eager to see the business section, Hammad made haste to the western gate and was greeted by the commotion of many caravans with their camels, mules, and donkeys. Some of the caravans arrived from Iraq carrying Persian textiles, some from Yemen with incense, myrrh, and gums while other caravans transported Roman goods and materials from Damascus. He stood for a moment and studied the tall, imposing gate designed in the Roman style. The stately pillars, supports, and engravings were appealing to the eye and supported an architrave which had Latin engravings etched on it that Hammad could not read.

Hammad passed through the open gate and found himself on a street paved with stones and crowded with people moving to and fro, so he decided to dismount and lead his horse the rest of the way. He was on the main east-west highway which intersected a similar north-south one. A short distance later, he saw an arch in the distance that was the width of the street. Hammad immediately recognized it as the Triumphal Arch which the Romans had erected to celebrate the glory of their conquest. He slowly approached the arch and saw two smaller versions of the central arch, the large arch stood in the center of the street and the two smaller ones were placed on each side. He estimated the stone arch to be more than forty feet high plus forty feet wide and twenty feet thick, erected on highly polished supports. At the top of the massive arch an inscription was engraved that Hammad could not read.

Hammad asked a man sitting nearby to decipher the inscription for him. The man was a Roman, so he called an interpreter who explained that the writing said that Julius, Julianus, the leader of the Alberite troop had built this arch. Admiring the lavishness of the Romans, Hammad was certain that they were nearer to greatness and luxury than the Persian kings. If this is any indication of their skill at the time of their uncultured age, how far advanced their extravagance and grandeur must have been at the time of their glory. He passed beneath the arch and reached a large crowd of people at an intersection. He strode toward the huge market where the merchants sold their expansive goods. At one corner of the crossing he faced an impressive building that was decorated with balustrades and pillars and etched engravings. This temple was originally built by the Romans who had practiced idolatry, having worshipped statues long before their descendents adopted Christianity. He learned from a local that the basilica was now being used as a church and as a residence for the chief Roman rulers who occupied Busra.

Hammad also saw that from the center intersection of the city, there stretched four wide roads that ended abruptly at the rampart. There was also, at each corner of the rampart, a door that opened to a specific compass point. He turned back to investigate the other streets and left through the east door. From there he rode to the monastery and examined the buildings along the way. There were tall mansions, many churches, and some heathen temples that were built in the days of the Romans, as well as the magnificent hippodrome where they performed plays, held wrestling matches, and conducted races. Engravings and paintings created in the Greek, Latin, and Coptic languages adorned these buildings. He studied the business streets and the market sections. These were occupied by the Syrians, Iraqis, Romans, and Persians. He passed the Roman and Persian goldsmith shops and the Damascene merchants with their silk goods. He noticed that most of the buildings had arched ceilings.

Hammad then recovered from his astonishment and curiosity and realized that it was now late morning. Pushing his horse, Hammad made his way up the mountain and came across a large building surrounded by orchards. He asked a native born man journeying on a donkey about the building. The man told him that it was indeed the Bahira Monastery.

Racing in that direction, Hammad became fearful that Hind might have arrived ahead of him. He reasoned, however, that the distance between her palace and the monastery would take several hours to cross, which meant that she would not arrive before noon. Exploring the monastery, he saw that it consisted of two buildings. The first was a very large dome-shaped structure with a cross atop it, the other was situated on the hill and Hammad assumed it to be the monk's residence.

Dismounting, he tied his horse to a tree and walked toward Bahira's church, which was built in the Roman style. He entered the yard and arrived at a temple which he realized was the abbey. He could hear the monks and priests chanting in Greek, the ancient and honorable language of the Eastern Church, from within the abbey, and as he continued on he heard others talking in Latin, the language of the ruling government, and others yet speaking Hebrew and Assyrian. He visited the temple and kissed the icons, and then asked directions to the monastery itself. After receiving directions, he realized that the monastery was the building situated on the hill nearby.

It was hard for Hammad to believe that the monastery was one solitary room made of five huge stones, four stones joined together to create the walls and one colossal stone which formed the ceiling. The door was hung on a strong hinge made of stone that could be opened and closed easily. This style of building was common in Hauran where the land was rocky and the wood was scarce. Hammad learned from an inhabitant that the hinges of their doors, windows and the frames of their rooms were chiseled from stone. They also built houses with numerous rooms, all of stone, without using a single piece of wood.

He stood looking at the strange building without an inkling as to where the entrance was until he saw some people exiting. He walked up to it and peered into the dark room. It resembled a cave and was devoid of all openings except for one small slit on one of its walls. As Hammad entered, he saw that the floor of the room was made of one immense slab of stone and that on the walls were hung pictures illuminated by the soft glow of a lamp. To one side of the room a monk, his face wrinkled with age, with an elongated nose and a beard that reached down to his chest, held beads in his hand and squatted on the polished floor. His lips moved in prayer, people entered the abbey to be blessed by kissing the palm of his hand, and after receiving their sanctification the pilgrims were then given a room at the church to rest in.

Hammad was moved by the sight of the old monk and noticed that his dress was the same as that of his home country. He approached the man and bent closer to kiss his hand. The monk contemplated Hammad as if he had known him and directed the young man to sit down. Hammad, who was very curious, wished to hear the story of the building and seated himself next to the monk.

"Are you from the Arabs of Iraq, my son?" the monk asked plainly.

With surprise, Hammad replied, "Yes sir, how did you know that?"

"I knew it by your facial features, for I have been in contact with the Arabs of Iraq for a long time." The monk continued, "Are you here to stay or have you come as a traveller?"

"I have come to perform a vow I owe to this monastery," Hammad answered him.

"What is your vow?" asked the monk.

"The vow," Hammad replied, "is that my first haircut is to be performed in this monastery and that it should take place when I am twenty-one years old, which will be this Palm Sunday. So I have come to get the blessing and to behold the sight of this monastery and talk to the monk named Bahira. Are you Bahira, sir?"

"No, my son, the one you seek was assassinated by the wicked!" the monk exclaimed woefully.

"Who would do such a thing?" asked Hammad with some astonishment. "I wish to hear this story," he continued, hoping to pass the time until Hind arrived.

"Bahira," said the monk, sighing with a stare and combing his beard with his fingers, "was without question a blessing from God to humanity that no other could resemble. His real name was not

Bahira, but John. The word Bahira was derived from the Kaldanian expression meaning 'the particular learned man'. They called him that because he was a learned man in every phase and degree of study."

"Did you know him personally?" asked Hammad.

"I am one of his disciples, along with many others including Solomon the Persian," the monk nodded. "I accompanied Bahira until the day he died."

"Would you tell me about him?" Hammad requested.

"Of course, my son. John Bahira was a Nestorian monk according to the sect of Urius and Nester. They had few followers because they were opposed to the sect of the Caesars."

"Yes, this much I know," said Hammad, "for I have read about that in school."

"What then do I have to explain?" asked the monk, "since you must know then that the basis of the Nestorian sect is the denial of the divinity of Christ and that to call him the son of God is not permitted. I have already told you that I am one of Bahira's disciples, I was his disciple in everything except for this belief. We would argue constantly about it, but I learned astronomy and mathematics from him. However, for his frank opinions, Bahira was discharged from his position in Iraq and subsequently from another in Egypt until he came to this monastery where he and I stayed together for a short time. He often travelled from place to place in Arabia but I could not give you all their names. Then word came to me that some heathens had assassinated him."

"Did he not tell you of his destinations?" asked Hammad.

"No, but I am convinced that he went to Hejaz," claimed the monk. "Forty years ago I witnessed something very strange with my very own eyes."

"And what was that?" asked Hammad.

"It was the habit of the caravans at the time," said the monk, "who journeyed from Arabia and other far off places, to stay here for a rest. Bahira sat among them and taught them to worship God, giving special attention to the heathens. He would tell everyone that God wished him to guide the Arabs for Him so they in turn could spread the teachings of God. So, about forty years ago, a caravan from Hejaz arrived overburdened with people from the tribe of Quraysh, who inhabited Mecca, the most decent people of Arabia. The tribe stayed here to rest under the large tree in the courtyard which shaded them all. They secured their donkeys and mules and had their camels kneel so they could be unburdened, and then proceeded to avail themselves of the water. Bahira walked over to them and began to lay his teachings before them. He saw a lad among them who had a very fine looking face and seemed to be intelligent and respectful.

"Bahira stared at him in awe and turned to me and said, 'Look, this young boy will soon occupy the highest position in the heart of humanity, he will guide the children of Ishmael to God.' Bahira approached a middle-aged man and asked him about the boy and the man replied that the boy was his brother's son.

"'Take care of him,' said Bahira, 'and watch the heathens, for they may want to snare him if they know about him.'"

"What is his name?" asked Hammad.

"'His name is Muhammad,' said the boy's uncle, whose name was Abu Talib ibn Abdul-Muttalib," continued the monk. "This nomadic tribe stayed with us some length of time before leaving for Damascus and then returning to Mecca."

"What of the prophecy of Bahira, did it come true?" asked Hammad.

"Yes my son, that Qurayshi boy became a great prophet and his religion is called Islam. His authority is spreading throughout the Arabian Peninsula and his followers are called Muslims. The merchants and travelers who come and go from Hejaz speak of his deeds, the wars he has fought, and of his victories. It is truly remarkable. Now, the inhabitants of the Arabian Peninsula are solidly united under his banner, while before many different militant divisions were fighting each other."

"I had heard about this prophet when I was in Iraq," Hammad remarked, "but not of the extent of his influence."

With tears in his eyes, the old man said, "Oh, my son, it is probable that Syria and Iraq will become his should it be the purpose of his coming. You see how we Christians are divided into many sects, our forts ruined by the war between the Romans and the Persians, and our government has become divided so we cannot accomplish anything."

Hammad would have liked to have listened to the monk all day if it were not for his meeting with Hind, and he began to worry about her lateness. He listened a short while longer, then bade the monk good-bye and made himself comfortable under the sprawling shade of a tree nearby.

The Rendezvous of Two Lovers

Since he had not sleep well the night before, Hammad dozed off under the tree. Aroused by the neighing of horses some time later, Hammad saw two riders approaching the monastery both dressed in similar clothes. He stood up and noticed that their faces were hidden behind silk scarfs but he immediately recognized Hind's horse and that of her maid-servant.

He sat up and waited for some sort of sign from Hind. She seemed not to take notice and instead walked toward the stone building and entered. Hammad hesitated for a moment and then walked in the same direction. As he neared the entrance, Hind's maid-servant exited the building, looked around for a moment, then spotted Hammad and approached him inquisitively.

"My mistress has asked me to locate a jewelry merchant," she asked, "Do you know one?"

"I am that merchant," Hammad replied. "What is it you desire?"

"My mistress would like to speak with you," she answered.

"Does she want to purchase anything now?"

"Have you any goods on you?" said the servant.

"They are in my store," answered Hammad, "the jeweled pieces which I sell are much too valuable for me to just carry around. If your mistress is affluent, however, I will gladly bring her whatever she wants."

With scorn, the woman smirked and said, "She is the most worthy among all the women of Hauran and Balqa and well can afford your jewelry."

"Oh, is that so?" asked Hammad, "Where is she then?"

"She is in the abbey!" said the servant, "Come this way."

Hammad's whole body trembled as he entered the abbey and saw Hind sitting on a stone bench. He greeted her and acted as though she were a stranger, "Madam, I have been informed that you are interested in purchasing some jewelry, is that correct?"

"I am," replied Hind.

"My selection is in my store nearby," he said.

"Shall I go with you?" she asked, "for I do not know exactly what I need and perhaps you have pieces I do not want."

"I do not wish to rouse you from such peaceful settings, Madam. Describe for me what you are looking for, and I will bring you the very best of its kind," Hammad offered.

"Very well," replied Hind. "I am looking for a pearl necklace and a gold bracelet set with precious stones. Have you any such pieces?"

"Indeed, I am at your service, Madam, I will get them for you and return presently," replied Hammad with a bow.

Hammad mounted his horse and left in a full gallop. Luckily, his purse was not empty since he had brought money for his travels. Arriving at the market, he selected a few of the finest necklaces and bracelets made of the best materials he could find on such short notice and returned immediately to the monastery. He was met at the door once again by the servant who asked if he had the jewelry and then showed him to the room where Hind waited alone.

While Hammad was searching through the market, Hind was trying desperately to calm her tremors and her wildly beating heart. She engaged Hammad as she would a stranger, fearing her maid-servant might suspect the true reason for being there. When Hammad returned, she handed him a cushion to sit on. Hammad gently placed the bracelets and necklaces in her hands. She looked them over carefully pretending to show great interest in one of them.

"What can you tell me about this set of bracelets?" she asked.

"They are handcrafted in Constantinople," he said, "and the connoisseurs much prefer them to those made in Khorasan."

"How much are these worth?" she inquired.

"They are very precious, Madam," said Hammad, "and worth five hundred dinars, but the price for you today is a mere fraction of that, only ten dinars."

"Do not concern yourself with the price," said Hind. "I will have to show them to my mother before I can buy them at any rate."

"Very well, where is your mother?" Hammad asked.

"She is in our palace a few miles from here, and since you do not know us and whether you can trust us to come back with your jewelry, I will send my maid-servant to my mother and I will remain here until she returns. If my mother likes them, I will buy them from you," Hind declared.

"As you wish, Madam," Hammad consented, then added, "but I cannot stay here long."

"Worry not. My maiden will ride as swift as the wind," Hind reassured him. "And if she does not come back in time we will return them to you as they are."

"Very well," said Hammad, "tell her to take special care of them lest they lose some of their stones."

"Do not be so apprehensive, they will be safe with her," Hind replied. Then, turning to her maid she said, "Take this jewelry to my mother and show them to her. Tell her the price as well. Go now, and return with the reply as soon as possible."

"I shall follow your instructions, Mistress," said the maiden with a bow, and then she left for the palace with haste in the hopes of receiving one of the trinkets as a present.

Hind and Hammad remained alone in the room, silent, with only their love beating between their hearts.

"You have understood my ruse well, Hammad," remarked Hind.

He gazed at her for a moment and said, "How could I have misunderstood you? For when you think, you think with my mind, and when you speak, you speak with my heart."

She kept her eyes lowered, shyly looking over the remaining jewelry and turning them around as if she wanted to speak. He continued to stare at her face, taking in her beauty and overawed at the freshness of youth in her face and the light of intelligence coming out of her eyes. He could see there was something she wanted to say, so he met her gaze so that she could see that he wished for her to open up.

"I am afraid that you might see my boldness in asking you here as insolence," she finally uttered.

Hammad sighed and said, "God forbid! The daughter of Ghassan is very precious to me and I do appreciate her kindness. How can I be blessed with the presence of the Princess of Ghassan and not consider myself the happiest of men?"

"This princess," said Hind, "has become a captive mute and knows not what to say."

"If my mistress will allow me to speak, I would say that I am her servant and prisoner, and I would consider her mere condescension a generous gift."

"Hammad, do you have any idea why we meet in this abbey, this house of God?" she asked.

"No, I do not. Perhaps you mean to rebuke me for my bold actions toward his Majesty," he answered.

"No! That is not my intention at all, you do not think with my mind nor do you speak with my heart," Hind murmured meekly.

"What is it, then?" he asked.

With a faint blush she answered, "I have come to congratulate you for winning the breastplate and to say that your magnanimous attitude proves that you rightly deserved to be the victor."

"The breastplate is the most precious thing I have ever received or will receive. It is a protective instrument and evil-proof, and the gift is a great honor for a stranger in your lands," Hammad replied. "But I am a stranger whom you know nothing about. That breastplate is my only possession of true value, and to be victor of your heart I must also be in the position to be in a king's position, which I am not."

She looked at him with a beguiling side-long glance, and in a sweet manner said, "A true king is the one who occupies the hearts and rules the feelings of his people, not the one who keeps pace with wealth and the vanities of the world."

He turned to her and saw the love she held for him.

"Such is the generosity the world has come to know of the Ghassan," he said. "Say something now to soothe the beating heart of your humble servant."

"What could I say? You control my heart," she sighed deeply. "Does Hammad not speak himself?"

"And what could I say? You know that every sign in my face betrays awe at your beauty," replied Hammad.

He took her hand in his and found that it was as cold as ice and imagined that she was melting in his fingers. No sooner had he touched her than he felt an electrifying sensation pass through his body and was positive she felt the same.

She kept her eyes lowered and said, "The hour grows late, and soon we will have to leave."

"I am a prisoner of your love," said Hammad, "and have nowhere else to go."

Hammad knew that she loved him but he feared the rivalry of her cousin, Tha'labah. Tha'labah may not yet be betrothed to Hind and she certainly did not love him, but if he were spiteful enough toward Hammad, Tha'labah could make plans for a betrothal. To be sure that Hind would be his, he asked, "What of Tha'labah?"

"I have nothing to do with him!" Hind exclaimed.

"Suppose he insisted on marrying you by the virtue of your relationship?" Hammad persisted.

"We will not recognize his kinship after knowledge of his vileness is made known," Hind spat.

"What have you seen that suggests such vileness?" he asked.

"It is the matter of the reed that marks his vicious nature," Hind answered, looking up at Hammad.

Hammad registered alarm and was surprised to hear her speak of the reed, but it appeared that she knew about it. To be sure, he asked her what she meant.

"The incident with the reed demonstrates what debase and dishonorable a nature the son of King al-Harith is made of," Hind restated bluntly.

"And what of the horseman whose lineage you know nothing of?" asked Hammad.

"One who is led by his heart will not stumble, Hammad. You cannot be a commoner, for you have the traits which kings and princes are destined to be worthy of," said Hind, praising him.

"And what if there is some hostility between your father and my tribe?" he asked.

"I love you," said Hind, breathlessly, "no matter how hostile your tribe is to my father's."

Shifting himself more comfortably in his seat, Hammad said, "Your captive sweetheart is not from the ranks of kings for is he from the ranks of the common people. He is a prince, however, though not equal to the lofty ancestry of your father."

Hind felt her whole body release at his declaration but was curious about the tribe he was from. Having noticed his accent, Hind asked, "Are you an Emir from Iraq?"

"Yes, my love," he affirmed. "Will that change your feelings in any way?"

"No!" she hastily replied, "you are more than I wished for. The tribes of Iraq are well known for their high principles."

"Your humility only makes our love stronger," Hammad said, adding softly, "I must ask, will you be mine?"

"Our love is true. It is not me you need to convince. You will need to find wisdom if you are to find a way to win the consent of my father, however," Hind replied.

He considered her words seriously and knew that gaining her father's consent would be no easy matter because of the breach between their tribes.

"Why are you hesitating, are you afraid of going down that path?" she asked.

"No!" exclaimed Hammad. "I fear nothing or no one in order to be with you, but I must be prepared for the road to be rocky and obstructed by the hatred and hostility that exists between our people."

"I am on your side, for whatever is hard for you is easy for me," Hind said valiantly.

"I am glad for that, my hope and my strength," Hammad said, reassured by her devotion.

Outside once more, they saw the sun was setting and the young couple stood close to each other and held hands to say good-bye. Their intimate mood was interrupted by the sudden, loud neighing of horses and shouting that sent the monks into a frenetic state of confusion. Both Hind and Hammad looked around in alarm at the startling scene, turning toward the sound of the shouting.

"That sounds like Tha'labah!" Hind cried in alarm. "He must have found out about our meeting and plans to do us harm. We had better go!"

No sooner had she stopped talking than a man snuck in close and dropped a piece of jewelry into Hammad's pocket and pulled it out pretending to find it there, exclaiming, "These bracelets are mine, they were stolen from my shop! Where did you get them from?"

Hammad's reply was a blow to the man's face which sent him falling to the ground. A group of soldiers rushed forward and restrained Hammed roughly. One of them grabbed Hammad by the shoulders and pulled him upright, sneering as he said "You are a thief and a spy. You are under arrest."

"Shut up, dog of the Arabs," Hammad yelled in a caustic voice.

"Leave him alone!" screamed Hind.

Hammad hastily whispered to her, "Do not reveal to them who you are!"

The soldiers engulfed Hammad and a voice was heard saying, "Seize that thief and bring him to me dead or alive! He is a dangerous spy!"

It was then that Hammad saw Tha'labah through the tumult. Hammad violently shook himself free from the guard's hold and strode toward the jeering figure of Tha'labah, the soldiers scattering every which way. Hammad shouted, "Come coward and let us see who the traitor is!" With a dagger in his hand, Hammad pushed at the crowd that had closed in once more, trying in vain to pursue his enemy. Suddenly, one of the guards pushed through the crowd and made a lunge at Hammad. Hammad turned swiftly and immobilized the soldier by grappling the man's shoulders. The crowd began to disperse to make room for the commotion.

Fearing that Hind's arrest would bring disgrace upon both of them, his only thought was to escape with her, but Hind had a different kind of courage in mind.

"No! I will not go and let you fall into the hands of these villains!" she cried in anguish.

Hind then valiantly grabbed a sword from one of the soldiers and attacked them with no thought for her own life until most of them had vanished, fearful of her undaunted bravery. As Hind fought, she kept shouting, "Be gone, you vile dogs!" while advancing relentlessly. The guards swiftly mounted their horses and rode off, leaving a cloud of dust behind.

The Escape

Earlier that day, back at the Stream Palace, Tha'labah's devious mind was plotting treachery. He snuck down to the kitchen to spy on the servants and overheard them talking about Hind's plans to visit the monastery that day. The devious prince then delayed the preparations for his own journey for as long as possible because Hind could not leave before Tha'labah had departed with her parents. He was obligated, after all, to accompany his aunt and uncle to ensure their safe escort back to the province of Balqa. Once Tha'labah had seen his royal family safely to the borders of Balqa, he left them to make haste for Busra and the monastery. He arrived with his men late in the afternoon, eager to seek out Hind and discover her reasons for the visit, but when he heard the voice of his rival Hammad inside the abbey, Tha'labah could not believe his ears! Jealousy raging in his heart, Tha'labah schemed with a local merchant to draw Hammad out to be arrested, but when he then saw Hind fighting valiantly with sword in hand and all his men hastily retreating from her, Tha'labah could not believe his eyes! With a cowardly snarl, Tha'labah ordered his men to retreat so that he could stage another trap, the next time for the both of his rivals!

Praise be to God, he was too late. Hammad and Hind rode their horses hard toward the Stream Palace until they had reached the edge of the desert, taking a road which they hoped the maid-servant would not return by, wishing not to get her involved.

"Woe unto that traitor!" cursed Hammad. "Would to God that he had been killed for his treachery!"

"As much as I wish it to, it was not God's will today," replied Hind to try and sooth Hammad's fury. "Tha'labah will receive his just reward, but I fear his persistence. He will have another trap in store for us somewhere."

"Fear not, my love," said Hammad, "there is not a prince or king alive who could harm a hair on your head while the blood flows through my veins. I have witnessed a courage in you today that made me despise myself for a coward. Glory to the Creator who blessed you with the courage of man and the compassion of woman. The moment I saw that sword in your hand and the soldiers scurrying away like beaten dogs I found an inner strength that I will never lose with you at my side."

"My love for you stirred me to action, Hammad," Hind replied. "I could not bear to see them harm you. That treacherous Tha'labah is my family, and I am also responsible for upholding my family's honor!"

"Then we share both love and truth and our bond runs deep," said Hammad tenderly. "No one can separate us!"

Hind halted her horse and gazed at him as if to speak. They clasped each other's hands in a vow to keep this love alive in their hearts. "I will keep your love in my heart for all the days of my life and in the life beyond," Hind promised, "no matter what stands in our way."

"And I will let nothing stand in our way," vowed Hammad, "in this world or the next."

Hind lowered her head, blushing as if she were echoing his words.

"We have vowed our love for each other," said Hammad, "let the bracelets be a reminder of our love. I offer them to you without a motive, they are just a small trinket. Will you keep them as a memento of me?"

Hind looked admiringly at him and said, "I will keep them for as long as I live, but I do not have a memento to give you in return."

"The breastplate which you bestowed upon me is my memento," said Hammad, "It is as priceless as our love and it will keep me safe from danger and aid me in fulfilling our vow."

"You honor me, Hammad, may God protect you," said Hind.

They rode side by side in silence until they reached the Stream Palace. It was encircled by the fires of hospitality, a sign which meant, "Here is a refuge for whosoever wishes food and shelter."

"There is your palace ahead," said Hammad. "Return to it and I will depart for my home. My father will be worried."

"Stay in the safety of the palace tonight, Hammad," Hind insisted. "I fear that the traitor will be out there somewhere, hiding in wait with his men to do you harm."

Hammad shook his head proudly and said, "I am equal to all of his father's soldiers, God willing."

Hind urged him once more to stay at the palace overnight and seek hospitality, but he refused again saying that it would be shameful for him to fear the prince and his men no matter how many there were. Hind reluctantly bade him farewell. Their hands clasped and they silently renewed their oath to remain steadfast and loyal to one another. Hind then passed through the palace gates and Hammad watched over her until she was out of sight. Turning to go home, he spurred his horse to a fast gallop leaving his heart back at the palace and his mind wandering with thoughts of Hind.

After riding for some time Hammad realized he had gone astray. He pulled his horse up short and looked around to determine where he was but did not recognize any of the landscape. Being unfamiliar with this country, but well-schooled in astronomy, Hammad looked to the stars for guidance. The path he chose turned out to be in the right direction, and he offered his praise to God for the stars and a solemn thank you to the science that had taught him to read them. Making his way through the orchards near his home, Hammad heard the sound of hoof-beats racing toward him. He slowed his horse to a walk, listening and staring in the direction of the sound. After a moment, he could make out the silhouette of a horseman heading straight for him. Hammad gripped the reins of his horse and brought the beast to a halt. Peering through the darkness, Hammad thought he could hear a familiar voice calling to him by name.

"Is that you, Salman?" he called back.

"Yes, Sir!" came the answer.

Salman materialized from the darkness a moment later, his face somber. "Come with me, Sir, there is much I need to tell you."

Hammad nodded, and Salman took the lead. They continued riding until they were in the desert again.

"What is it, Salman?" Hammad asked, "What is so important that we had to come all the way back out here to discuss?"

"I have come by the order of your father, Sir," Salman replied, "to tell you to leave Hauran and go to Amman immediately."

"What? Why?" asked Hammad, not believing his ears.

"Because the governor of Busra has sent a company of his men to arrest your father and has taken over the household," Salman answered, bravely hiding nothing from his Master.

This news sickened Hammad but he was certain that Tha'labah had something to do with it since Busra's governor was a Roman official who was a close friend of the treacherous dog's father, King al-Harith. Trying to ignore the distress welling in his heart, he asked, "Why have they done that?"

"They arrived under the pretense that your father is a spy sent by the King of Iraq," said Salman, "and an armed guard has taken him to Busra. But they did not come for your father, Sir, they came asking for you. They searched the house thoroughly but found no trace of you, and they took my Master prisoner before pillaging the house. Your father ordered me to find you and take you to safety in Amman and await him there."

"Did they harm him?" ask Hammad.

"No, Sir, but they bound his hands and you can be certain they will come searching for you. Let us disguise ourselves and make haste for Amman," Salman implored, "without delay!"

Hammad frowned in anguish and then choked up with tears. He was so depressed at the thought of running away but he knew he could not disobey his father. As they rode together, Hammad asked Salman if he was familiar with the way to Amman.

"Yes, Sir, I know it," answered the servant, "for I have traveled it many times with your father years ago."

Amman, a venerable city sixty miles south of Busra, had endured since the thirteenth century BC. At the end of the first century AD,

Amman came under the rule of the Romans who had continued to occupy the city long after the adoption of Christianity. The two men rode hard until they were overcome by an oppressive fatigue and were forced to stop and rest. The moon began to throw its light upon the uninhabited plains and cast a purple-hued glow across the peaks of the mountains on the horizon. The land between Busra and Amman was rich with forests, olive and walnut trees grew in abundance, so the two men took shelter in a reasonably concealed grove. Salman seemed content to sleep, but Hammad's thoughts and anxieties beat in his heart for Hind and he feared for his father, recalling the enemy and his devious nature.

"Tell me, Salman," asked Hammad, "what did those villains do to my father and the house?"

Salman sat up against a tree and told the whole story to Hammad as truthfully as he could recall. "We were taken by surprise. My master had been in an anxious state all day because of your absence, he did not know where you had gone. The sun was setting and you still had not returned, so he," Salman paused thoughtfully before continuing, "well, Master became more agitated and ordered me to ready the horses to begin a search for you. As we were about to leave, dozens of armed men surrounded the house, demanding your presence, Sir! Your father asked them what their business was and their reply was nothing more than utterances of insults and curses. We echoed the same to them, but alas, their reply was to draw their arms and arrest your father, even though he was unarmed. They bound your father's hands behind his back and secured him by the door. They proceeded to pillage the house, searching it thoroughly. While they were busy I had a chance to talk to your father and he bid me run to find you to bring you the warning not to return home. I found you, Sir, and here we are, God be praised for our safety."

"Did they find the valuables?" asked Hammad.

"Luckily, no," Salman answered, "the money is well hidden, Sir."

"Did they take the breastplate?" asked Hammad, worriedly.

"No!" replied the servant with a smile, "It is right here on my horse in the saddlebags, let me fetch it for you."

Hammad was pleased to find the breastplate had not been taken, and the two continued talking about what to do next. They decided to carry on at a slower pace toward Amman, and so they mounted their horses and made way. It was not long, however, before they noticed a fire far off in the distance.

"What is that?" said Hammad, "are we approaching an encampment?"

Salman stopped and looked and thought, then answered, "The flame you see is a light from a city on the edge of the Zarqa River. It is not far from Amman. If you wish to go there we can, Sir, but you should know that we will soon reach a spring where we can gratify our thirst and satisfy our horses. There is a lodge along this road where we can rest for the night."

"We should not show ourselves in the city," said Hammad, "Tha'labah will have spies everywhere searching for me. Let us find this spring of yours."

The Land of Lions

Hammad and Salman rode until they reached a valley through which a river coursed from east to west banked on each side with trees. They surveyed the valley, awestruck by the sublime calmness of nature, and stood listening to the quietude of the night, watching the gossamer shadows of the leaves' reflection on the water. As they approached the river, they heard the evening-song of the frogs and the calm rustle of the saplings bending with the gentle breeze. They dismounted and carefully led their horses down the slope toward the river, making their way slowly by the poor light of the moon.

Salman was apprehensive of this area, not because it was late at night in a strange land, but because he knew that the lands near Zarqa were inhabited by fierce beasts. They were still some distance from Zarqa, so he said nothing to Hammad for he felt that there was no reason to alarm his master. From their view by the river bank they could see that they were sitting at the head of the valley near the base between two mountains. The valley was lush with plants and magnificent trees. Salman tied the horses to a nearby tree and accompanied Hammad to the water where they washed and drank their fill. Hammad removed his head wrap and arranged his hair so that it would not be in his way. Salman spread his cloak on the soft dirt beneath a tree and they both sat down for a rest.

Salman began talking, but Hammad was not listening to the words. Hammad was listening to the croaking of the frogs, the crowing of the ravens, the rustling of the leaves, and rushing of the water. Were it not for his preoccupation with his father's calamity, Hammad would have felt serendipity at the sight of the valley. Their horses made neighing sounds and pawed the earth with their hooves, sensing that water was near. Salman saw his master's distraction and left his side to tend to the horses' needs. He untied them and led them to a lower bank of the river and joined their reins with a knot. Salman toyed with the handle of his sword as his sharp eyes scanned the tops of the mountain range and the ridges of the valley, keeping vigil while Hammad was lost in his thoughts.

The horses drank their fill and Salman led them back to a nearby tree, securing them for the night. He then returned to Hammad and sat with his back resting against the tree. Hammad stretched out and fell asleep wrapped in his cloak, the fatigue finally hitting him. Sleep escaped Salman, so he kept watch while saying his prayers for God's protection. He remained awake until dawn when he finally gave in to the weight of his eyes.

Before Salman could enjoy his slumber, however, he heard the whinny of the horses and the rattle of their bridles. Looking over to them, he could see them pulling frantically against their reins with fear in their eyes. He spun around, hearing stones rolling down the mountainside, and saw them plunging into the water on the opposite bank. The horses began panicking, increasing their distressed whinnying. Hammad woke and jumped to his feet in alarm as Salman yelled, "Hurry, Master, we are in great danger!"

"What is happening?" asked Hammad.

"We must be much closer to the land of Zarqa than I thought, the land of the great lions! They must be coming for the water, but do not worry, the stones fell from the opposite side of the river, the water separates us. Let us mount our horses and go!" At that moment, a great lion emerged from the brush on the opposite bank and sauntered with great pride toward the water, his eyes glowing like two large beacons. The beast saw them and let out a great roar that echoed and shook the entire valley.

"Fear not, the water stands between us," Salman whispered reassuringly as he slowly backed toward the horses. Hammad did the same and they mounted quickly and rode their horses hard over the summit in the direction they had come from, their ears still ringing with the lion's roar, the fierce echo betraying their sense of direction. When they reached the crest of the valley, the morning light revealed another lion placidly drinking water. Thankfully, this beast was also on the opposite bank of the river.

"What have you done, Salman?" asked Hammad, "why have you brought us to this dangerous place?"

"We were forced to come this way," came Salman's reply. "When I traveled this path years ago, there were no beasts. It would seem that the lions have wandered far from their home in search of water. They will soon go, God willing."

They stood for a while and gazed at the constant flow of the river at the bottom of the valley and watched the lion turn his massive head from right to left. The lion then noticed them and roared such a roar that Hammad and Salman were left dumbstruck and horrified. It was the first time Hammad had ever seen a lion this close but Salman knew the feeling well. Salman had seen them in captivity in the parks of Khosrau I, the Persian King who kept a court in the city of al-Mada'in where Salman had spent a great many years. Hammad watched the lion's show of great pomposity with fascination. At last, the beast laid his tail on his back as he majestically ascended the slope and disappeared from sight.

The sun began to beat down, and Hammad realized he was very tired. "Do you want to sit here and take some nourishment?" he asked.

"We had best not linger here, Master. You can see that it is not safe," Salman answered. "Let us go a little further so that we might sooner find some shelter. We can rest there for the day and stay for the night so we will be well rested for the next day's travel."

After a somewhat lengthy ride down the valley, they arrived at a monastery. The building's only adornment was a globe and cross erected high atop the roof. They entered the gates and were warmly received by the monks. They spent the day there as guests, resting and eating. The food, plain but delicious, consisted of fresh milk, artificially soured milk, cheese, and fried lamb with eggs, dried fruits, walnuts, and very old wine. They enjoyed the monks' hospitality, the generosity of these pious men helped the two to forget their anxieties for a time and find some rest. They lodged for the night and talked mostly about the lions. The monks informed them that the land of the beasts was far from the monastery but in the direct path of Amman. With the monks' directions, Hammad and Salman had two choices ahead of them, either a shortcut through the land of the beasts or the long way around. They chose the latter although Hammad was not entirely happy with the delay in reaching Amman.

The Imprisonment of Abdullah

We must remember to be mindful of what had happened to
Abdullah while Hammad and Salman made their way to Amman.
On the march to Busra, Abdullah's thoughts weighed heavily on the
unnecessary violence used in arresting him. Charged with spying, he
knew that he was innocent, so Abdullah became certain that he
would be released as soon as he stood before King al-Harith. Once
freed, he would hurry to meet Hammad in Amman, from where they
could proceed together to Bahira Monastery in order to consummate
their vow. But the soldiers drove him to Busra and imprisoned him
in one of the castle's cells in the dungeon south of the rampart.
Abdullah spent the night in his cell wrestling with anxiety, worried
about Hammad. Should the boy make it home without first meeting
Salman, he would most certainly fall into a trap. The night passed
without further incident, however, so Abdullah gave thanks to God,
certain that Hammad had escaped.

Late the next morning, two soldiers dressed in the uniform of
the Roman Army came to Abdullah. Their brass helmets were
adorned with horsehair braids that flowed downward and their steel
breastplates were highly polished and shone like mirrors. They were
each bearing a small steel sword and shield adorned with two
embroidered ribbons affixed with a golden letter H, the initial of
Heraclius, the Roman Emperor. Behind the Roman soldiers were
two men standing at attention in Arabian dress. The two soldiers led
Abdullah to a higher level of the castle, and showed him into a room
that was decorated with the finest Roman furniture. Across the
room, a great man was sitting on an elevated gold-plated chair. It was
clear that he was the governor of the Roman guard in Busra.

This imposing man wore a narrow gown reaching below the
knees and a breastplate with brass ornaments, plated with gold.
Sitting nearby were men dressed in the same attire who formed the
Roman council. One of the councillors stood out from the others,
dressed in Arabian clothes. It was Tha'labah, the son of King al-

Harith. Arriving in front of the governor, Abdullah stood at ease, his manacled hands clasped before him. The governor introduced himself as Romanus and addressed Abdullah through an interpreter.

"State your name," Romanus ordered.

"Abdullah," he replied.

"And which country are you from, Abdullah?" he asked.

"I come from Iraq, Sir," he responded.

"What is your occupation?" the governor inquired.

"I am an Emir of Iraq," Abdullah replied. "I live by means of my properties and trade."

"What brings you to this country?" asked Romanus.

"To perform a vow I have made to Bahira Monastery, Sir," he explained.

"And may I ask what that might be?" said Romanus.

"To have my son's hair trimmed during a ceremony on his twenty-first birthday, Sir," Abdullah said earnestly.

Romanus turned to Tha'labah and talked privately to him, then turned back to Abdullah and asked, "If your sole purpose for coming here is for your son's ceremony, why have you lingered here for months without doing so?"

"Because the ceremony is not to be held until this Palm Sunday," answered Abdullah truthfully.

Romanus laughed scornfully and said, "That tender pretext does not exonerate you from the charge of treason. You are accused of being a spy sent by the kings of al-Hira. If you were truly here for a religious ceremony, you would not have stayed in a distant village hiding behind the guise of a wealthy Emir of Iraq. Furthermore, anyone as privileged as you claim to be would not avoid a city like Busra, with its beautiful vistas and comfortable lodgings, only to conceal themselves in a poor village such as Ghasam. Confess, or your lies will only make your punishment worse."

"I have told you the truth!" Abdullah implored. "There is nothing more to profess."

"Are you incapable of speaking the truth?" asked the Roman governor. "You claim you are related to the Emirs of Iraq, but only yesterday our guards caught your son stealing jewelry from a merchant at the monastery."

Abdullah remained quiet for a moment, he speculated that the governor was trying to extract some news from him regarding Hammad's whereabouts.

"Perhaps there was a misunderstanding," Abdullah finally answered. "I know nothing about these crimes. My son and I are not in need and we do not follow or condone such foul conduct."

Tha'labah shook his head disdainfully, and toying with his moustache, haughtily remarked, "We are certain that you are spying and we will open all eyes to it."

Rising indignantly, Tha'labah walked over to Abdullah and searched the pockets of his robe. He pulled out a fancy little box and opened it. It held a ring set with a large ruby which Tha'labah examined. On the inside of the band he noticed Arabic lettering unlike any he had ever seen before. Tha'labah held the ring up, astonishment very apparent on the face of Abdullah even though he tried to control his nervous reaction. Tha'labah rotated the ring in his hand and scrutinized it but was still unable to decipher the inscription. He turned to one of the interpreters, "Can you read what is written on this ring?"

The interpreter took one look at the ring, swiftly glanced at Abdullah, and then returned his gaze to the ring once more. Signs of fear were evident on Abdullah's face while all the audience waited to hear.

Tha'labah wearied of waiting so he repeated his request, "Can you read the inscription or not!?"

"This ring bears the name of King al-Nu'man III, the son of King al-Mundhir IV ibn al-Mundhir, the great Lakhmid king. It bears King al-Nu'man's personal inscription."

The audience was taken by surprise and each in turn looked at the ring and flashed a look at Abdullah.

Romanus became very stern and addressed Abdullah, "How did you come by this ring?"

"I bought it from a jeweler," Abdullah answered, trying not to hesitate.

Tha'labah rebuked him saying, "You still insist that you are not a spy and you claim that you bought the ring of the King of Iraq from a jeweler? Why on earth would a king's personal ring be sold on the market? Tell me how this ring fell into your hands at once!"

There was no answer from Abdullah. Tha'labah repeated his question again and again without receiving an answer. Infuriated, Tha'labah consulted with Romanus privately. When they had concluded their conversation, Romanus turned to Abdullah and spoke, "The discovery of this ring in your possession will add to the charge of treason unless you relate the facts of how you came to possess it."

Abdullah remained silent.

"Answer the question!" Romanus said angrily.

Abdullah's silence infuriated Tha'labah, who started to shout, "Talk! Answer me!"

"I told you that I bought it at the marketplace and that is all I know about it," Abdullah replied once more. "It would seem to me that the interpreter was inaccurate in deciphering the writing or perhaps the name is similar to that of the king."

With a laugh, Tha'labah said, "That is a weak lie! And were my father present, he would confirm that the inscription on this ring belongs to King al-Nu'man, for he has seen the seal many times himself. You will remain prisoner until you confess the truth. If you do not, we will execute you."

"I have no fear of death, for I am innocent," said Abdullah. "You must do what is right in your judgment."

Tha'labah's eyes almost bulged out in anger. "You will regret your impertinence when we find your son and bring him here to answer for his treason!" Tha'labah turned to the four guards who were posted at the door and addressed them, "Take him, by order of Romanus, to the tower cells and hold him there under heavy guard!"

The tower in the castle of Busra was used solely for the confinement of prisoners because there was no way for prisoners to escape. If a prisoner attempted to escape through a window he would fall to his death, and if they broke out of the door they would have to exit through the guard's room. The four guards ascended the two flights of stairs to the tower prison, escorted Abdullah into a small cell with two windows, and then locked the door behind him.

Abdullah was alone now and began to consider what had happened to him. The threat that Tha'labah had made toward Hammad kept repeating over and over again in his head. He could not understand the theft charge against Hammad and thanked God for his son's escape, knowing now in all certainty that his son had not fallen into a trap. The discovery of the ring, however, complicated matters. Abdullah got up from his pallet and went to the east window. He had a sweeping view of the entire city of Busra, its buildings and streets, of the ramparts surrounding the city, and the cisterns brimming with water beyond it, with the sun shining brilliantly over it all.

He took in the breadth of the horizon, a mountain rose up to the north and he could see a building which was other-wise hidden from sight at the ground level. He guessed that it was the Salkhad Citadel, and between it and Busra, Abdullah could make out a great road that ran straight as an arrow and was paved with massive stones, a remnant of the great Roman thoroughfares. Before him, he could see that Busra and its outlying villages were a lively park in the midst of a desert given that the country of Hauran was made of barren land littered with mountain ranges. The scenery did little to ease the anxiety that Abdullah was feeling over his son, however, and he feared dying before he could explain everything to Hammad, to let go of the burden of secrecy that he had kept in his heart for more than twenty years.

As Abdullah pondered his fate, the guards brought him food which he did not eat. On the second day, he thought of jumping from the tower to escape, thinking he may yet survive the fall. Taking another look out the window, Abdullah reconsidered, it was an unwise thought indeed. On the third morning he awoke to the sounds of the bells pealing from all the churches and monasteries. He looked down through the window and saw people cheering and hailing as they moved through streets decorated with palm and olive branches. There were many people walking through the streets all dressed gaily and carrying flowers, candles, and olive twigs as they made their way to gather around the churches and monasteries.

It was Palm Sunday. Abdullah woefully remembered his vow to his son and he grieved deeply and wept. Abdullah passed that day, and many more, eating very little but doing what he could to keep a positive mind, always hoping that matters would take a better direction. Abdullah was beginning to think that he might lose track of time, when one day the guards came and ordered him to accompany them to the council chambers. He obliged and accompanied the guards without objection, preparing to defend himself. He stood once more in the presence of Romanus and Tha'labah, the latter of which asked, "How do you find yourself today?"

"I find myself a prisoner in the presence of a governor and a prince," answered Abdullah.

"More empty words," said Tha'labah. "Confess your true purpose for being here and we promise to release you."

"I have told you the truth," Abdullah replied, "but you will not believe me."

"Tell us where your son is and we will pardon you," Tha'labah urged.

Abdullah shook his head in surprise, "How am I to know where my son is when, during your violent raid on my house, he was absent? Since then I have been locked away in your tower."

Then Romanus spoke, his voice booming, "Hear me well! If you insist on silence, I will have you sent to the Emperor in Homs, and he will be swift in delivering severe punishment for your treason. When you stand before him there will be no one to save you from his judgment. You would do better to confess your crimes now and you will be granted a pardon."

"My lord, I have spoken the truth to you as it is in my heart, but you will not believe me," Abdullah said solemnly. "Do with me as you wish."

Romanus, vexed by now, gave the order to the guards to deliver Abdullah, along with the ring, to Homs and escort them personally to Emperor Heraclius.

Abdullah's only hope was that the emperor was a more reasonable man than Romanus had implied. He was thrust over the back of a horse with his hands bound in front of him so he could man the reins, and accompanied by ten guards, five of whom were Roman soldiers, Abdullah set out for Homs.

Emperor Heraclius

Emperor Heraclius had arrived in Homs only a few days prior, returning from his campaign against the Persian armies in Nineveh, a victory which he had not expected. He had made a vow to march from Homs in Syria to Jerusalem in Palestine to honor the success. When Abdullah arrived in Homs, Emperor Heraclius was prepared to embark on his journey with King al-Harith, the son of Abi Shimr of the tribe of Ghassan and ruler of Busra. King al-Harith had travelled to Homs to pay homage to the emperor for his victories in Persia and join the emperor on his triumphal march.

Emperor Heraclius walked with the patriarchs and archbishops in his attendance. He wore a crown and carried a golden scepter which he used as a mock cane, and was dressed in a rich, green, silk robe. King al-Harith and his men preceded the emperor and spread carpets in his path. Abdullah marched with the guards behind the procession. Every soldier that returned from Nineveh was in the procession marching in their detachments. Each battalion had a standard bearer marching in front of them with a banner that bore a silver eagle and a cross. There was one company bearing a golden cross set with rubies and diamonds who marched in circles around the whole procession.

As they passed through each village, the peasants flanked the roads and enjoyed the colorful spectacle. They watched the emperor and his attendants as they walked over the carpets which had been abundantly covered in flowers that gave off a medley of aromatic perfumes. After three weeks of marching, the procession arrived at the Holy City. Jerusalem had been decorated in preparation of the procession's arrival, and all the bishops, and the city's Patriarch had assembled to welcome them with torches and banners in hand, incense hanging by their chains. They greeted the emperor and his company on the outer limits of the city with songs and prayers. The streets of the Holy City were crowded with onlookers and people converged on their roof tops and in their windows as far as the eye could see. The clergy and the choirs from every church were taking part in the celebration by offering prayers of thanks to God for the victory over the Persians. Through all the commotion, Abdullah could not help but notice the traces of battle and age amongst the buildings of the ancient city, or how the ramparts of the city were nearly in ruin. When the entourage arrived at the government house, the guards directed Abdullah to the jail, isolating him there until the next morning.

At the break of dawn, the guards delivered Abdullah with a note from Tha'labah to King al-Harith's audience chamber along with the ring, which the king kept to show to Emperor Heraclius. Abdullah was then confined to his prison cell for nearly a month while waiting for his case to be brought before the emperor, who had to meet with dignitaries from all over the land who had come to congratulate him in his success. His duty to the emperor coming to an end, King al-Harith was becoming eager to return home to Busra and finally turned his attention to the imprisoned Abdullah. King al-Harith asked Emperor Heraclius to hear the charges against Abdullah and decide the man's fate. Abdullah was led by the guards to a large hall near the church which was prepared for the emperor and his council, all of whom were surrounded by armed guards in uniform.

King al-Harith entered first then beckoned for Abdullah to follow him. Abdullah was astounded by the lavish furnishings and opulent decoration of the Roman hall. At the head of the room he saw Emperor Heraclius sitting upon a throne of solid gold, his crown set with precious stones. He wore an elaborate scarf over his shoulders, and held a long, golden rod set with the most beautiful stones with a granite encrusted eagle at the top. Heraclius was an imposing figure, large in stature with a commanding countenance. To his right, the Patriarch of Jerusalem stood in his official attire holding a stately rod, and to his left Sergius the Patriarch of Antioch stood casually observing the room. Flanking these men were the leaders, the clergy, and the council of the Empire, sitting upon gold chairs. The floor of the hall was covered with rugs woven from palm branches and expensive wools. Taken aback by the grandeur at first, Abdullah managed to maintain his calm by recalling the ramparts of the city which had shown him that all the appearances of greatness would wither and nothing remained alive in this world except truth. Had it not been for the ring, such an affair as this would be a trifling matter unworthy of the emperor's attention. So when Abdullah was brought before the great man, the emperor ignored the matter of treason entirely and asked first about the ring.

With King al-Harith interpreting, Heraclius asked while examining the ring, "Where did you get this?"

With his eyes lowered, as if to be engrossed with something on the ground, Abdullah replied, "I found it in the market, and thought it lovely, so I paid its price and bought it for its uniqueness."

"It is highly unlikely, nigh impossible, that a ring such as this could be found in the market," the emperor declared. "Tell me, even if you found it on the street somewhere, would it not be wiser to give it to the owner whose name is scribed within?"

"Sir, if it is correct that this ring belongs to King al-Nu'man III, rest assured that he is long dead. About twenty years, if I had to guess," replied Abdullah.

"Did the Lakhmid King have no sons to give this ring to?" asked the emperor.

Abdullah remained silent.

"Why do you not answer me? You may speak openly, even if you were spying on us, God has granted us victory over the kings of Persia."

"Your victory brought peace with Khosrau III, the King of Persia, and there is no need for spying, as you declared," Abdullah replied. "Your Majesty, pronounce my innocence of being a spy through your own benevolence and we may praise God together."

"We just said that!" barked Emperor Heraclius, "but we are anxious to know how this ring came into your possession. Tell us as well why you have been staying at Busra for so long a time when your supposed vow was to be held on one specific day."

Abdullah kept his head lowered without answering.

"Speak up!" bellowed the emperor. "Heraclius, the Emperor of Rome has asked you a question!"

Aghast at the thunderous blast from the emperor, Abdullah knelt at his feet to kiss them and said, "Your Majesty, I know what you have asked but I cannot say more than I have."

"Then you are hiding something that you will not tell!" declared Heraclius.

"Yes, Sir," said Abdullah, with some resignation.

"What is it that you would hide from your Emperor?" urged Heraclius, "Do you not fear his power? Do you not fear death?"

"I do not think there is a man alive who does not fear death," answered Abdullah humbly, "but I prefer death to revealing this secret."

This stoic resistance intrigued Emperor Heraclius, who mused aloud, "How strange – you say that without fear."

"I am certain, your Majesty," said Abdullah, "that my life or death is nothing more than a whisper from your lips, but I cannot disclose any other information to you."

Turning to the clergy and council, the emperor asked, "What do you have to say about this man's boldness? It fuels a burning curiosity in me to know the secret of the ring!"

The Patriarch of Jerusalem himself turned to Abdullah and urged him to confess, as did the Patriarch of Antioch, but to no avail. Abdullah was adamant and uttered not a word. Emperor Heraclius, frustrated, threatened Abdullah with death and called the executioner to decapitate him. The executioner marched Abdullah to the church courtyard and ordered him to kneel on the ground. As the blow was ready to be felled upon Abdullah's neck, the emperor intervened and ordered the guards to remove the blindfold from Abdullah's eyes. The guards thrust Abdullah on the ground before the emperor, who said, "Do you still insist on this secrecy?"

"I swear by the honor of my Master the Emperor, by God, and His Son, and The Holy Ghost that there is nothing about this ring that is of concern to your Majesty and that this secret is my sacred duty and I must take it to the grave."

Turning around, the emperor asked with some exasperation, "What is to be done? I must know the secret of this ring."

"If your Majesty wishes me to bring some ease to him, I may know of a way," said Abdullah.

"What is it?" Emperor Heraclius inquired.

"We are Christians, your Majesty, and we have a great respect for confessional secrecy. If you wish," Abdullah suggested, "I will confess my secret to the pious Patriarch of Jerusalem on the condition that he may advise you regarding this matter of the ring without relating its story. If he assures you that I speak the truth and that this ring in no way concerns you, would you then pardon me for not revealing it?"

Considering for a moment, the emperor responded, "I have no objection to so reasonable a suggestion."

Then, turning to the Patriarch, he ordered the confession to be held in the church. Remaining for over an hour in the confessional, Abdullah revealed his entire story to the Patriarch. Returning to the hall, Abdullah noticed the guards at the entrance engaged in light conversation with a stranger. The stranger was dressed in desert-dwelling attire with a scarf covering his head and a turban over the scarf. His face, dust-covered and deeply tanned from the sun, showed signs of having traveled widely. Around his waist, hanging to one side, he wore a curved sword, and he bore a large knife and a spear upon his back. As soon as Abdullah took a look at him, he knew that the man was from Hejaz and wondered why he was here. The man's attire was unlike anything in the Holy Land. Abdullah was accompanied by the Patriarch as he entered the hall and stood to one side. Emperor Heraclius addressed the Patriarch, "How did you find the prisoner?"

"He is true in his dialect and story. I believe that he has the right to keep the secret of the ring," the Patriarch declared. "Abdullah divulged all to me and there is nothing about the secret that would touch your Majesty or cause concern for the Roman Empire."

Convinced, but regretful that the secret would remain a mystery, Emperor Heraclius turned to Abdullah, who bowed his head respectfully, and said, "The conditions have been met, and we grant you our pardon." The emperor personally returned the ring to Abdullah and then called upon King al-Harith to write him a note of security.

Muhammad the Lawgiver

Abdullah knelt before the emperor and thanked him before retreating to the door. He was accompanied by King al-Harith who was intent on leading Abdullah back to his quarters to prepare the letter of security. At the entrance to the emperor's hall, however, they were approached by the stranger of the desert whom Abdullah had seen earlier, he was requesting entry to the hall.

"Absolutely not!" declared the king, "state your business here."

"I come bearing a note for the Emperor. It is my duty to deliver it to him," the stranger replied.

King al-Harith took the note and examined it. The paper was plain, and it was sealed with clay. He scrutinized the stranger once more, then ordered him to wait at the entrance. Abdullah found a spot in the crowd to observe unseen while the king returned to the emperor to deliver the note. Abdullah watched the emperor open the missive and study it, but he could not read the writing and gave the note to his interpreter. After a moment, after reading it twice, the interpreter explained that the note was written in the Arabic language, and read as follows:

> *In the name of God, the pitiful and merciful, from Muhammad, the Messenger of God, to Heraclius, the chief among the Romans. Peace be to whosoever turns to guidance. Do join Islam and be saved, you will be rewarded by God twice. Otherwise, you will be held accountable for the sins of all great men.*

A seal was affixed with the signature of Muhammad followed by, "the Messenger of God." The audience hall stood silently aghast at the calm severity of the note. Turning to his council, Emperor Heraclius consulted them, not fully comprehending the purpose of the letter. Never in his life had the emperor heard of such a demand.

"What do we know of this Muhammad, Messenger of God?" the emperor asked his council. No one replied, so the emperor scanned the audience hall and spotted Abdullah whom he beckoned to approach. Abdullah made his way slowly and deliberately then knelt at the emperor's feet.

"Do you know anything about the author of this note?" asked the emperor, handing it to Abdullah.

After reading it, Abdullah said, "Yes, Sir. The sender of this note is a prophet who appeared in Mecca, Hejaz, from a tribe called Quraysh. It is he who called upon the people to worship God, since most of the Arabian tribes have always been idolaters. His family persecuted him for his beliefs and he was spurned by his native city, so he travelled to Yathrib with his followers, seeking refuge. The people of Yathrib helped him, supported him in his time of need, and so his message began to spread across all of Arabia. It seems, your Majesty, that his influence has grown and now the Prophet Muhammad is calling upon you to follow him as well."

The moment of silence before the crowd erupted in speculation was almost serene. Shouts of disdain at so presumptuous a decree came from some in the assembly, and as the opinion began to gather momentum a spokesman declared, "The letter shows great boldness and contempt for our Emperor!" Another agreed, shouting, "This is impermissible!" Frowning in thought, Emperor Heraclius raised his hand to silence the crowd without a word and turned to the Patriarch of Jerusalem for advice.

"There is confidence in this note," said the Patriarch, "which is incomparable. The decree is delivered with calm ease and the author begins first with the mention of his own name and then mentions the name of your Majesty. He already places himself above you, do not underestimate this man."

"Then we must learn more about this prophet and his disciples," declared the emperor. Turning to the council he asked, "Do we know anyone from Mecca or of the Quraysh tribe?"

"I know of an Emir from Mecca named Abu Sufyan who arrived in Gaza to trade," answered King al-Harith. "He may know more about the prophet and his followers."

"Bring him here," the emperor commanded.

"At your order," answered King al-Harith with a bow. "I will bring Abu Sufyan here within several days."

The emperor then turned to Abdullah, "You have earned your pardon and your innocence. If you truly are a friend of Rome as you say, then you will assist King al-Harith. You know the Arabic language and would be of great use to us."

Abdullah bowed, kissing the ground before the emperor, "I am at your service, your Majesty."

Abu Sufyan

As they left the audience hall, Abdullah's thoughts were consumed by regret that he was not yet able to leave and see his son. He was, however, very eager to see Abu Sufyan. Abdullah had met the man when he travelled through Mecca many years ago and wished to hear his account. King al-Harith had sent a detachment to bring Abu Sufyan to Jerusalem. Abdullah decided to go to the monastery to partake of their hospitality until the man had arrived. During his stay in the Holy City, Abdullah roamed the city for some sightseeing and he encountered a great diversity of people, Jews, Assyrians, Egyptians, and more, but it was clear that the Romans were the masters of the city.

On the day of the audience, Abdullah joined King al-Harith and they went together to the Church of the Resurrection. They found there a company of desert-dwellers whom Abdullah recognized as Arabs of Hejaz. Abdullah even recognized a few of the men and then spotted among them a man who was dressed in fine robes, wearing a large turban, who Abdullah knew was Abu Sufyan. He had on a knitted cloak and wore a sword at his side with his head covered in a large turban, while his soldier's heads were bare. Abdullah did not speak as King al-Harith advanced toward Abu Sufyan. He stood up as a show of respect, knowing of King al-Harith's importance, and greeted the king warmly. King al-Harith explained that Abu Sufyan had been summoned to Jerusalem by order of the emperor and that he was requested now for an audience. Abu Sufyan ordered his men to follow. When they arrived at the hall, they were greeted by guards at the door. Abu Sufyan was asked to remain outside and the guards admitted Abdullah and the king. Entering the hall, they approached the emperor and announced Abu Sufyan's arrival. Emperor Heraclius bade King al-Harith to bring the man from Quraysh to him. The king excused himself, but he came back alone explaining that the man would not enter without his sword.

"Let him enter," said the emperor. A moment later, Abu Sufyan entered the hall with his men, all of whom were dazzled by the lavish furniture and decoration of the room. Standing before the emperor Abu Sufyan knelt down, kissed the ground, and spoke his greeting, "God forbid you the curse." With kindness, the emperor asked him to be seated. He did as the emperor directed, but sat on the floor instead with his legs folded. Abu Sufyan removed his sword and set it upon his thighs and then his men sat down behind him. Emperor Heraclius knew this to be their customary way of sitting and addressed Abu Sufyan through an interpreter.

"Who are they?" asked the emperor pointing to Abu Sufyan's entourage.

"They are from the tribe of Quraysh, the Defenders of al-Ka'aba," replied Abu Sufyan.

"What do you mean by al-Ka'aba?" the emperor prompted.

"It is the place of pilgrimage for the people of God," Abu Sufyan answered.

"Do you know the man who calls himself the Prophet Muhammad, the one who appeared among your tribe calling the people to a new religion?" asked Heraclius.

"Yes, I know him, for he is related to me, but I am not interested in his calling," Abu Sufyan said flatly. "He came to us with this new religion of his, but we continue to worship the faith of our fathers. We forbid him to stray from our teachings, but he would not heed us."

"I have a great interest in this man," said Emperor Heraclius, "I would like to know more about his philosophy. Would you tell me about this man and his teachings, and about who he is calling the people?"

"Of course," Abu Sufyan complied. "We have always worshipped the idols of our gods, and it is from our idols that we maintain prosperity, because pilgrims from all over the land come to worship, and during their stay they trade with us. He cursed our idols and evicted them from al-Ka'aba! We have shown him great enmity

ever since, as he has with us, but in the long run he has gained many
supporters. Even though he is illiterate, he attracts the attention of
great learned men and his influence reaches far. He even has
connections with a monk as far as Busra, from what I hear."

Abu Sufyan went on to relate the long story of the Prophet
Muhammad's desecration of their idols and of his tireless endeavor
to spread the word of God all over the world, to spread his belief in
what he calls 'the unseen God who sent him to this world to guide
the people of the Earth.' After Abu Sufyan had revealed all he knew,
Emperor Heraclius thanked the man for his narration and reached
for the note from the Prophet Muhammad, folded it, and put it in a
reed of gold which he presented to Abu Sufyan with a silk robe and
a few pieces of gold.

Abdullah slipped from the hall as soon as Abu Sufyan was
dismissed by Heraclius and approached him in the courtyard. Abu
Sufyan did not remember Abdullah, but Abdullah related to him
how they had met a few years earlier in Mecca. They talked together
and shook hands. When asked where he was going, Abdullah told
Abu Sufyan that he was leaving for Amman.

"The road is very rough and difficult," remarked Abu Sufyan,
"have you ever taken that route before?"

"Yes, many years ago," replied Abdullah.

"Since we have had our introduction, let us travel together,"
offered Abu Sufyan. "Since I will be on my way home to Hejaz, it
would be nice to pass through Amman first. From there I may bid
you farewell. Our caravan is still travelling from Gaza with our
camels, packs, and horses so we will have to wait here for a couple of
days until they arrive before we can depart."

"Most agreeable," said Abdullah, "for I wish to bid King al-
Harith farewell and handle some other business before we depart.
Let us meet again in the church courtyard this evening."

"As you wish," said Abu Sufyan as they parted ways.

Abdullah returned to the audience chamber and ran right into King al-Harith, who happened to be seeking Abdullah out as well. Abdullah offered an excuse when he was asked where he had been.

"Will you come back to Busra with me tomorrow?" asked the king.

Abdullah was at a loss for how to reply, for fear of King al-Harith's annoyance if he were to outright refuse, so he thanked the king and praised his courtesy. Abdullah explained that since he was here, however, he would like to stay a few more days to enjoy the sights of the city before returning to Busra.

"In that case," King al-Harith responded, "where ever you go you shall be under the wing of my protection and the guardianship of our master, the Emperor." At that, King al-Harith presented Abdullah with the promised note of security and bade him farewell. Abdullah walked through the city until it was time to meet Abu Sufyan and then passed a few days in Jerusalem until the caravan arrived. On the third day, the horses were prepared for Abu Sufyan and his men.

"Have you a horse?" asked Abu Sufyan.

"No," answered Abdullah, "my horse was left in Busra."

So Abdullah was given a fine horse to ride compliments of Abu Sufyan, and the pair rode out of the city to meet the caravan.

Hammad's Stallion

They found the caravan just outside the city limits and sat down to rest for a while. Abdullah, though restless, had to show homage to them as their guest. They brought him a choice and swifter horse, outfitted with an expensive saddle. Examining the horse and appraising the saddle, Abdullah's heart started beating rapidly for it looked exactly like Hammad's horse! Approaching the beast he touched the animal between the eyes. The horse was gentle and nuzzled under Abdullah's touch. Abdullah was positive that it was Hammad's steed and he turned and regarded Abu Sufyan, who had been standing and watching what had transpired.

Abu Sufyan asked about the horse's familiarity with Abdullah, who answered, "It is my son's horse, I am sure of it."

"How do you know this?" responded Abu Sufyan.

"He is easily recognizable by his color, his size, and this saddle is unmistakable. We have had him since he was a colt," Abdullah replied. "I owned his mother, and he clearly knows me."

Showing great surprise, Abu Sufyan asked, "Where is your son?"

"The last I knew, he was travelling from Busra to Amman," said Abdullah, beginning to worry. "Where did you find his horse?"

"We found him astray near al-Zarqa," Abu Sufyan said gravely, "the land of the beasts."

Abdullah immediately feared that something horrible had happened. He asked again, "How did you find him?"

"We were coming from Hejaz on our way to Damascus a few weeks ago and were ourselves near al-Zarqa. We saw this horse running wildly and feared for the beasts. My men caught him and brought him to me and we rode him to Gaza, as you can see," explained Abu Sufyan.

Abdullah stood in silent astonishment, overcome with the fear that he may have lost his son. He knew the horse was from good stock and loyal to his master, he would not run unless the master were captured or worse. The tears welled up in Abdullah's eyes and they rolled down his cheeks slowly. Still in control of himself, however, he vowed, "I will not rest until I see the place where you found the horse."

Abu Sufyan nodded. "It is on our way to Amman. If you wish," he added, "my men and I will help you in your search. We are most concerned for you."

Onward they rode, but Abdullah refused to use Hammad's horse. He rode another while Hammad's stallion stayed in the company of Abu Sufyan's caravan. Abdullah uttered not a word, fearing the worst for Hammad. They pressed on for two days and Abdullah refused all food and did not sleep until they had reached al-Zarqa. Abu Sufyan informed the caravan that they were very near the land of the beasts and advised them to set up camp here so that they may leave the loads and camels safely behind while the horsemen moved on into the plain where the horse was sighted. Accompanied by eight riders, Abdullah and Abu Sufyan carried on with caution, fearing an encounter with a lion. After a short while, Abu Sufyan stopped and announced, "This is the place where we first saw your horse."

"Where is the land of the beasts from here?" asked Abdullah.

"It is to the east," answered Abu Sufyan, "we will take you there if you wish."

"Please do," implored Abdullah gratefully, "I cannot leave this land until I know something about my son."

"We will find him," Abu Sufyan reassured Abdullah. Turning to his men, Abu Sufyan instructed them to search the area very thoroughly. They dispersed and a short time later a man returned saying, "I found traces of people near a copse of trees by the river," and pointed out the direction.

Abdullah and Abu Sufyan followed the man until they came to the grouping of trees where they found a dead horse. The only things that remained were his skull, his saddle, and some bones. Abdullah immediately recognized the saddle to be the one belonging to his servant, Salman.

He cried in anguish, "This is the horse of Salman! But where is he? Where is Hammad?" He looked around and saw a cloak that had been torn to shreds that had belonged to his son. He started to sob and pull at his face, succumbing to grief and the fear that his son had been devoured by the beasts. Holding the pieces of cloak tightly against his breast, with tears rolling down his face, he said, "Woe unto me if the lions devoured him!" Unable to stand, he sank to the ground, despair overcoming him. The hearts of Abu Sufyan and his men were greatly touched by the sight of Abdullah's pain.

Abu Sufyan tried to console him by telling him not to fear, that what they had found did not mean that Hammad had been slain. But Abdullah's suffering was so great that he would not listen and kept crying, "Is this the end of your life, my son? I curse the teeth that bit you to crumble into pieces and the claws that tore your flesh to fall from the paws of that beast. Oh! My son, is this how I fail my vow, is this the end of twenty years of waiting?"

Abu Sufyan was deeply troubled with Abdullah's state of mind and he pitied and feared for the man. He sat close to Abdullah and held him in his arms. Abu Sufyan noticed some easing in Abdullah at the reassuring words that his son might still be alive and chose to continue this encouragement.

"There were no human remains, wouldn't we have found his sword and spear?" he suggested. "Surely the lion could not have swallowed them. It is likely your son escaped the lion's pursuit."

"But the horse..." insisted Abdullah.

"Return your mind to the thought that he escaped. Be sensible. And besides, crying will do you no good," Abu Sufyan said resolutely. "It will accomplish nothing, so let us look around and we might uncover what may have been missed."

"You speak the truth, brother," said Abdullah with a deep sigh, "crying will not help my situation. Yet, I fear failure in my search and with it more desperation. So let me weep for my son and kiss his cloak in this desert until I see the lion who devoured him! Either I will avenge myself of the lion or be eaten by him!"

"No!" insisted Abu Sufyan, "Come with us and look the land over."

Seeing that he had little choice, Abdullah reluctantly mounted his horse and joined an exhaustive search that left everyone mentally and physically fatigued with no results to show for their efforts. Abdullah, who had doubts about the search all along, felt compelled to relinquish it and so he thanked Abu Sufyan and his men for their indulgence and begged for it once more as he asked for them to leave.

"I am going to Amman to inquire about my son. Peace be upon you, and I hope to see you someday soon. I will not forget your help," Abdullah remarked, thanking the men once again, shaking their hands as they departed with Abu Sufyan.

On his way to Amman, however, Abdullah crossed paths with a company of Arabian soldiers dressed in Hejazi garb who arrested him and detained him for questioning.

Hammad and Salman

When we last left Hammad and Salman, the two men were enjoying the hospitality of a monastery while deciding whether to make a shortcut through the land of the beasts or to go the long way around. Salman urged for the latter, but Hammad was unconvinced and became determined to take the shortcut.

Salman, fearing the risk involved, advised Hammad, at the very least, to wear the breastplate under his clothes. The two rode on until they reached another part of the river where they dismounted and prepared lunch. Hammad took off his cloak and arms and sat down with them at his side while Salman, fearful of the area, paced around anxiously and surveyed their surroundings. Once they finished their repast, Hammad and Salman pulled their horses behind them and worked their way up a hill to where they could better see their surroundings. Stretching out before them was an expansive plains land that was rambling with hills and sparse copses of trees. They took this to be the land of the beasts.

Suddenly, a roar from far off startled the horses, who began to paw furiously at the dirt.

"We must escape!" yelled Salman. "There is danger here, just as I had feared!"

"Where can we go?" asked Hammad, looking around frantically. Spotting a large tree, Hammad grabbed Salman and led the horses to it, explaining, "We can climb the tree to where the lion cannot follow us!"

Trembling with panic, Hammad and Salman bound their horses to the tree and began climbing, weaving through the branches. The horses whinnied frightfully as the beast approached. Hammad and Salman clung tightly to the branches, hidden amongst the leaves, hoping not to be seen by the lion. A moment later, the beast leapt over the crest of the hill near the horses, sending them into a frenzy to free themselves. Hammad's horse's reins fell lose and the animal bolted straight for the desert. Salman's horse, unfortunately, could not loosen himself before the lion descended upon him.

The beast jumped on the horse's back, biting the neck while its claws ripped at the animal's chest until the horse toppled to the ground. The lion tore at the horse's throat with his fangs and finished his cruel work. The beast let out a fierce roar and then, turning, saw Hammad's cloak hanging between the branches and took a swipe at it, tearing it to shreds. Slowly, he stalked around the tree and circled it with pride, rubbing the trunk vigorously with his back to shake his new prey to the ground. Hammad and Salman held their branches even more tightly, hearts beating rapidly with fear as their branches waved to and fro. The lion occupied them until nightfall, pacing and roaring loudly, feasting on the horse. When night fell, and hid Hammad and Salman in the darkness, the lion left the tree for the plains, and he continued to roar until finally disappearing over the hillside. Hammad and Salman did not move until sunrise, and praised God for his mercy when they reached the ground.

They surveyed the carnage that the lion had wrought upon the horse and Salman turned to Hammad and said, "We will have to carry on to Amman on foot. It seems to be God's will that we have no means of transport but ourselves."

"I am unarmed," said Hammad, "we should go down to the river and retrieve my sword and spear."

Salman shook his head, "We left them farther behind us than you think. All these hills look alike and I cannot remember which leads to where we took our rest. We should leave now." Hammad reluctantly agreed and they set out for Amman. They arrived in Amman two days later and then stayed quietly for a month waiting to for news of Abdullah. When his father failed to arrive, Hammad became troubled with despair and frustration, and he ordered Salman to buy two horses.

They rode for Busra, taking the long way around the plains to avoid the attention of the beasts. Likewise, they slipped into the city unseen and unannounced to avoid the attention of Tha'labah.

Hind and Her Mother

On the night of the ambush at Bahira, Hind returned to the Stream Palace to find her mother in a very anxious state over the lateness of her arrival. Hind argued defensively, blaming her mother for the delay of her servant with the bracelets. Queen Saada became earnestly concerned, replying that the jewelry had been approved and the servant was sent back with orders to hasten Hind's return. Hind shook her head and told her mother that she had waited until nightfall without the servant's return, so she enlisted the help of one of the monastery's servants to bring her home. Believing Hind's story, Queen Saada apologized and suggested that perhaps the servant went back in the wrong direction and would hopefully return soon. Feigning exhaustion, Hind went straight to her room, anxious and fearful of Tha'labah's treachery. She passed the night sleepless and finally dozed off toward daybreak.

Later that morning Hind learned of the capture of Abdullah and the escape of Hammad. The good news about Hammad did nothing to quiet her anxieties, however, and Queen Saada worried about her daughter. Hind would not eat anything and did not seem to be sleeping. She passed her illness off as fatigue from her time spent at Bahira, but the queen remained concerned, dubious of this excuse. As the days passed from one to the next Hind continued to get thinner and more pallid without any real explanation why. Queen Saada was determined to find out the cause of this noticeable change in Hind, but her daughter would not tell the truth. Then, King Jabalah approached the queen one day and told her that King al-Harith had just come to him with a proposal to betroth the Hind to Tha'labah. Queen Saada hoped that the weight of this news would draw out the problem that was causing her daughter's malaise and bring to light the heavy burden that was hanging over her.

The next morning, Queen Saada asked Hind if she would like to enjoy a picnic and Hind agreed. The queen ordered the servants to prepare a light lunch for them to bring along. Hind wove her hair into a thick braid that hung straight down her back and then fashioned a scarf around her head to give the appearance of suffering from a headache. She walked in silence and with an easy stride. The train of her dress was dragging the earth behind her, occasionally giving Hind an excuse to fuss with the hem to protect it from thorns, and she would often stop to casually observe the birds fly from tree to tree. Late in the afternoon they settled in a pleasant pasture under a shady tree, and Hind relaxed on a carpet and leaned against a pillow made of silk and embroidered with lace. Queen Saada gathered a bouquet of mixed flowers and handed them to Hind, who said nothing.

With a whimsical smile the queen said, "Accept these flowers, for I have hidden a meaning within them. Do you know what it is?"

Hind accepted them without comment, and instead admired their color and perfume.

"Why do you not answer my question?" asked Queen Saada.

"Ask me a question and you will get an answer," replied Hind.

"I asked you and you answered with nothing!" the queen remarked.

"How could I answer without speaking?" Hind countered.

"Then you did answer!" Queen Saada replied, raising her voice.

Hind sighed and said, "You asked me nothing and so I answered nothing."

"Taking the flowers from my hand was an answer," her mother said irately.

"Well, I did not understand you, mother," Hind offered, "please explain."

"I asked a question in my heart, and offered it to you in the flowers. If you accepted them it would have answered my question," Queen Saada answered.

"Why do you still use tokens?" asked Hind, somewhat vexed. "I did not say anything."

"Well, never mind," said her mother. "I want to ask you another question and hope you will tell me the truth with a straight answer."

"Of course I will, mother," Hind sighed.

"Do you love your cousin Tha'labah?" the queen asked directly.

Hind blushed and then turned pale after hearing the question. She said nothing.

"You promised to answer," Queen Saada reminded her.

"I do not see any reason for your question," said Hind. "You know what my relationship is to Tha'labah. I do not understand your intentions."

"Why do we still joke? I ask you again," said the queen firmly, "and speak plainly! Do you love Tha'labah?"

Hind collected herself and continued to ignore the fact that she understood the real meaning of her mother's question. "Is it not enough that he is my cousin and I love him because of that, even if he is not worthy of it?"

"Does your love for him go deeper than the bonds of blood?" the queen pursued. Again, Hind did not answer. Queen Saada moved to sit next to her daughter and asked softly, taking her by the hand, "Why do you not answer me, your father wants me to bring him your answer, what shall I tell him?"

Hind shifted her position and looked at her mother with astonishment. "Tell me plainly, mother, what do you mean by asking me if I love that mean man in spite of my will?"

Dismayed, Queen Saada finally understood the enormity of the hatred that Hind held in her heart for Tha'labah. The queen had noticed it before, but chose to ignore it to allow Hind's opinion to grow unbiased on its own. "Do not be so hasty in attacking your cousin, for he may yet be of closer relation than that," she warned her daughter.

Showing her distaste, the flowers falling from her hand, Hind looked at her mother accusingly, saying, "I do not want you to injure my feelings, so I tell you now that Tha'labah has no place in my heart. You know this, so why do you keep up this absurdity?"

"No, my daughter," Queen Saada sigh, "I am not being absurd. Your Uncle al-Harith has approached your father about a betrothal, and he expects an answer. What shall we tell him?"

Taken aback and speechless, Hind could only stare at her mother in disbelief.

"I mean everything I say," her mother continued, solemnly.

Hind, without commenting, rose to her feet and collected the flowers. Her mother, understanding Hind's behavior, pretended to ignore it to discover the cause of Hind's crossness the night she returned from the Monastery. So she persisted, "Why do you keep busy to avoid answering me, does your silence mean my question is not worthy of a reply?"

Anguished, Hind laid her head upon her mother's breast and kissed her hand, blushing at the rebuke. She said, "God forbid, mother, I would never suggest that, but your insistence does surprise me, knowing as you do that I want to get rid of the old ties that bind to forge new ones."

"I take it you have chosen another, then?" her mother asked softly. Hind did not reply, but her face turned a deep shade of red. Keeping her smile hidden, Queen Saada persisted, asking, "Why do you still not answer me? I see your face talking and your eyes confessing, so why does your tongue keep quiet?"

Thinking about her beloved, and picturing the harm that Tha'labah could have done to him, Hind became greatly touched and tears welled up in her eyes. She turned away from her mother to hide her feelings, pretending to watch a deer loping through the hills. The misdirection was unsuccessful, however, and Queen Saada saw her opportunity to uncover her daughter's malaise.

"Why do you turn your face from me, Hind?" she inquired gently, "Are you hiding something from me?"

Hind kept her face averted and wished to be alone to weep. This unnatural behavior on her part made her mother quite sure that something very serious was bothering Hind. What Queen Saada had not prepared for was that it was breaking her heart as well. She took her daughter by the hand and endeavored to draw her closer, but Hind disengaged herself and covered her face with her sleeve to hide her weeping.

"Why, Hind! What makes you cry, my child?" the queen asked with concern, "am I right in my imagination?"

Hind sobbed deeply, trying vainly not to let her mother hear her cries, until her sleeve was soaked with tears and she was unable to control her feelings.

"So there is someone who turns your mind away from Tha'labah," the queen remarked.

Hind went mute and buried her face in her sleeve again to hide the blush that rapidly over took her. Queen Saada stopped provoking her daughter and wondered who it could be that preoccupied her daughter's thoughts with such severity. She also feared that more insistence may make Hind too timid to finally confess the truth.

"I am your mother, my child," the queen said, "you may tell me all you hold secret and fear not for what you have hidden in your heart. Your cousin cannot touch a hair on your head and even though your father may accept him, I will not!" She hugged Hind reassuringly and kissed her tenderly. "Confide in me, Hind," Queen Saada gently urged.

Soothed by her mother's words, Hind's trepidation faded and she lifted her head and looked at her mother, her eyes swollen with tears from a heartache too shy to talk of. She lowered her head to her mother's breast once more. Queen Saada took her face in both hands and asked once more, "Tell me, dear, do you love somebody?"

With a deep, penetrating sigh, Hind nodded back in silent resignation, for it was the truth.

"Who is the man whose love goes so deeply into your heart that it controls your will like this?" Queen Saada asked. "Your father and I have always known you to be more courageous than men!"

"It does not matter," said Hind, lowering her head again, "I am in love with someone, but I wish to rid myself of this world for I have been so miserable since the day I was born!" she cried, dramatically falling to tears once more.

Near heartbreak, Queen Saada hugged her, asking "What kind of talk is that, are you in such despair over the one you love?"

"Yes, mother," answered Hind with courage, "I am so miserable, weep for me!"

"What could be the cause of your misery? You are the Daughter of Ghassan, the flower of this country," her mother said with pride. "You are the envy of all."

"What do they envy me for?" asked Hind with a tearful voice.

Queen Saada, saddened for her daughter, tried soothing her by saying, "Tell me your troubles and I will help. Rest assured, my child, for your cousin will never be able to touch you."

Gritting her teeth at the mention of Tha'labah, Hind finally answered, "That man is the cause of my misery. Do you think he proposes because he loves me?"

"Why then, otherwise?" asked Queen Saada.

"He does it to wreak havoc on the noble man who saved his life," answered Hind, "a man who has nothing but generosity for all."

Like a flash of lightning, Queen Saada remembered the race and the unselfish nobility of Hammad and was struck with surprise. She had been blind and only now realized the true cause of her daughter's odd behavior. Hind was in love with Hammad. She felt dumbstruck and could not reply. Not only was the young man a stranger, but the queen also knew of the story of Hammad's flight from custody and of the arrest of his father, Abdullah, who had been charged with treason. The queen was troubled, but she was not disdainful at the mention of the young man. On the contrary her recollections of his conduct left Queen Saada feeling at ease, his character was exemplary. And yet she still felt a touch of strangeness at the thought of Hind's love for him.

Hind observed her mother closely to discover what, if anything, she was thinking about Hind's last remark. Queen Saada was still silent, so Hind said, "Did I not tell you that I was miserable? Yet the mere mention of the cause of my misfortune leaves you pitiless and perplexed!"

"No, darling, I promised you my support and I will honor that promise but I received this astonishing news without expectation. Hammad is a very generous and noble man, you have known of my opinion of him since our conversation after the race. Hind, do you really love this man?" the queen asked softly.

Hind's continued silence confirmed Queen Saada's suspicion. But the queen still repressed her astonishment because she considered the matter of her daughter's wedding to the stranger very seriously. She knew nothing of his heritage not to mention that he was now a fugitive charged with treason in connection with his father. There was also the anger of King al-Harith and Tha'labah toward the young man. It seemed to Queen Saada that, with all these complications, if Hind were to persist in her devotion to this man, it would surely bring about a severance of blood ties between her husband and his cousin. She certainly could not confide her thoughts and fears to Hind without worsening her daughter's depression, so she decided to be lenient with Hind of her feelings. In the meantime the queen decided to discover the full extent of Tha'labah's campaign against Hammad. So she said to her daughter, "Hammad is worthy of your love, but how did he reach so deeply into your heart? He is a stranger and so distant from us…"

Hind interrupted her mother and sobbed, "Did I not tell you that I already know my fate for I know what is hovering in your mind! But what is the use of it all? Hammad has disappeared to God knows where, perhaps already victim to the treachery of Tha'labah!"

"Do not be impatient, my child," said the queen consolingly, "for God is against the tyrant and I am indeed surprised at Tha'labah. Why should he have set a trap for this young man when there is no affiliation between them?"

"It is his wicked jealousy and meanness, and by God, that traitor is not worthy to walk in Hammad's shoes!" Hind exclaimed, drying her eyes.

Queen Saada wished to know more about when this love began, so she asked Hind, "How could you deliver your heart into the arms of a man whose ancestry you know nothing about? This is a serious matter, Hind. You cannot judge one's ancestry by their looks, my child."

"I know that he is an Emir of Iraq and that is enough! Even if he were not, he has controlled my feelings through the power of God and that is what lies in my heart," Hind proclaimed, lowering her head in modesty despite her heart bursting with cheer as her mother's expression softened.

"How do you know his ancestry?" her mother asked.

Hind became aware of her inadvertent slip of the tongue. She grasped her mother's hand and kissed it, saying, "I beg your pardon, for I have sinned against you."

"What you do you mean?" asked Queen Saada.

Hind related the story of her meeting at the monastery and confessed what happened between her and Hammad. Her mother listened intently to the tale, and after hearing the full account of Tha'labah's treachery, promised to aid Hind however she could. Hind became tranquil after hearing her mother's promise, but still feared for Hammad. The sun had begun to set, so they rose from their carpets and slowly walked home, each deep in their own thoughts. Hind wrapped her arms around her mother's shoulders and asked, "Tell me mother, how are we to stop Tha'labah from setting more traps for Hammad?"

"Be at ease, my daughter, and take comfort knowing that I will guarantee his escape," the queen promised. "Let us have patience for now so that we can find out what has happened to Hammad." Queen Saada wanted to placate her daughter even though she had doubts of his being found alive. She struggled within herself more and more as she thought about the grave consequences of her daughter's humble acceptance of the love of a stranger. She also held herself accountable for being easily swayed in the matter.

Queen Saada sincerely hoped that Hammad was still alive. She relaxed slightly and continued to soothe Hind's anxiety until they arrived back at the palace. The first thing that the queen set out to do the following day was to find out what had happened with Hammad and his father. It took her a few days, but she finally learned of Abdullah's pardon by the emperor and his certificate of security. Queen Saada brought this happy news to Hind, who joyfully looked forward to telling Hammad when he was found.

The Caller of Bahira Monastery

Weeks had passed when one day while Hind was sitting in her room worrying about Hammad, she thought she heard a voice coming from the courtyard below calling the name of Bahira. Looking through her window, Hind saw a horseman wrapped in a cloak with a monk-like hat on his head clenching a silver cross in his hand. He looked like the monk who came by every year calling to collect alms for Bahira Monastery. When she heard the monastery's name, her emotions began to stir within her as memories of her true love and the conversation they had flooded back. She saw the caller as a good omen, this monk roamed the land in his duty, so she wished to talk to him to see if there were any news concerning Hammad. She sent one of her servants to bring him to her and within a few moments the man entered, bearing a saddlebag in his hand. He greeted the princess and offered his cross for her to kiss and then sat down on a cushion, placing the saddlebag to his side. Hind looked at the monk and saw that he was not the same man who usually came every year.

"Where are you from, father?" asked Hind.

"I have travelled from Busra to collect the alms," he said.

"Have you collected many, father?" she asked.

"Yes, Mistress, the faithful have made more vows this year than in the past, for my saddlebag is full," he shook it to demonstrate its heaviness, the rattle of iron resounding.

"What manner of alms are you collecting that they are made of iron, father?" Hind asked, the sound catching her interest.

"I have gathered many inconspicuous items," he answered with a smile that suggested something more.

"How did you come by iron though, alms are usually paid in silver, gold and precious stones are they not?" Hind inquired, perplexed by his answer.

"This is my first time collecting vows. I have never done it before, but I think that I have worked wonders," he proclaimed.

Hind then noticed that his accent was forced, but she was more curious about the secret which the monk had just hinted to her. "What are these wonders of yours that you collect vows like no one before you?" she asked him inquisitively.

"I have redeemed a vow to the monastery never before collected upon, not because it is precious and valuable, but because it is very unique," he explained as he untied the saddlebag. He lifted a large wrapped object out of the bag and uncovered it for Hind to see. Hind turned pale and gasped in shock, instantly recognizing Hammad's breastplate! She stared at the monk in disbelief, his gaze averted and the suggestive smile still upon his lips.

"Who gave this to you?" Hind demanded.

"The owner did, Mistress," replied the monk.

"Do you know the owner's whereabouts? This breastplate was taken from my family!" Hind exclaimed eagerly.

Turning to her, he replied, "I do not think its owner is a thief, Mistress. I know him to be a faithful man, and he has paid a high price for his vow."

"Perhaps he is as you say," Hind said, "but I know this breastplate belonged to my family, I must meet the man who gave it to you. Is he close by?"

"He is very near," the monk reassured her with a smile, "and, if I am not mistaken, you know that he did not steal this breastplate."

Hind realized that this monk knew more about her and Hammad than he was letting on. Ignoring his last remark, a deep blush flashing across her face, she said, "I see that you talk nonsense!"

"No, Mistress!" he insisted. "I am certain of it, you wear your confession upon your face."

Hind was overjoyed at the thought of Hammad being nearby, but her vivid imagination could not shake the fear of Tha'labah's treachery, and so she suspected deception. "Please explain to me what you are talking about," she requested. "I do not understand you, perhaps you are mistaken in your imagination!"

"I am not mistaken at all, and if you still doubt what I say, ask the bracelets, they will tell you the truth," instructed the monk with a grin.

"What bracelets do you mean?" Hind inquired.

"I mean the bracelets that were purchased at the monastery, it is for the same vow that the breastplate was given as alms," the monk answered. "I can fetch the merchant of the jewels himself, if you like."

Hind was taken aback and asked to be excused for a moment. She stood up and went directly to her mother and told her everything that had just occurred. Hind asked her mother to come meet the monk for herself but cautioned her not to reveal anything until they were sure of the monk's true purpose. The queen followed Hind through the door and as she approached, the monk stood up to greet her respectfully.

With reserved composure, Queen Saada asked, "Did you come from Bahira Monastery?"

"No, Mistress, I have come from Busra," he replied.

"Show me the breastplate," the queen demanded.

Queen Saada recognized the armor immediately as Hammad's prized breastplate, and took it from the monk, declaring, "This breastplate was bestowed upon a noble man by the King himself. Do you know the one to whom this belongs?"

Smiling with a hint of skepticism, the monk answered, "I think I do."

"Where did your paths part?" asked Queen Saada.

"I left him in one of the villages of Busra a few hours ride from here."

"Is he staying there or is he travelling on?" the queen asked.

"He awaits my return, your Majesty," the monk explained.

"Why would he await your return if he bestowed this breastplate upon you to fulfill a vow?" asked Queen Saada. "I find you are talking contrary to what you said before."

"Nothing contrary, Mistress, for the owner of this breastplate made a condition that the vow would not be consummated until I returned the breastplate to him along with news regarding a matter that greatly concerns him," the monk explained, and turning, he gave Hind a sidelong glance as if he expected something from her.

Seeing her face brighten, he smiled, and his eyes flashed her a curious look as if to ask, "Shall I reveal our secret in the presence of your mother?"

The queen asked the monk to wait outside of the room so that she could speak with Hind alone. When they called him back in, Queen Saada looked at the monk in a straightforward manner and requested that he speak plainly about his business and ask what he wanted to know. Hind concurred, so the monk reached into his saddlebag once more and revealed the matching gambeson and said, just to be sure, "If you do not know the man on whom you bestowed this garment, then what I am about to tell you will be in vain."

Hind's heart skipped a beat at the sight of the padded jacket, and she blushed a deep crimson as she replied, "Yes, we know him, please, tell us his name!"

"His name is Hammad," said the monk.

The maiden's mood took a cheerful turn and the monk was pleased to see the joy on her face. He waited for a reply, which she returned with a question, "Tell the truth, where is he now?"

"He is in hiding, not daring to reveal himself for reasons we all seem to be aware of," the monk replied gravely, with a bow to Queen Saada.

"Then tell us who you are," she asked, "for I still do not believe you are a monk."

Taking the tall hat off his head, he bowed again and said, "I do not think you know me, Mistress. I am your servant Salman, retainer for my master Hammad."

The revelation enlivened both mother and daughter and Hind began questioning him about Hammad and what had happened to them. Salman related their troubles in great detail and explained that he had come in disguise and left his master in much anxiety over the well-being of his father and his beloved Hind.

"Did you not get the glad news about your master, Emir Abdullah?" inquired Queen Saada cheerfully.

"No, Mistress!" he exclaimed. "Please, tell me the news."

The queen happily explained, "We have learned that the Emperor pardoned him and gave him a certificate of security."

This was wonderful news for Salman and he wished the ability to fly so he could inform Hammad immediately. He requested from the queen to take his leave and was told to make haste with the good news to Hammad.

"Tell him to be at rest concerning Hind and that I send my regards. And Salman, beware," she warned, "let no one know that you have come here. Tell Hammad to look for his father and we shall send news whenever we have any."

Pleased and satisfied, Salman placed the hat on his head, collected his bag, and bid them both farewell.

Queen Saada now saw the full consequences of her indulgence with Hind. Hammad was still alive and she now had to carry out her promise to help the two lovers. Only now did she realize how serious this matter had become. She pictured the trouble that would erupt between her husband and his cousin King al-Harith should they reject Tha'labah's proposal, not to mention the tension that existed between Tha'labah and Hind's beloved Hammad. Remembering the treachery of Tha'labah and Hind's loathing for him, however, Queen Saada quickly strengthened her resolve and saw that she was righteous in her support of her daughter regardless of the hardships ahead.

Hind, seeing the troubled look on her mother's face, welled up with despair and ran to her room to cry, certain that her mother only dealt tenderly with her on the outside. Queen Saada followed her in frustration, but put her own anxieties aside when she entered the room and looked on her daughter with pity. She smiled as she approached Hind, who was looking to her for reassurance. Hind recognized the indulgence and sympathy, and lowered her eyes without speaking.

"Why are you still anxious, my child? Are you not pleased with the news about Hammad?" she asked. Hind gave no reply, so Queen Saada put her arm around her daughter and asked, "Why are you silent, my child? Are you not thankful to God for his grace?"

"I have thanked him reverently over and over but I cannot see the end of my misery! Whenever my hopes are lifted, I am thrown again into sorrow," cried Hind.

"What makes you sorrowful?" her mother asked.

"What I read in your face makes me grieve," said Hind standing before the mirror, untying her braid.

The queen became overwhelmed by her maternal tenderness and hardened her resolve to support Hind in every possible way. "Lock your doubts away, my dear daughter, I am as you want me," was her reply.

Pleased with what she heard, Hind teased, "You are mocking me, mother!"

Queen Saada laughed heartily saying, "How typical of young lovers, your moods are never restful!"

With a sly glance, Hind studied her mother and let her unbound hair cascade, falling through her fingers. Seeing her mother laugh she smiled, hope returning to her once more. She turned to the mirror and busily braided her hair again.

"Let me finish your braid, we have something more important yet to discuss today," Queen Saada said, approaching her daughter.

"It is absurd that there would be something more important," mocked Hind.

"Why?" Queen Saada asked, "Is it absurd to rid ourselves of Tha'labah's demands?"

Hind cringed in detest at the name, crying out, "Would it be to God!"

Queen Saada took Hind by the hands, forced her to sit on the bed, and looked deeply into her eyes. Hind understood that her mother meant to take serious action so she listened carefully.

"Let us discuss this matter with a far-sighted approach," stated Queen Saada.

"Say what you will, mother, but remember your promise. I cannot lose sight of your neglect in discovering the state of Hammad's well-being," Hind proclaimed.

"As you say," the queen consented. "I congratulate you and my help is yours, but we have to use our wisdom in order not to do harm to the interests of your father."

"Then do you want me to accept Tha'labah?" asked Hind, frightened.

"No! I will never give my consent to Tha'labah but we have to proceed slowly and wisely," Queen Saada cautioned.

"I will leave everything to you, mother," said Hind, kissing her.

Queen Saada returned her daughter's affection, as yet unsure how she ought to proceed.

The Search for Abdullah

Hammad was hiding securely in quarters not far from Busra, impatiently awaiting Salman's return. When Salman arrived, they greeted each other and Hammad asked Salman if there was any news of his father. Salman's encouraging smile foretold of the favorable news and he informed Hammad of the amnesty granted to his father and of the strength of Hind's love for him, complete with Queen Saada's consent. Hammad was greatly overjoyed by the turn of events, but his thoughts still lingered on his father. He consulted Salman about a search and they both agreed it was the right thing to do, but where would they start?

"Remain here and let me go alone to our home in Ghasam," Salman offered, "perhaps I can gather some information."

"What did you have in mind?" asked Hammad.

"I want to return to the house to look for our valuables. If they are not there, then perhaps my master has already collected them. I will then begin to look for him throughout Busra and its suburbs," Salman explained, "otherwise, if I find them, then it is likely that he is still in the Holy City where I would then head to continue my search."

Hammad approved of Salman's plan, and the two prepared to part ways. In the morning, Salman mounted his horse, disguised as a monk once again, and departed. Two days later, however, Salman returned with the treasure of precious gold, silver, and antiques which they had left hidden at their home. Salman's face indicated that he had no luck picking up Abdullah's trail in Busra.

"I worry that Tha'labah has been up to no good," Salman said worriedly, "he may yet have set a trap for my master after the pardon."

"I fear you may be right, Salman," agreed Hammad.

"In Busra, I learned that the pardon was issued more than a fortnight ago from Jerusalem, and that my master left the Holy City in the company of a caravan which was heading to Hejaz," Salman said.

"Do you think he really might have gone with the caravan?" asked Hammad. "How conceivable is it that he had gone to Hejaz when we had planned to meet in Amman?"

"He might have accompanied the caravan to the outskirts of Amman and then finished the trip alone to the city," Salman theorized.

"He must realize, though, that the time for our meeting has long since passed, in fact, nearly two months have passed since we departed," reasoned Hammad. "Maybe he wished to pass through Amman in order to be sure that we had left, and reassured of that, he might return to Ghasam. Let us wait for a while to find out."

Salman said nothing but still feared for the safety of his master, so he appeared convinced for the sake of Hammad's peace of mind.

The owner of the house they were staying in, who always seemed around, left for Busra on an errand, so Hammad and Salman took the opportunity to discreetly secure their valuables. They quickly stuffed the treasure in their pockets and other items of clothing and began the search for a safe location as if carrying bundles of clothes to be laundered.

The King's Arrival

When we last left Hind, she was filled with the hopes and dreams of Hammad being hers, but shades of doubt continued to intrude upon her thoughts. Tenacious as ever, Hind's intuition and intelligence uncovered her mother's concerns regarding the king's acceptance of Hammad. Queen Saada had to repeatedly remind herself that she must keep her promise to Hind in the face of constant opposition from her inner conscience.

One day while they were visiting the Stream Palace, one of the queen's servants announced a visitor from al-Balqa. Making haste, Queen Saada met with the man as he was dismounting his horse. As he drew near to her, he kissed her outstretched hand and she recognized him as one of her husband's attendants.

"My master, King Jabalah, sends you his regards and asks me to announce his arrival on the morrow," he declared graciously.

"He is welcome," Queen Saada replied, "we will prepare to receive him." Returning to the palace, Queen Saada began to dread, for she knew that the visit was to discuss the matter of the betrothal between Hind and Tha'labah. She suddenly felt a cloud of gloom settle over her at the thought of how soon she would face the consequences of her support for Hind and Hammad. While she agonized, Hind came and stood in the doorway to ask about the horseman, even though she had already guessed the reason for his arrival.

Hind's heart beat faster as she approached her mother's room, doubts about her mother's resolve were already crushing her hopes and she half expected to find her mother's embarrassment. Aware of her mother's fondness for solitude, Hind nevertheless entered the room and saw her mother's frustration knit upon her brow, worsening Hind's fears. As she approached her mother, the queen changed her expression and endeavored to smile at Hind to hide the turmoil that was raging within.

Hind spoke with a choked voice, and asked, "Do not be so troubled mother, what could be so terrible that you seem so upset?"

"My child," said Queen Saada, "I feel ill."

"I am the cause of your illness!" Hind cried despairingly.

"No! God forbid, you are my delight, the source and the growth of my happiness. Do you not see how more relieved I am since you came in?" consoled her mother.

"Yes, I saw your smile," said Hind, "but I also see that you felt obliged to, there is no need for embarrassment or strain in concealing it." She was testing her mother's resolve, knowing full-well that her future depended upon this meeting.

"Why do you address me with hints," asked her mother, "are you not certain that I will stand by my promise?"

"I never doubted that, but I see that I have caused you a great deal of trouble," said Hind.

"Your trouble is my rest," the queen reassured her, "so dispel your doubts and let us plan a course of action. Your father is coming tomorrow and be assured he will bring up the subject of Tha'labah."

"What are you going to say to him? You know what is in my heart, so let your reply be as your wisdom finds best," Hind stated. "As for me, if I am asked I will be replying in the negative."

"Your father will surely ask your reasons for refusing," cautioned Queen Saada. "Shall I mention Hammad?"

"I do not know what you should say on my behalf, mother, but you know all that my heart desires and you promised to honor that," Hind declared, "so say what is best."

The queen remained silent, lost in thought, so Hind took her leave. Queen Saada then resolved once more to follow the road her daughter has chosen, and leaving her room, she directed the servants to prepare tents and ready the butchered livestock for King Jabalah's reception and the meals for the king and his entourage the next day.

The following morning at the Stream Palace was a flurry of activity while servants carried out their chores to prepare for the King. Queen Saada and Hind dressed in their most elaborate robes, richly embroidered in flattering hues. Excitement was high, and late in the morning dust could be seen from the direction of al-Balqa. Queen Saada stood by an open window peering at the plain while Hind reclined on her bed. Hind's whole body trembled as she imagined her father's angered reaction when he learns of the trouble his Hind has caused. She soon heard the rattling sounds of the chains on the horses in the courtyard indicating her father's arrival. Summoning what bravery she could, Hind rose from bed and peered out the window at the horsemen below who were now entering their tents.

King Jabalah dismounted outside the park and made his way to the palace. He wore a scarf wrapped around his head that was decorated with a finely twisted ikal, and a short jacket and lavish cloak topped his elegantly flowing robes. He smiled at the queen as they greeted each other and noticed that her face showed signs of depression as he drew nearer. When he saw his daughter he kissed and hugged her joyfully. The king was surprised at the leanness in Hind's face and asked her what the reason might be. Queen Saada explained that Hind was suffering an acute ailment as she escorted her husband into the hall, walking with him hand in hand. The main hall had been decorated with the finest carpets and cushions, and pleased by the efforts of the servants, the three sat down on pillows together.

The king sat at the front of the room and led Hind by the hand to sit beside him. A feeling of sympathy awakened in him as he looked at his daughter's unhappy face, and as soon as the three were alone King Jabalah questioned the two about Hind's health. They reassured him that it was not serious and urged him to change from his traveling clothes and take a rest. Queen Saada could see a distant melancholy in her husband's face which she had never seen before, and Hind was the least of his worries. The queen made up her mind to find out the cause before dinner, but this was not to be, for the king decided to take a tour of the rooms for an inspection and then went to the stable to check his horses. Queen Saada noticed that the king was keeping himself unusually busy in order to avoid her inquiries. When evening came they sat down for supper together but everyone sat silently, each lost in their own worries with nothing to talk about except the particular manner in which the food had been prepared.

When the meal was finished, their guests cleared the hall while the servants busied themselves with clearing away the dishes and left the king alone with his wife and daughter. King Jabalah leaned against his cushion with Hind at his side and Queen Saada in front of him. Examining Hind's face, he said, "We have been absent from you for a long time because some important matters kept us busy, and while I promised myself I would return to you a few days ago I could not finalize those matters until today. I thought coming here would relieve my gloom, but I find myself more depressed than I was before."

Extending herself forward, the queen said, "There is nothing about Hind that should make you feel sad, everyone is subject to illness from time to time, but I have seen a look of dispirit in your face since your arrival this morning. I thought I might have been mistaken, but since you acknowledge this depression I hope you will talk to us about it."

"My depression is nothing for you to worry about, it is only accidental," the king explained.

"Anything of such importance to you has the same importance to us. No matter what the problem could be, we cannot rest if we do not know what it is," implored Queen Saada.

"Let us not talk about it," the king replied wearily, "it might be a summer cloud that may soon drift away."

But the Queen's curiosity was peaked, and she could tell that he had heard some news which caused him this uncertainty, so she pried further, "I can only suppose that you are not sure about it, so why not confide in us."

"A man from Hejaz," the king sighed, "came and told us that an Arabian army was on its way to wage war with us."

"Why would they have done that?" asked the queen. "There has been nothing amiss between our nations to cause this breech!"

"Well, as you know, Saada," said King Jabalah, "those Muslim soldiers are a strong group led by the Prophet Muhammad. He sent a man with a note to the Holy City calling us to his new religion. Later, he sent another messenger to Damascus and my cousin, al-Harith, tore the missive to shreds, insulting the bearer and the sender, plunging us into this catastrophe. Yesterday al-Harith approached me with this news and we had a lengthy discussion about it."

When Queen Saada heard about the meeting between King al-Harith and her husband she became certain that something was said about Hind. Knowing that he would not discuss the matter of their daughter in her presence, Queen Saada pretended as though she was making ready to retire for the night so that she and King Jabalah could speak privately. Hind, falling for the ruse, also took her leave and retired for the night.

The Disclosure

Queen Saada sat on the king's bed as he stretched out to relax. The room was softly lit with candles and the night was quiet, a calm prevailed over the palace.

"I asked you to speak with Hind several days ago and I need an answer," King Jabalah began. "al-Harith has approached me again about the betrothal and wishes us to make haste with the wedding of the young couple before the arrival of the warring soldiers."

Queen Saada remained silent, now facing the full difficulty of her situation.

"Why do you not reply?" King Jabalah asked. "Is there something I should know about?"

"I do not know," said Queen Saada. "But I know that Hind's health did not improve after I mentioned it."

"What did she say?" he asked.

"She said nothing," the queen replied.

"Then she has accepted him?" King Jabalah asked again.

"Silence is not always the sign of acceptance," cautioned the queen.

"What then?" the king asked with some surprise. "Did you take it to mean she refused?"

"I do not know," she said, "maybe I am mistaken."

Showing bewilderment toward her behavior, the king said, "Mistaken about what? Explain. Hesitation in this matter could bring great danger."

"What danger do you fear?" she asked.

"Are you not aware that the refusal of this question will bring on an unsavory predicament between our family and al-Harith?" the king replied indignantly.

Ignoring his intonation, she said, "What has the one matter to do with the other? Is marriage compulsory?"

King Jabalah sat upright in his bed, quite perplexed, and asked, "Has Hind become so wayward that she refuses what her parents have chosen for her?"

"Do not say 'parents'," the queen corrected, "say her 'father' only!"

With a caustic stare, he shouted, "Are you tolerating her rudeness, Saada?!"

"No!" she replied, tears in her eyes. "I am not tolerating her rudeness, but I fear for her life, and if you are willing to endure that, to make her the victim of that man, then so be it, proceed with the marriage!"

Utter disbelief swelled within him as he listened to his wife's words. He gathered himself and said, "What do you mean, Saada? Are you sure of what you are saying?"

"I didn't bring it up before but I am certain now after a long discussion with Hind, and if you do not believe me, call her and talk to her face to face," offered Queen Saada. "As for me, I have nothing left to say to her."

King Jabalah wrestled with this news for a moment and began to reason with himself because the love he held for his daughter was boundless. Yet, the consequences of her rebellion in this matter were grave indeed, so he said, "Call her to me, I want to address her and hear her arguments."

Queen Saada stood up to leave, but stopped, knowing that the arrival of Hind while her husband was still angry might bring about a bad reaction, so she sought to lighten his anger. Approaching him with tears still in her eyes, she said, "I am going to call her but I want to direct your attention to a matter you should not forget."

"What is that?" he growled.

"You know of Hind's tender heart and generous feelings. Her illness is a direct result of my conversation with her regarding Tha'labah. And," Queen Saada implored, "she knows, as we do, that he is not a gratifying companion for her. We have both long known of his churlish vindictiveness and treachery. Do not fool yourself into thinking that he loves her – he only wishes to possess her or kill her. If what I have said is true, you will use wisdom in addressing her by using a mild tone. Do not coerce her lest you drive her to her fate. Regretting it later will not do us any good."

"You are right," the king agreed. "I see that I have little choice but to face these troubles directly, though I cannot begin to comprehend what would bring Hind to fear for her life. Tha'labah is her cousin and I know of no other person in the tribe of Ghassan better than he, nor anyone more equal to her position. Why does she hate him so?"

"She detests him for his pretentious and shameful conduct, and has known him for these many years without seeing a shred of the self-respect or generosity that we of Ghassan possess," she said, adding haughtily, "deny that, if you can."

With some dismay, the king replied, "I do not deny that, Saada, but you know that there is a rivalry between our families which is kept together only through blood kinship under a veil of courtesy, and without doubt, the refusal of this betrothal will bring us war with him while we are more in need of unity now in the light of the news from Hejaz."

"The same worries have been haunting me these last days, but I know in my heart that we will regret forcing her to go through with this marriage," Queen Saada repeated. "She does not love him and she will never accept him. Shall we deliver her to a vile man who cares nothing for her?"

"You are certain that he holds no love for her?" King Jabalah asked doubtfully. "If it is as you say, why, then, does he ask for her?"

"I am sure of what I say, and we can talk about it later. For now I will call Hind to you so that you will have the truth from her own lips," she replied, departing.

Queen Saada took a lamp with her to light the way, and when she reached Hind's door she found it locked and heard a low, almost inaudible sound from within. She knocked on the door and called Hind's name. After a moment, the soft light of the lamp fell upon

Hind's face as the door opened slowly, revealing her swollen eyes and the great duress she was under. The sight tore the queen's heart asunder, and she set the lamp down to hug her daughter and kiss away the tears, cooing, "Cry not, my child, mourn not, for nothing will take away what you desire."

"I have had enough consoling, mother," Hind said wearily, "and I heard my father's angry voice with my own ears."

"How is it possible that you over heard his words when you were in your room?" asked Queen Saada.

"When I passed by your room," Hind explained, "I heard him yelling at you, insisting on the wedding! If he remains adamant then we should say goodbye now, forever!"

Queen Saada kissed Hind and said with a smile, "You are mistaken, child, for your father will soon agree with us in refusing Tha'labah. Come now, let us go to him."

The Remarkable Stand

When they both entered the room, King Jabalah was leaning against his bed. When he looked up, he saw his wife hand in hand with their daughter. Hind, eyes fixed on the floor and silent, acted in much the same manner as when her mother had found her in her room. Stricken with pity, the king asked simply, "What do you think of it, Hind?"

She remained silent, her fingers toying with her braid.

"What do you think of your cousin Tha'labah?" he repeated.

At the mere mention of his name her legs began to tremble and she started to cry again, trying vainly to hold back the sobs, but the tears coursed down her face uncontrollably. The pitiful sight softened the king's heart.

"Why do you not speak, child? We called you here in order to hear what you have to say," he said, a trifle impatient.

She could not control her sobbing, and turning to flee the room, Hind fell to the floor in a faint before she could reach the door. Her mother rushed to her with orange blossom water and sprinkled it on her until she rallied.

"Well," the king glibly remarked, "I understand that you do not love Tha'labah, but I ask you, do you love your father and your tribe?"

"Yes, I love you father, and I love my tribe!" she cried. "If you foresee tranquility for yourself and for your tribe by delivering me to that traitor, I will accept death as a redemption for our tribe. Here is my soul between your hands, do what you want!" She stretched her hands out to her father, nearly falling over him, and he clasped her to his chest with tears welling up in his eyes.

"Do not be so impatient, my child. I am as you wish, so be at ease and gather your senses," he continued, sitting down with her at his side.

She gathered her hair which had come loose and let it fall down her back. Hind felt the tender sensitivity in her father, but they only reminded her of the obstacles standing between her and Hammad. Since her father might vouch for him more affirmatively than for Tha'labah, she took advantage of this moment while he was still in an affectionate mood and started to weep again.

Surprised by her renewed anguish after having just reassured her regarding Tha'labah, he surmised that she did not understand so he tried to placate her fears by saying, "Calm your anxieties, we have precluded Tha'labah."

Yet, she continued to weep so her mother, who had guessed the girl's designs, drew her by the hand and led her to her room. Back in her daughter's room, Queen Saada dried the girl's tears, kissed her cheek, and asked, "Why are you doing this?"

"Let me cry, mother, I brought this misery upon myself," said Hind.

But Queen Saada knew that Hind referred to the alliance with Hammad and said, "Thank God instead, for we are almost there!"

"We may have crossed the plain," replied Hind, "but we have yet to cross the stony path."

"Take ease," the queen reassured her. "Go to your bed and I will take care of all you desire. In the morning, you will find things as you want them to be."

Hind felt relieved and looked at her mother with a smile like an infant who had contrived to get what she wanted by crying about it.

"Rest easy, child," Queen Saada said indulgently. "Good night."

The Revelation

Hind lay exhausted in bed and urged her mother once more to do her best.

"I said I will," the queen repeated, heading for the door.

Queen Saada reached her husband's room and found him waiting for her. He questioned her about Hind's last outbreak and asked, "Do you think that Hind will continue to refuse Tha'labah? Will you not help me to convince her?"

She smiled sweetly, trying to show astonishment, "Do you think that I tolerate or condone Hind's actions? Needless to say, did I not tell you that I have done it unwillingly because I feared the loss of her life? Is Hind not the fruit of our lives and the flower of our age? Is she not our consolation in our old age? Is she not the bravest of all our horse-riders? Is it right that we deliver a worthy maiden like her to a man who is hardly worthy of her shoes? You talk about Tha'labah, but who is Tha'labah? Is he not the coward who holds a grudge like an elephant, plays tricks like a fox, and commits treachery like a scorpion? Did you forget the day of the race when that stranger crushed him twice and the third time the stranger returned with the reed rendered short?"

While she went on, King Jabalah remained silent, admiring his beloved's eloquence and the way she remarked on each point, but when she mentioned the reed, he recalled that he had indeed seen it cut. He furrowed his brow, and interjected, "I remember that now!"

"Did you not wonder what caused the damage? By God, if I had told you what had transpired, you would have cursed the hour Tha'labah was born," she carried on, gaining momentum. "You would have wished to have the stranger for blood instead because it is he who displays the magnanimity of Ghassan!"

With rapt attention, King Jabalah asked to hear the whole tale and the queen was favorably inclined to tell all including the generosity of Hammad's nature and conduct, and she made sure to intensify the mean and vile character of Tha'labah. As soon as she finished speaking, the depression written on the king's face was plain to see. "What Tha'labah has done is unspeakable!" he exclaimed. "God bless Hammad and woe to Tha'labah! I wish Hammad had killed him and saved us from this shame!"

Queen Saada saw her husband's bewilderment, so she took a deep breath and said, "Since the door of our conversation is still open, there is something that I wish to ask you that may be the answer to a question which you posed this evening."

"What is it?" King Jabalah asked, his attention focused again.

"Do you know what prompted Tha'labah to request the betrothal to Hind after all these years of non-communication?" the queen inquired.

"What do you mean by non-communication?" King Jabalah responded.

"Is not Hind his cousin from birth?" she quizzed.

"Yes, of course," he replied.

"Then was it not proper for him to make the betrothal request long ago as is the custom of cousins," she asked, adding to press the point, "a tradition arranged in infancy?"

"Of course, Saada," he replied. "What of it?"

"Do you know what made him hold off the betrothal until now?" she asked insistently.

Amazed at her words and eager to hear the rest, he said, "I do not know, so tell me what you think about it."

"It may be that he believes himself superior to her in rank, or perhaps he expects us to push her on him, thinking that he will be doing us a favor by accepting her," hinted Queen Saada.

"To hell with that insidious coward and his father," said Jabalah, highly agitated.

"To hell, is right!" she answered. "He had no intention of asking for Hind, as I have learned, if it were not for a circumstance that made him jealous and incited him to revenge, and if you will permit me, I will relate this matter to you."

"Relate this matter to me," he said, with his complete attention on her.

"But I ask you, by God and for your love for Hind, to pity her youth and to excuse her for what you have seen or will see in her," the queen pleaded.

"We have excused her already, my queen, so there is no need for an oath," he said.

"I ask for your oath in a matter you are not aware of yet," she said.

With more alacrity he said, "Speak up, woman. I grow impatient!"

Cringing at the outburst, Queen Saada began, "You have now learned about Tha'labah's envy of Hammad's victory in attaining the reed and Hind's awarding the breastplate to him by your order."

"Yes!" said Jabalah.

"And you, being an honorable man, I saw how you admired the magnanimity of this stranger, and as you know, this display of admiration for the magnanimity of men exists more particularly in women, especially one who, like Hind, is in the prime of her youth," Queen Saada explained gingerly, expecting his reaction.

With a wild stare, King Jabalah sat straight up, saying, "What do you mean?"

"I mean," she continued, "that when Tha'labah saw Hind's admiration of Hammad, the fires of jealousy and vengeance flared within him and…"

Hoping to elicit the facts from her without duplicity, the king cut her off and said, "I think you mean more than that, Saada!"

"I mean that Tha'labah thought that Hind loves Hammad, so he premeditated this marriage scheme to deprive her of having him, and in so doing, do you not see, he will have avenged himself on both of them?" Queen Saada announced plainly.

Amazement again registered on his face, but there was also doubt at the words the queen spoke. He asked for more clarity, "And all of this is only in his mind?"

"I do not know the limits of his imagination," she answered.

"I see that you are steering me toward one conclusion while hiding some part of the truth," King Jabalah mused. Queen Saada kept silent, fearing to tell more clearly. He urged her to talk, saying, "Tell me what you are hiding!"

"Suppose I have something to hide, what is the use of telling it?" she answered.

Realizing for certain that there was something secret which she could not divulge for fear of his outrage, he said anxiously, "Answer me, Saada, do you know that Hind loves this young man?"

Lowering her eyes, without talking, she shrugged her shoulders.

"Do you not reply because she loves him?" the king asked again.

Looking at him to speak purely and simply to him, the queen decided to hold back because she saw an angry stare under a pair of furrowed brows glaring back at her. She stood up, pretending to delay the conversation to another time, and said, "I do not know. I will find out and tell you."

Holding her by the hand, he gently forced her to sit down again, speaking softly, "We have had enough of will and shall, tell me now. You know everything, this as much I have ascertained by virtue of your words."

"If you have learned this," she countered, "why do you question me again?"

"Then she loves him and wants to be wedded to him?" the king asked directly.

"Perhaps this is so," she said. Turning away from her husband, she busied herself arranging her bed, trying to show an uncaring attitude.

Fury built within him and King Jabalah spun her around and held her arms and pulled her to him roughly, his words sharp this time, "Why do you treat my anger with indifference, as if you see nothing in the matter worthy of your attention?" He continued, "Do you not care about your daughter? Or if she marries a stranger? We have no knowledge of his forefathers! He may be a commoner!"

She looked at him disapprovingly, dismayed by his physical display of anger. "This harsh attitude is the very reason why I kept the affair from you! I feared your knowledge of it would put you in just this mood, believing in your tribe only," she replied, rebuking her husband sharply. "Rest assured, however, Hammad is not from the common people. He an Emir of Iraq and his tribe is called Lakhum, which I am sure you have heard of."

King Jabalah flushed a deep crimson at his unmanly actions and enclosed the queen's soft hand in his, asking apologetically, "Do you not believe in the honor of Ghassan as I do? Suppose he is a prince, what about the enmity between the Lakhum and our tribe?"

"I will not hide the fact from you," she said, "that I have taken this matter seriously since the moment I found out, but I have had to use wisdom and patience in order to find a means of resolving it. If you had seen the seriousness of Hind's condition as I had, you would have acted in much the same way. But, what is the use of talking when I see that you have forgotten your pity, so do as you will and if Hind dies, you are to blame," she concluded with tears filling her eyes.

Seeing his wife's despair, the king tempered his anger and his patience returned. He said, emotionally upset at the sight of his wife, "Then what is to be done?"

"If you will consider to accept this problem with wisdom, I will plan a means by which it could be easily dismissed," she answered, gathering herself.

"What is your plan?" he asked.

Sitting down next to him she said, "What I think we ought to do is pretend that we give our consent to Hind's wishes and then plan a means to sever ourselves from Hammad that will not harm her sensitivity."

"How might that feat be accomplished?" he asked in disbelief.

"Like so," she said. "I will tell Hind tomorrow that if Hammad asks for her hand in marriage, you will turn down his proposal. Then I will talk with her and explain in no uncertain terms that she is much too lofty to marry a stranger whose ancestry is unknown – for she does not deny this. Then, I will persuade her to ask him accomplish some deed, of my own suggestion, which will be impossible for him to carry out. And, if he should succeed, then his wedding to Hind is his destiny which we will have to accept as the will of God."

King Jabalah, nodded and felt content with this plan of action and asked her what she would suggest to Hind.

"We will have to think it over until tomorrow," she replied.

Very pleased with her judgment, King Jabalah praised his wife for the intuition and wisdom she displayed, and apologized again for his ignorant behaviour.

She stood up and said, "Let me go to Hind and set her at ease lest she spend the night troubled and wakeful." She left for Hind's room, who was indeed restless, waiting for her mother to return.

Seeing her mother enter the room, Hind got up to meet her. She immediately recognized the good omen in her mother's face. Her mother smiled and all of Hind's anxieties subsided. Hind asked if there was some word, and Queen Saada responded by telling her that her father will not stand in the way of her will.

Despair for Finding Abdullah

Returning once again to our friends in Busra, we find Salman making haste for Hammad's quarters. Hammad, still wrestling with unease over the fate of his father, asked Salman if there was any news.

"Just as before," Salman shook his head. "Sir, I ask you to let me journey to Jerusalem or Amman to look for my master."

"Yes, you may," replied Hammad, "and I will be going with you."

"There is no need to go with me," said Salman. "It would be better for you to stay here until I return."

"Are you going to visit the Holy City or Amman?" asked Hammad.

Salman thought for a moment, then vowed, "I shall go to the Holy City to follow my master's trail and won't return until I am sure of his whereabouts."

"Go then. May you be protected by God," Hammad consented, adding with a grin, "and do not be gone too long. You know I get anxious."

Bidding him good-bye, Salman put on his traveling clothes and left for the Holy City. He arrived a few days later and wandered through the streets until he came upon an Arabian owned hotel. He sent his horse to the stable and took up lodgings there. After changing his clothes, Salman sat near the proprietor who then conversed with Salman about whatever came to mind. Their conversation eventually turned to the topic of Emperor Heraclius. "Did you see the Emperor?" asked Salman.

"Yes, I did," explained the innkeeper, "but only on his arrival. We were unable to see him later on because there were too many travelers to attend to here at the inn."

"Do many Arabs come here?" Salman questioned.

"We seldom have Arabian visitors anymore," the man replied, "but this year far too many have come."

"Why this year in particular?" asked Salman.

"Because the Emperor summoned Abu Sufyan, who came with his entire caravan. They lodged here for a length of time and the city derived much benefit from their presence, at the least. They seem to be a prosperous people," the innkeeper added.

"Why did the Emperor summon him?" Salman asked.

The innkeeper narrated the story of the note up to the departure of Abu Sufyan. To try and elicit some information about his master, Salman asked, "Are all the Arabs that come here from Hejaz?"

"We have visitors from all parts of the world but they are only seasonal, it seems. This year we had a visitor from Iraq, in fact," the innkeeper added, "an Emir came to my hotel not much more than a week ago to meet with Abu Sufyan, and then left in his company."

"Do you remember this Emir?" asked Salman.

"I think I recall that his name was Abdullah," the innkeeper answered.

Salman was positive that it was his master the innkeeper spoke of, so he asked, "Did you hear anything about this Emir after his departure?"

"Oh, yes," replied the innkeeper with a sad face, "something that would break the heart happened to him."

With the sign of horror written on his face, Salman asked, "What happened to Abdullah?"

"I heard that Abdullah lost his son," the man answered. "The poor boy had been devoured by a lion!"

"And how did you learn this?" Salman asked, much relieved.

The innkeeper told him the story of the search for Abdullah's son, including the visit to the land of the beasts. Salman listened intently until he had finished.

"What happened next?" Salman asked eagerly.

"I heard that when Abdullah was certain of the death of his son, he decided not go to his residence in Busra but joined the caravan to Hejaz instead."

"Are you sure he went to Hejaz?" Salman inquired.

"That is all I heard," said the owner. "I do not know for certain whether he did or whether he changed his mind later."

"Have you no more details?" asked Salman.

"Well," said the innkeeper, "since the news of this story is apparently of great interest to you, I will ask my muleteer to join us. He accompanied the caravan and is the one I heard the story from."

Summoning the man, he asked him to relate the story of Abdullah's despair. The muleteer told them the same story of Abdullah's discovery of the horse's remains, the shredded cloak, and of Abu Sufyan's generous offer to take him to Hejaz even though Abdullah was hesitant to go. "When we reached the land of the beasts, Abu Sufyan had us set up camp while the horsemen went in search of the missing boy. I returned here after assisting with the tents, having finished my duties, and heard nothing else," the man concluded.

"Did you hear him talk about going to Amman?" asked Salman.

"No, I did not," was the man's reply.

Salman was surprised, and thinking over what he had learned he reasoned that his master could not stand this strain about his son so he may have gone directly to Hejaz with Abu Sufyan. Thanking the innkeeper, he went to his room and in his own despair began to imagine many ominous tidings without knowing what to do next. He passed the rest of the day and all the night in anxiety, but after a great deal of pondering Salman realized that he should follow the footsteps of his master by himself and preferred to start in Amman. In the morning, he went to the innkeeper, told him of his intentions, and asked him to allow the muleteer to accompany him, which both men did graciously.

Following the same route as the caravan, they arrived at the land of the beasts and from there to the point where the muleteer left Abdullah.

"Will you go on with me to Amman?" asked Salman.

"Yes, I will," he answered reluctantly, "but I have heard that there are great hordes of men from Quraysh near Amman readying to fight us, so we may not be safe if we go there."

Salman remembered that he had heard this before he left Busra and with that in mind, they took a different route which few people knew of. When they arrived in Amman they could find no trace of Abdullah. Salman, suffering mental anguish, did not know how he would face Hammad with the news, but reasoned that no matter how depressed Abdullah may have been at the thought of the loss of his son, he would at least return to Busra and renew the search for his son's remains. Salman wished to go to Hejaz to look for his master, but doubted that Abdullah would be there, so he returned to Busra where Hammad awaited good news.

Hammad at His Tent

After Salman had left for the Holy City, Hammad recounted all the problems that had befallen him. But whenever he envisioned his beautiful Hind, he was once again consoled, and so he continued to pass the time in his quarters with his mind wavering between hope and despair. One night, he heard the sound of an ox and knew that his host had returned from grazing.

Hammad envied him for his uncomplicated, simple life, and wished to be in the man's shoes, with nothing to boggle his mind, nothing to depress his spirit, and desiring nothing but a good crop from his farm and the reproduction of his cattle. But in retrospect, Hammad suspected that the old man had never known love, having spent more time with his farm than his fellow man.

While his thoughts lingered, Hammad heard his host's footsteps approaching. Before he could rise to meet him, the old man entered the tent barefoot with a scythe still in his hand, dust covering his beard and turban, and his shirt wide open showing the curly hair on his chest. Greeting him, Hammad stood up out of respect for the man's age. The old man threw the scythe down at the door and entered with a smile on his weather-beaten face. Hammad could not remember seeing him smile before, although he never showed any depression or worry either. When Hammad saw the smile, a feeling of contentment filled him. He made room on the carpet and asked the man to sit down. The old man refused politely and sat on the bare earth, rubbing the palms of his hands together to remove the dirt, repeating the same process with his beard.

"How are you today, my old man?" Hammad asked.

"Very well," said the old man, shaking the dust from his turban. "I thank God for his blessing! My cow gave birth to a calf today and within a year or two I will be able to use it for ploughing. It has freed me of the need for children."

Hammad was surprised at the simplicity of the desert dweller and said, wishing to jest with the man whose tribe had once ruled this land, "Are you satisfied with this life, caring for cattle while the tribe of Ghassan hold the power and rule over everyone else?"

With a wry smile, the old man said, "No grace lasts forever. As we speak, someone is coming to take that authority from the Ghassan and compel them to follow in the footsteps of their forefathers and flee like those refugees who came to this land from the floods caused by the collapse of the great Ma'arib Dam."

"What do you mean by 'take that authority'?" asked Hammad.

"Have you not heard about the Muslim army coming from Hejaz to punish the tribe of Ghassan?" the man asked, somewhat surprised.

"No, I had not" Hammad replied, suddenly very worried. "What brought on this reckoning? What sort of quarrel could there be between the Muslims and the Ghassan? Hejaz is a great distance from Syria."

Laughing, the old man said, "It is the will of God. The wrath of these people comes as an answer to the disrespectful conduct of King al-Harith of Ghassan. He tore to shreds a note from the Prophet Muhammad and insulted the apostle who delivered it. This insulted the Prophet himself, and he has sent his men to destroy this tribe for their misconduct."

Hammad took the news seriously for he knew that this war would put yet another obstacle in his way and bring danger to Hind, especially since her father would have to side with his cousin.

Turning to the old man, he asked, "Are you sure that the armies of Hejaz are coming?"

"Without a doubt," he said. "The downfall of Ghassan is of great importance to me, for they are my enemies as you so cleverly attested a moment ago," he continued. The old man belonged to the Nabataean tribe who held these land before the arrival of the Ghassan. He thought Hammad would be glad of these tidings, unaware that Hammad's life was wrapped up in the princess of the palace.

Hammad remained silent, not knowing what to do and grew more concerned as his thoughts turned back to Salman and his father. Looking at the old man, Hammad saw that his eyes were closed and that he had let drowsiness overtake him. The old man suddenly woke up with a start at the sound of his oxen clamoring, and he left, commenting that the animals were warring.

Hammad followed him out into the dark night, and when they reached the oxen they found that the animals had not been fighting, but had instead been joined by a camel. The shepherd grabbed the camel by the neck and pulled it to the campfire. While Hammad looked on, the old man laughed and said, "This she-camel is from Hejaz. She must have gotten loose and went astray. I bet she belongs to the army I told you about."

"How do you know that?" asked Hammad.

"I recognized the saddle on her back," he answered, "it is the shape they use in Hejaz."

"Then it would be safe to assume that the army is nearby?" Hammad said.

"They may not be near yet," he answered. "This she-camel could have lost her way many days ago," he stated, giving the animal some food and water.

Hammad went back to his tent to dwell on the gravity of the situation.

Salman's Return

After many days of searching, Salman returned very worried because of his failure to find his master. He told Hammad all that he had heard and of his supposition that Abdullah might have joined the caravan of Abu Sufyan.

"I do not think he would have gone before he looked for the treasure we left in Ghasam," said Hammad.

"How do we know that he did not search for it after we had taken it? Anyhow, he is not in Palestine or in Balqa, nor did I find him in Amman," Salman recounted with dismay. "So it seems that all I have heard is that he may have left for Hejaz."

Hammad's face grew into a grimace and utter frustration filled his body and his soul.

"Will you now allow me to go to Mecca to search for him?" pleaded Salman.

"If we were sure about his departure for Mecca, I would have gone there by myself but our trail that leads us there is only hearsay and guesswork," Hammad sighed. "Besides, I grow restless regarding this war between the men of Hejaz and Ghassan."

"Yes, the Muslim army," Salman nodded. "I know all about it and have seen their encampments on the outskirts of Amman with my own eyes. Hopefully my master traveled to Hejaz. Or perhaps something has simply delayed his return to Busra," he reasoned further. "If he does not make an appearance after a few days it would mean that he has likely gone with Abu Sufyan to Mecca."

"I leave it up to you, Salman," said Hammad, "to have a look around Busra one last time. Maybe you will hear something of my father. And, do not forget to ask about Hind and her father, since we have seen how the Ghassani are stricken with insensibility at the threat of war. I feel the vanishing of our hopes if the war becomes too heated."

"I had already intended to check on Hind," Salman replied. "She is now the cause of much gossip."

"What gossip do speak of?" asked Hammad, highly surprised.

"I have overheard while the people of al-Balqa and the outlying districts discussed Tha'labah's request to be betrothed to Hind," Salman explained.

Hammad became distraught at this news and felt every hair on his head stand straight. With a tremor in his voice, Hammad asked, "Who did Tha'labah ask to intercede for him?"

"I understand that Tha'labah asked his father, the king, to propose the union to Hind's father," Salman paused, "who in turn gave his promise."

"What promise did King Jabalah give?" asked Hammad.

"Why are you so impatient?" Salman rebuked. "Take ease and listen to what I have to say!"

"You have my patience," apologized Hammad, gathering himself. "Please, tell me the promise that Hind's father made."

"He promised to talk to the girl, or rather to consult her mother," Salman answered, "for you know the marriage of girls never depends upon their own wishes."

"What did her mother say?" asked Hammad.

"Nobody knows," replied Salman, gravely adding, "but I heard from someone in al-Balqa that King al-Harith urged King Jabalah again to give him an answer. He would like to have the ceremony held as soon as possible, before the advance of the Hejazi armies."

"What has all this been for, Salman, our hopes and our dreams?" Hammad lamented. "Have our struggles all been in vain? Should Hind just accept her cousin?"

The depth of despair that showed on Hammad's face twisted like a knife in Salman's heart. He clasped Hammad around the shoulders tightly and said, "Hind is too esteemed to degrade herself with that coward's empty love, and being more familiar with her pride and her loathing for the man, it would seem to me that her slow reply suggests her unacceptance."

Hammad's spirits revived some, but he was still afraid that she would be forced against her will.

"Her refusal to accept her cousin will be a difficult and precarious situation for her to handle," complained Hammad, "not to mention the position it puts her father in."

"No difficulty is too great for her to overcome," proclaimed Salman, "for she has an ally in her mother, and that woman has the courage and great cunning of a lioness and will be able to persuade the king to see her way of thinking without any difficulty."

Hammad remained lost in thought until he fell asleep.

The News

Hammad tossed and turned all night and could not fall asleep. Salman, on the other hand, stayed up for a while planning what he and his master should do next. He awoke the next morning after only a few of hours of sleep intent on visiting the Stream Palace, for he was certain that the answers were with Hind. He put on his monk's clothes, mounted his horse and rode to the palace. When he arrived, he inquired who was within and was told that King Jabalah had left several days ago for al-Balqa. Salman then approached the gate of the park where he was met by servants who asked him the reason for his visit, to which he answered, "I have been sent on a mission to Queen Saada by the abbot of Bahira Monastery." After acquiring her confirmation, the servants admitted him to the palace.

The queen recognized Salman as soon as they were alone and he told her that he had come to secure some information regarding Hammad's position. Hind was in her room thinking of Hammad when she overheard the servant announcing the arrival of a monk from Bahira. She hurried to where Salman and the queen were meeting, her face etched with signs of dismay and uncertainty. Salman stood up as she entered the room, and Hind greeted him and immediately asked about Hammad. He eased her anxieties and answered her questions while he watched the queen for any outward signs of bias, and what he noticed was promising. He wanted to find out about Tha'labah and his demand, so as he talked with Hind and her mother, he learned that King Jabalah had rejected Tha'labah in favor of Hammad after great consideration of Tha'labah's conduct. This good news elated Salman and he wished to ride like the wind to tell Hammad. He then asked what date had been set for addressing the king concerning the betrothal.

"We have set a date for an introduction to the king a few days from now," Queen Saada explained, "and at that time Hammad may come and ask for Hind's hand in marriage to which we will give our consent."

Hind listened to the exchange with a joyful heart and was bashfully silent.

"Who will inform us of the exact time?" asked Salman.

"We will have a servant accompany you back to your residence and when that date arrives we will send him back to fetch you."

"Very well," Salman said, rising up. He thanked them and bade them good-bye. Hammad was only too glad to see Salman and all the more ecstatic to hear the good news.

Meanwhile, on the other hand, King Jabalah was regretting his lack of practicality regarding his wife's persuasiveness with respect to his daughter. The anxieties churning within him left the king in a quandary as to how he should approach his cousin, so he thought it best to keep it secret for now and petition his cousin to delay the betrothal until after the conflict with Hejaz had been resolved.

Tha'labah

Tha'labah had started to plan his engagement to Hind in the belief that she would accept whether she was compelled to or not. He later learned from his spies that Abdullah was missing and there was a great possibility that Hammad was dead. That was the news he had wished for, so his jealousy for Hind began to subside. The thought of Hammad's death led Tha'labah's devious mind to scheme a way to jilt Hind in order to make her feel more wretched, alone, and unloved. He began to look for an appropriate opportunity to delay the wedding and then work out a means of revenge on Hind. He decided to postpone the marriage as long as possible to keep Hind waiting and wondering. But, his father was not aware of his son's malice, so the king continued to pressure his cousin in the hopes that it would please his son and make him happy.

After the news of the coming war spread, King al-Harith insisted that King Jabalah have the marriage take place at once. Dispatches reached their ears that the Muslim soldiers had reached Amman and were already moving on to al-Balqa. The king had ordered his son to fortify the citadel with arms and to get ready for the wedding without a ceremony for the time being. Once they had won the war, the ceremony would be double. Tha'labah remained silent for a time, ruminating, then said to his father, "I see no hurry for the wedding, I would rather put it off until after the war."

His father was aghast at this declaration, and praised his son for his intelligence and unselfishness at a most critical time for Ghassan.

"What shall we reply to your uncle if he accepts our request?" the king asked.

"Tell him," said Tha'labah, "that we are in a difficult time of war which does not permit marriage."

"But we were in the same situation when I asked him to hasten the wedding," King al-Harith explained with some irony. "He, at that time, was in favor of putting it off until the end of the conflict!

How can I approach him with this excuse? It might bring him ill-feelings for us."

"I care little if he thinks ill of us," Tha'labah countered dismissively, "I would rather put off the wedding!"

King al-Harith was surprised by the sudden rashness of his son and his uncaring attitude toward the relationship between the two cousin kings. Turning to Tha'labah, he said sternly, "Are you not aware, my son, how such thinking could cause a war between our families? Even if you aren't, I am. This problem needs keen intuition and subtlety."

Tha'labah thought for a few seconds, more sensitive to the injuries it may cause to his family, but still blinded by jealousy and vengeance. After a moment, he said, "Today is not yesterday, and yesterday our enemies were in Amman. But today they move closer to our city. We must prepare for conflict. Make that your excuse for the postponement of the wedding."

King al-Harith saw it a plausible reasoning so he decided to follow his son's advice when he next met with King Jabalah. While they discussed the details, a messenger arrived and announced that his cousin wanted to meet with him to discuss the coming war.

"I am going directly to al-Balqa," the king said to his son, "to gain his council regarding war tactics, and if he addresses me about Hind we will excuse ourselves, as you said. Otherwise I will not bring up the matter again. So while I am gone, prepare our soldiers and write to each of the princes to mass their men under their banners and be prepared when the time comes."

Jabalah and al-Harith

After his argument with his wife, King Jabalah left the palace and returned to al-Balqa. Upon his arrival, he heard that the Muslim army had left Amman and was coming directly to his door. He wrote to King al-Harith to come to al-Balqa for tactical discussions.

As soon as they met, they went into seclusion, with King Jabalah beginning the talks. "I called you, cousin," he said, "so that we might coordinate our efforts to repel the enemy. The reports that have come to me have the army advancing from Amman northward, no doubt aiming at this land. I have sent scouts to track their movements and detail where their camps lie, so prepare your men as I have mine."

"I have seen many tribes arriving here to aid us," said King al-Harith, "and I have instructed Tha'labah to write to the other tribes to concentrate their men in the area of Busra. Then when they are all massed, we will attack first and take them by surprise! I do not think we will encounter much difficulty in defeating them for I have learned they are barefooted people and wear only wide robes to cloak their bodies, you cannot tell between the prince and the coolie," he continued. "I also think that if we encounter any difficulty in fighting them, we can offer them money to disperse. It is money that they are after, I suppose, for the riches of Syria and the Roman Empire are vast."

"We will not offer them money," King Jabalah shook his head, "not unless their opposition is mightier than ours, but I am betting that they cannot hold out for a single day if your information is accurate." His thoughts turned to the protection of his home, and then to his daughter and the betrothal, so King Jabalah asked, "You said that our son Tha'labah is writing to the tribes, is he now in Busra?"

"Yes," his cousin nodded, "he is there, and we feel badly that this serious conflict interferes with our hopes for a wedding."

"It is a sorrowful thing," said King Jabalah, inwardly pleased, "perhaps we should consider postponing the engagement until after the war, for when that time comes we can celebrate double joy for both of our children."

King al-Harith, glad to see that the wedding was resolutely postponed without further issue, praised his cousin, "Thank God that we are unanimously agreeable, for I think that this is the right thing to do for now. This war still requires our full attention"

"It is for the best," King Jabalah consented, adding, "I wish to leave for the Stream Palace to see Queen Saada and tell her our agreement lest she be preparing for the wedding. I will return."

"Of course, do as you please," said King al-Harith, "and may God straighten your path."

King Jabalah mounted his horse and rode back to the palace. He was warmly welcomed by his wife who was greatly surprised to learn that King al-Harith and Tha'labah had decided to postpone the wedding without argument. Sitting next to his wife, King Jabalah asked, "Well then, heart of my heart, what trickery will you plan now to rid us of the next hurdle?"

Mary's Earrings

"I've already thought of something," Queen Saada smiled, "we will ask Hammad to offer Hind a marriage endowment which will be most difficult for him to obtain. If he cannot furnish it for her, then he is clearly not entitled to wed her. In this, we will then be able to maintain our innocence with our daughter. I spoke to her about this plan and she is inclined to accept its resolution. She prefers to see Hammad occupy higher esteem in the eyes of her parents, and would be more proud of him if he can gain something not obtainable by any other. Should he succeed, Hammad will have certainly proven his worthiness."

"Have you talked to your daughter about what this endowment might be?" asked King Jabalah.

"Not yet, but I think I have an idea that you will find quite satisfactory husband," Queen Saada replied. "If you do not like it we will find another."

"What is it?" Jabalah asked.

"As you know," she said, "your great grandmother Mary, the daughter of Zalim bin al-Harith, is the grandmother of all the kings of Ghassan."

"Yes, of course," said the king, "She was renowned the world over for her beauty, and her magnanimity is the example we still follow today."

"Indeed," continued the queen, "and she wore a pair of earrings which no other queen on this earth has ever worn. These earrings have a glorious pearl set in each piece that was as large as the egg of a dove, the likes of which no one has seen since, and are truly priceless."

"I have heard of them, they are certainly very precious," King Jabalah remarked. After a moment of thought he added, "My father told me that my great-grandmother, to fulfill a vow, gave her earrings as a gift to the al-Ka'aba in Mecca before she died. It is the holy place where the Hejazi go to make their pilgrimage to the idols that they worship as gods. It was presumed then that she was a heathen, for if she were not, she would not have given that treasure to the gods of al-Ka'aba."

"Well," Queen Saada wondered, "heathen or not, would her earrings still be in al-Ka'aba?"

"Yes, as far as I know," he answered.

"Then I suggest that we ask Hammad to bring those earrings to Hind as the endowment so she may wear them for her wedding," the queen proposed. "What do you think?"

Admiring her wisdom, he smiled with relief and said, "God bless you, it is a fine suggestion. The earrings are at the heart of our enemy's lands and most unattainable. They are likewise a treasure worthy of our daughter. Let us suppose that Hammad should secure them, he would indeed be worthy of Hind. Do you think she will agree?"

"I think she will," Queen Saada answered. "Otherwise, we will object to her union with Hammad."

"This is a very clean solution," said King Jabalah. "Speak to Hind, and if she consents, summon the young man and give him his instructions for me, for my time will be occupied with dealing with the Muslim army marching to our door."

"Very well," Queen Saada replied before leaving the room.

Meanwhile, Hind had busied herself with a leisurely stroll through the park after learning of her father's arrival. She was certain that his visit concerned her betrothal. She continued walking to ease her nerves but was overly anxious to know what was transpiring. As soon as she saw her mother, Hind hurried over to inquire but her mother asked her to wait until her father had left. Queen Saada gave the servants orders for preparing dinner and King Jabalah walked into the park looking for Hind. He met her with a smile on his handsome face and kissed her, asking her about her health. They talked about many things as the day tarried on, but he avoided the subject of marriage. After dinner, King Jabalah bade his wife and daughter good-bye and started out for al-Balqa.

The moment he was past the gates, Hind hurried to speak with her mother. With a sly smile, Queen Saada said to her daughter, "Good news, my child, your father is showing his resolve. He refuses to accept Tha'labah and instead welcomes Hammad as I told you before. He and I see the need for Hammad to accomplish some deed that would close the mouths of gossiping people regarding his forefathers and prove his honor to all."

Hind had heard all this from her mother before and said, "As you wish, mother, I would be proud of Hammad for doing something great for me. Have you and father found a task that you both find worthy?"

"Yes," said her mother. "I envision for your wedding an item to adorn for your head, one that would also adorn your honor, an item of unmatched beauty and worth."

"What could it be?" asked Hind excitedly.

"We will ask him to retrieve Mary's Earrings from al-Ka'aba," her mother proudly announced.

As her mother related the whole story of the earrings, Hind was dumbfounded and became very doubtful about the whole idea, but her pride prevented her from objecting. "I believe that Hammad will overcome any obstacle, God willing," Hind finally said.

"Then let us summon Hammad openly and offer this challenge to him," Queen Saada declared.

Hind's heart started to leap with joy. "Call him and rely on God to speed him on his way," she replied.

The mother called the servant who had accompanied Salman and instructed him to send for Hammad and return him to the palace.

Hammad and His Hopes

When we left Hammad and Salman, both were thinking of Abdullah, torn between hope and despair. Salman had been hunting back and forth between the cities of Busra and al-Balqa for signs of his master without any luck. He hoped desperately that Abdullah had in fact gone to Hejaz. Hammad's mind, however, was mostly preoccupied with anxiety as he waited to hear again from Hind. One morning, he awoke in good spirits and uplifted hopes expecting to hear some joyful news.

Salman was busying himself to occupy the time and distract his mind when he noticed a horseman riding in a great hurry, and from the cloud of dust it seemed as though the rider was headed straight for them. Salman's keen intuition told him that the rider was coming from the palace and became hopeful of the good omen. He recognized the servant as soon as the man dismounted and walked toward him to take the horse's reins. They shook hands as they met and Salman asked what news he brought with him.

"I have come to call Prince Hammad to Queen Saada who is at the Stream Palace, her Majesty would like to speak with him," he answered.

"Do you know what the audience is about?" asked Salman.

"I do not know," replied the servant with a laugh. "Perhaps you know more about it than I, but most of the attendants of the palace suspect that our mistress, Hind, will soon pledge her hand in marriage and we are all awaiting the happy day. We shall receive fees that day!"

With a smile, Salman said, "Do you know to whom she is to be betrothed?"

"Yes, it must be her cousin Tha'labah," the servant answered, "for who else among the Ghassani would be worthy of the princess? I have heard from some of the servants, however, that the fair princess does not love him."

"Could she refuse his betrothal?" asked Salman.

"I do not know," the servant speculated, "but it seems that she wants to."

Salman nodded and asked, "Any other news from the palace?"

"I have heard nothing else of note," replied the servant. "My master, King Jabalah, had a happy talk with the princess during his visit, and as soon as he departed for al-Balqa, my Queen Saada sent me to you."

Salman realized at once that the visit by King Jabalah must have been for the engagement and seemed to him that must have been for Hammad after all. If that were not the case, Salman reasoned, he would not have been summoned to the palace. Salman entered the tent and saw his master relaxing after having returned from hunting. Hammad smiled at his servant and Salman returned the smile in greeting.

"What is on your mind, Salman?" Hammad asked. "You seem to have something to tell me."

"I have good news, master," replied Salman, "I hope it will please you."

"What is it?" asked Hammad, his attention divided between Salman and the hem of his robe.

"The King and Queen of Stream Palace have sent for you. Are you going, or are you too busy to go!" said Salman, with a boisterous laugh.

Hammad bolted up, and thinking Salman was only jesting, said, "I care not about being called by the owner of the palace, for I feel too happy today."

"Would it harm you to have more happiness today?" teased Salman with a bow. "The servant of the palace has arrived, shall I bring him to you?"

The words had a sobering effect on Hammad, and he stammered, "Yes! Let him in!"

The horseman entered the tent with his dusty travel clothes on and knelt to greet the prince before explaining the reason for his visit.

"How were the King, Queen, and princess when you left them," Hammad asked, "were they well?"

"Very well, Sir," answered the servant. "They are wishing you to be in good health as well, and hope to see you soon."

Hammad received the news with elated cheerfulness, returning the courtesy, "I send my homage. Please inform them that we will arrive at the palace tomorrow morning, God willing."

Kissing Hammad's hand, the servant left the tent with Salman following him. Salman bid him farewell and gave him ten dinars, explaining it was to pay for feed for his horse.

"You will see more from us, if it pleases you," Salman added graciously.

After the servant had gone, Salman returned and saw Hammad deep in thought. "Why is my master so troubled?" he asked. "Is he surprised at this unexpected call?"

"No Salman," Hammad sighed. "I am thinking of my father and wish he were with us."

"Who can tell where he is now? Let the anxieties lie dormant, Hammad," Salman counseled, "for I feel certain that my master has gone to Hejaz. After we are finished with our affair here, I will take up the search until I find him. So worry not, and let us now get ready to go the Stream Palace in the morning."

"I know, we must leave before dawn so we will be at the palace by morning light," nodded Hammad.

"Very well," said Salman.

As they prepared for their departure, Hammad's thoughts turned more and more to meeting Hind again, and his heart raced as he remembered the first time he held hands with her at Bahira Monastery so many months ago, now certain that it had not been the last.

The Hour of Meeting

The servant returned to the palace and relayed the message to Hind that Hammad would be arriving early the following morning. With a fluttering heart, she counted the hours and the minutes and passed the day without resting.

In the morning, she went to ask her mother where the meeting would be held. Queen Saada told her that she had informed the servants to prepare the reception room and to let no one enter it on that day. She also made arrangements for the butchering of a lamb and the preparation of other dishes for their refreshment.

Hind dressed in a heavenly blue robe that she had saved for just such a day and combed her lustrous black hair into a braid. She kept herself busily occupied, trying to quiet the impulsive beating of her heart as it swayed between the joy of meeting her sweetheart openly and her apprehension at the thought of being so near him, and then to the dread of the trap her parents had set for him by sending him to al-Ka'aba for the earrings.

The queen had dispatched a group of her attendants to meet the guests before their arrival at the palace. As the morning wore on, Hind peered through the window, looking toward the field where the race was held a few months ago, and beyond that to the hills and forests that had cast long shadows across the plains in the early sun. For a moment she thought that Hammad had arrived, and her heart beat wildly, bringing a rosy glow to her face. She continued to watch until noon when a small trail of dust rose over the hills and then cleared to reveal a swiftly moving pair of horsemen. With a fullness in her heart, she watched the horsemen approach. A fair distance ahead of the other, she recognized her noble horseman riding boldly across the plain.

Hammad was practically flying toward the palace, his head and face wrapped in a colorful scarf, with Salman following not far behind him. Overwhelmed with excitement, Hind's knees began to tremble as the hour of their meeting drew near, and she did not remove her gaze from the window until Hammad had reached the palace gates. Her mother, who was at her side, said as she went to greet him, "Stay here until I call you to the reception room."

While Queen Saada made her way to the park, the two horsemen dismounted and entered, leaving their horse's needs to the servants. Hammad was wrapped in his cloak with the ends of his head-scarf falling upon his shoulders. He walked slowly with Salman, who was close by his side. Salman bowed and introduced his master to Queen Saada. Hammad greeted her graciously, expecting to see Hind. Not seeing her, however, he suspected that the princess may be overcome with modesty.

Queen Saada escorted them to the reception room where they relaxed while the servants waited on them.

"Would the prince care to wash and change his traveling clothes before having dinner?" the queen asked.

"Yes, I would," he replied thankfully. The queen left to gather Hind, and Hammad stood up to wash his hands and face and exchanged his travel-worn clothes for the rich silk robes that Salman had brought for him. Hammad sat down again after grooming himself, his eyes on the door of the reception room.

Salman tended to Hammad's clothing, then took his leave as well. Turning in the direction of the stables, he saw Hind standing there, toying with the bracelet that had started this all as it hung around her wrist, her mind clearly unsettled. Salman quietly coughed to gain her attention but startled himself at the artificial sound that he made. Hind spun around surprised and looked at him, and he smiled back at her. She returned the greeting and walked toward him.

"Is my Mistress pleased with the monk who collects the vows?" he asked.

Timidly smiling, she said nothing.

"Behold! I brought the thief who stole the breastplate! Would you like to punish him?" Salman teased. "I hope you will not sentence him to imprisonment."

Remembering the day he came dressed as a monk, she grinned, still playing with her bracelet. Salman approached her asking, "Why do you not talk? Am I guilty because I came here surrendering without the thief? Shall I call him here for you?"

She still said nothing but he saw that she was glad.

"I see that you pretend as if you care not of his arrival," pressed Salman, "though your face tells me differently." He turned to go, adding, "I am going to call the man to you."

She rebuked him with a glare because of his joking and teasing prattle, but he turned away from her laughing and entered the reception room where he intruded upon Queen Saada and Hammad who were speaking alone. Salman asked, still motivated by his mischievous manner, "Why do I see this with little light as if it is far from the sun's rays?"

"Do you not see the ray entering through this window?" the queen asked in return.

"No, I cannot see any light at all and it appears to me that your sun rises in the south," he said laughingly, his hand gesturing in the direction of Hind's room.

The corners of Queen Saada's lips curled upward in a smile as she understood what he meant. Hammad's face turned scarlet at the implication.

"I see that you are laughing at my words and I also see that I know more than you as to where your sun rises, Mistress," Salman carried on boldly. "I noticed that the tables are set for dinner, may I ask you to allow your daughter to come down, for she is the pivot of our amusement!"

"You are too pressing, Salman," the queen said sharply. "You have no interest in the matter!"

"Quite right," he said. "I have no interest, but speak on behalf of the feelings of another." He winked at Hammad, who gave Salman a disgusted and disapproving look.

Bemused, Queen Saada stood up and announced, "I am going to fetch Hind now."

Hammad battled his anticipation of Hind's arrival as he heard footsteps nearing the door of the reception room. Raising his head, he saw Queen Saada enter with Hind following close behind, her eyes lowered. Hammad stood up to meet her, his eyes also downward, neither having the courage to clasp the other's hand. They were both glad-of-heart to see one another, but Hammad nervously straightened his attire and headdress, and Hind fiddled with her bracelet, her knees trembling and knocking together, causing her dress to move in a peculiar manner. Hammad noticed her cheeks growing paler as though she were about to faint.

Opening the conversation, Queen Saada asked, "What has become of your father? Did you find him? Do you know where he is?"

"No, Mistress," said Hammad remorsefully, "our minds are deeply preoccupied with thoughts of him. We have looked for him everywhere without result. Our most promising lead is that he may have gone to Hejaz, according to the story of an innkeeper in the Holy City."

Queen Saada asked him to relate the story of the lion and Hammad obliged, relating the story of the dangers of al-Zarqa, his words reaching their way into Hind's heart. Then Salman told the story of his search through the Holy City and what he had heard there. When Salman finished, Queen Saada said, "The reports from our scouts also agree that it seems your father has traveled with Abu Sufyan to Hejaz."

Hammad and Salman were overjoyed to hear her encouraging words, but were politely interrupted when one of the servants announced himself and asked Queen Saada if the food could be put on the tables since it was now the noon hour.

"You may begin serving," she replied, and turned to Hammad with a hint of a smile, "We will finish our talk after dinner."

While they adjourned to the dining room, Hammad preoccupied himself trying to figure out what was behind the queen's smile. After they had taken their dinner together, they sat and rested and conversed with her and the princess. With a subtle hint from her mother, Hind retired to her room, and when they were alone, the queen said with a joking smile, "I suppose from your rapt attention that you are expecting me to speak."

"You seem greatly pleased about something," said Hammad, "would you confide in us?"

"I am pleased, young prince," said the queen, "because it is presumed that your father is in Hejaz and what we are about to propose will hopefully bring you face to face with him in that land."

Hammad did not quite understand what she meant by this so he asked her to clarify, "What is your suggestion?"

"Our son Hammad does not ignore that we are proud of his generous character and his magnanimity, and we consider him worthy of our Hind. The matter of relationship is of great importance to the Ghassani, therefore it should be no surprise to you to learn that King al-Harith has asked us for the betrothal of Hind to his son Tha'labah. He is her cousin and he has more right to marry her than anyone else in the tribe," the queen explained. "That said, we prefer you to her cousin by the will of our daughter, and in consideration of your highness's spirit and traits."

This grand praise from Queen Saada sent Hammad's spirits soaring and he felt that his hopes and dreams might at last come true.

"But her father, the grand King Jabalah," she continued, "is of the opinion that if you agree to our proposal then we shall be in a position to escape the gossip of relatives regarding this matter and offer a prideful union to us all."

"Speak your command, my queen," said Hammad, "and I will do as you request."

"We request that you carry out a mission that a brave man such as you will not fail to accomplish," Queen Saada proclaimed, "and in doing so will quiet the scorn of our opponents."

Hammad became bolstered with zeal by her continued words and offered, "Mistress, I will do whatever you bid me to do."

"Hind is a flower in the desert and for her wedding we command that you bestow upon her a gift equally as rare and beautiful," the queen explained. "You must retrieve for her a pair of earrings with a pearl as large as a dove's egg in each."

"Where would I find such a treasure?" asked Hammad in amazement.

"I am speaking of Mary's Earrings," revealed Queen Saada. "Do you know of them?"

"Regrettably, I have heard the Ghassani grandmother Mary, but nothing of any earrings," Hammad said plainly. "Can you tell me more about them?"

"It is said that she gave the earrings as a gift to al-Ka'aba in Mecca and we believe they are still there to this day," answered the queen. "They are in the heart of the Hejazi kingdom. There will have to be bravery and cunning in retrieving the earrings from al-Ka'aba. We are sure you are worthy of this challenge."

Salman became troubled and fearful for his master as he listened to the queen issue her commands, since he knew the danger that lay at the door of al-Ka'aba. He turned to Queen Saada and asked, "May I propose a question to your majesty?"

"Do ask," she answered.

"Do you want us to bring the authentic pair of Mary's Earrings or a pair similar to them?" asked Salman, apparently still jesting.

"We will not accept any substitute. We wish to be proud among our cousins that we married our daughter to a man who brought this treasure out of the heart of al-Ka'aba," she replied flatly. "It is a happy coincidence that Abdullah's journey took him to Hejaz. I believe in my heart that it is God's wish that Hammad go there to meet with his father."

Bursting with pride, Hammad rose and announced to the queen, "I will do as you command. There is nothing that can stop me from earning the pride of your family and the regard of Hind."

Afterward in her room, Hind was contemplating the danger this challenge would place Hammad in and regretted supporting her parents, so she began to weep. Her cries were interrupted by a servant who summoned her to her mother. She quickly wiped the tears away, but signs of depression still showed on her face. Hind entered the room, and Hammad was greatly touched when he saw her anxieties.

With great chivalry he said, "Do not let misgivings or impatience make you worried. I will bring you Mary's Earrings and prove my worth."

Hind said nothing but was moved with admiration for his bravery and tender traits. With tears brimming in her eyes, she bowed her head and adjusted the pleats of her sleeve but Hammad still saw her troubled face. He realized the words in her heart and anxiety in her mind and wanted to encourage her. He said to her mother, "I have always been eager to visit al-Ka'aba to see what this worldwide pilgrimage is all about. My father has often told me of the erected images and the great sacrifices those Arabs make to their gods." Hammad got to his feet and continued, "We will depart without delay, but we would first like to see his majesty and bid him good-bye."

"As you wish," replied Queen Saada, "he will be glad to see you before your departure. He has left for al-Balqa to prepare for the conflict ahead"

"Then we shall stop in al-Balqa tomorrow morning before we leave for Hejaz," Hammad decided. "Do you know the way, Salman?"

"We can send some men with you to show you the way," the queen offered.

They spent the remainder of the day resting at the Stream Palace, but Hind could not enjoy her time because she could not shake the mounting fears she felt for Hammad. He had become the whole world to her.

The Farewell

Salman rose before sunrise to prepare the horses for the ride to al-Balqa. Hammad, already dressed in his traveling clothes, went to find Hind and her mother for a last farewell. He found them in the reception room, and as he entered Hind respectfully stood up and Hammad put his hand in hers. She was cold to the touch and her face had taken on a pallid hue. As Hammad uttered his words of farewell, he could not help but notice the tears rolling down her cheeks. Hind gently withdrew her hand from his and bowed her head in silence. He knew the fears she held for him by her quiet dignity.

"Why so worried? Are you not the brave Hind who fought off a whole garrison of armed guards?" Hammad asked.

She looked at him with a sidelong glance and sighed deeply but remained silent. Hammad then bid his farewell to the queen and Hind began to weep. Queen Saada wished to dismiss her because the sight of her crying was slowly becoming unsightly, but said to Hammad instead, "Go, my son, in the company of God, he will guide you on your journey. We hope to see you soon with your father."

Thanking her for her courtesy, Hammad kissed her hand and left for the park where Salman was waiting with the caravan. Hammad thanked them both once more as he mounted his horse and departed with the caravan for al-Balqa. Hind and her mother watched them until they had passed out of sight. After they had gone, Hind fully realized the consequences of what her parents had planned for Hammad, and began to weep once more. As she retreated to the palace, her mother consoled her with her arm around Hind's shoulder, "Be at ease, my child, he will come back victorious."

"You know that is not so," Hind cried. "He is gone forever!" Her eyes began to overflow with tears of sorrow for Hammad.

"Put that imagination of yours to rest," the queen chided her. "Hammad is brave and his servant has great experience in every matter. They will surely return with the earrings and we will have our means of escape from Tha'labah and his father." Hind could not think of a thing to say and remained silent.

Hammad continued toward al-Balqa, keeping his unease regarding his mission hidden. The news reached King Jabalah regarding Hammad's journey to see him, and he knew the reason for the visit. After requesting entry, Hammad met the king and bowed to kiss King Jabalah's outstretched hand of welcome. In return, King Jabalah kissed Hammad on the forehead.

"I have come to thank you, Uncle, for your consent," said Hammad, "and to let you know that I am now on my way to Mecca, so pray for me."

"Peace be with you as you go and during your stay, my son," said the king, "but please keep this matter concealed until its conclusion, lest we fall into trouble."

"I shall," said Hammad, adding, "I have a servant outside who wishes to kiss your hand. He is a good companion to me."

"Let him enter," said the king.

Hammad called Salman who humbly kissed King Jabalah's hand and asked for God's protection for the men. Then they rode hard for their tent back on the outskirts of Busra. The old man who was their landlord was surprised and happy to see them, having been worried by their long absence. They joined him by the fire and planned their journey. Then they retired for the night, exhausted from their day of riding.

The Departure

The next morning Hammad and Salman asked the old man where they could purchase supplies, and he gave them directions. After a day of preparations, they had purchased two camels for bearing the water, clothes and provisions for the trip, and secured two servants to assist with the journey. They asked the old man to hire a guide for them to which he answered with a smile, "I know just the man! He arrived with the Muslim army to destroy the rule of Ghassan. He plans on returning to Yathrib which is his home and near Mecca, so I will ask him to take you with him and tell him you will pay him for his guidance."

"Is he here now?" Salman inquired.

"Yes, he is," replied the old man.

"Call him," said Salman.

"Abu Sa'id!" cried the old man.

"Yes, brother?" answered a voice from another tent.

"Come unto me!" called the old man.

A moment later, a desert man emerged from the nearby tent. He was a tall man with broad shoulders and a slim beard. He looked about forty years old and was cloaked in a sheet of white woven material, half of which wrapped his neck, the other wrapped around his head. He carried a spear and an arrow in his hand and his feet were unshod. Salman immediately recognized the Hejazi dress the man wore. Abu Sa'id was astounded at the sight of Hammad, who was elegantly dressed, and surmised that he must be an Emir. He smiled at Hammad and thought to himself, "What providence, he must be the prince of Ghassan!"

Seeing the look in Abu Sa'id's eyes, the old man said to him, "This prince is not Ghassani, as you are thinking, but Iraqi. Do not be fooled by his appearance."

"It does not matter even if he was a Ghassani," replied Abu Sa'id. "Since he is your neighbor, he is all right with me."

"God bless you," said Hammad, "where are you from?"

"I am from the people of Yathrib," he answered.

"The people of Yathrib are mostly Jews, are they not?" Salman asked casually.

"Yes, they are," said Abu Sa'id, "have you been there before?"

"I was there ten years ago," Salman nodded, "but great changes have come about since the sun of Islam has begun shining upon it. Does the Prophet of Islam come from your tribe or from the tribes of Mecca?"

"The Prophet, peace be upon him, left his home of Mecca under persecution by his tribe," Abu Sa'id explained, "but we from Yathrib came to his aid, so he calls us al-Ansar meaning 'the helpers'."

"Are you heading to Yathrib?" asked Salman.

"Soon, yes," Abu Sa'id replied, "where are you traveling?"

"We are on our way to Mecca," Salman answered, "would you bless us with your company on the journey?"

"I would, if that were possible," Abu Sa'id declined, shaking his head.

"What prevents you from joining us?" Salman asked curiously.

"Mecca is home to our enemies," Abu Sa'id frowned. "I fear their reprisal."

"Who are your enemies in Mecca?" Salman inquired.

"I speak of the tribe of Quraysh, the uncles of our Prophet, peace be upon him. He was exiled from Mecca after evicting the idols from al-Ka'aba, and his uncles are looking for an opportunity to kill him," Abu Sa'id explained. "He came to our city as a refugee, and we welcomed him with open arms. Regrettably they are no longer our friends. Some of his relatives came with him but the rest are still in Mecca pledging their opposition to his cause with Abu Sufyan the great merchant at their side."

"Suppose we left you in Yathrib," Hammad offered, "would there be any danger to you if we were to leave you there?"

"No, no danger to you either if you take well-known routes, since you are strangers and neutrals," Abu Sa'id answered, "but it will be safer for you to travel with the caravan than alone."

Salman exchanged looks with Hammad and asked his opinion.

"Let us go with him to the city of Yathrib," Hammad decided, "and once there we will decide what to do."

Preparing for their departure, Salman began to load the water and provisions on the two camels with the help of two hired servants. Hammad retrieved their hidden valuables to take with them and left some clothes and items of unimportance with the old man. Once ready they departed for Hejaz and after several weeks they came upon the mountains of Yathrib.

"We will soon be in Yathrib," said Abu Sa'id to the men.

"I remember the city and its main routes," said Salman, "for I visited some years ago now."

"Much has changed since the Prophet, peace be upon him, arrived and brought his followers with him. More people and more buildings now, more business," Abu Sa'id continued, "a result of the mass migration from Mecca."

The city of Yathrib came into view as they passed over the mountains. It was nothing but a plain of land surrounded by orchards and forests.

"This is Yathrib," Abu Sa'id announced. "Would you lodge here until you find someone to take you to Mecca, or have you other plans already?"

"I would prefer to stay here for a while," said Hammad, "to see the city and her people. I would also like to see the Prophet of Islam and meet his followers after hearing so much about him and his ways."

They descended from the mountains, and rode toward the city's ramparts. With Abu Sa'id at their side nobody thought ill of them, in fact many thought that they had come to join the Prophet and Islam. Nearing the city walls, Salman announced, "I think we should erect our tents here and rest for the night. Tomorrow we can leave our horses and supplies in the charge of the servants and enter the city unencumbered."

"I cannot linger any longer," Abu Sa'id said apologetically, "for I have some business that I need to tend to. I will leave you and hope that I might see you again inside the city."

"Very well," Salman and Hammad echoed. "God be with you."

He bade them farewell and left.

Hammad turned to Salman, "We should head for Mecca as soon as we can to retrieve the earrings." Salman nodded in agreement. It was late in the afternoon, so they sent a servant to buy some provisions. He returned close to sunset, so they ate, fed the horses and camel, and remained there for the night.

In the morning they filled their vessels with water and mounted, departing for Mecca. The only route to Mecca that Salman knew of ran along the Wells of Bad'r, west of the city, so they led their caravan to the wells. Knowing that the wells weren't far from Yathrib they rode slowly and arrived late in the afternoon. They unloaded their cargo and sat down to eat lunch under the shade of a tree on a grassy knoll. Once they had eaten and rested, they erected their tents and made a fire for guidance in the night. They arose the next morning and filled their vessels from the well, loaded their camels, mounted their horses, and rode straight on to Mecca which they reached the following week.

"Where should we start?" asked Hammad.

"Let us first go to an inn where we can stay and have our horses and camels cared for," Salman suggested, "then we can rest for the day, and tomorrow I will search the city for news."

They came upon an inn on the outskirts of the city and stayed that day and night. In the morning Salman dressed himself in Hejazi garb, and began his investigation around the city for some news. He arrived at a chapel and at one side of it he saw a crowd of men who wandered around naked, some were sitting, some standing, and some kneeling and talking to each other. He observed the odd behavior of the men for a while, and then left to look around some more.

His eyes caught a square building covered with thick curtains, which he guessed must be the al-Ka'aba. The pilgrims seemed to be aimlessly wandering around the cube, but on closer inspection, he found stone statues placed around the plaza and on top of al-Ka'aba itself between which the pilgrims would move back and forth. He also saw huge idols here and there with people nearby shaving and washing. The behavior of these people surprised him. It would be a great service, he thought to himself, if nothing else was achieved by the Islamic religion other than the enlightenment of these people and the end of the worship of idols. Salman stood off to the side of the plaza and regarded al-Ka'aba, thinking of the earrings. Was it possible that they were still here in Mecca? If so, where would they be kept?

These questions left Salman feeling perplexed, so he departed al-Ka'aba and walked through the streets lost in thought. After a time he came to a beautiful, stately mansion surrounded by a throng of people milling about. Salman suspected this to be the home of an Emir, so he asked one of the people who the owner was and learned that it belonged to Abu Sufyan. Thanking God for delivering him to this doorway, Salman was overjoyed by the belief that he finally had a favorable chance of finding his master Abdullah. He looked at all the faces in the crowd without recognizing anyone, so he asked the same man about Abdullah and received the reply that Abdullah had left Abu Sufyan's caravan near Amman and had not been seen since. Dismayed by this news, Salman made his way back to the inn, the world dark in his eyes. The sun was setting as he returned to the inn, and Salman found Hammad restlessly awaiting him. Salman showed signs of worry but didn't feel that it was the right time to tell Hammad the news about his father, so he said instead that he had not learned anything new. Hammad and Salman remained in Mecca for several months, searching from one end of the city to the other for word of Abdullah but all was in vain.

One day as he passed by the house of Abu Sufyan, Salman found it vacant and asked a local about it. He was told that Abu Sufyan heard about a march of the Muslims on Mecca and had left to parley with them and perhaps join the Prophet's religious cause. Inquiring about the Muslim soldiers, Salman was told that they were very close. Looking around, he saw the looming signs of failure in the eyes of the locals. He overheard some praising Islam and assailing Abu Sufyan, and some blaming the Quraysh tribe, the uncles of the Prophet, for their stubborn resistance to Islam. As he continued to look around, Salman saw people in flight and women sobbing their woes. Then he heard the thunderous sound of hooves in the distance and a monstrous cloud of dust began to form on the horizon. It continued to grow and when he could feel the thunder of the hooves beneath his feet, the cloud of dust finally settled to reveal a wide army of cavalry and infantrymen with flags. Behind each flag stood a Muslim tribe.

Salman hurried back to warn Hammad of the invasion just as a detachment led by Abu Sufyan entered the city, calling the people to join Islam, declaring that whosoever closes his door shall be spared the indignation of conquest.

The Conquest of Mecca

They lodged at the inn that night and arose early the following morning to get an early start to their activities for the day. Salman left Hammad and rode outside the city to a nearby hill to see if anything was happening. He saw the Muslim army approaching them and could see that the army was made up of several different tribes. There were over ten thousand men marching in a solid formation across the plain. They were advanced by horsemen and standard-bearers, and a man dressed in red robes and a burnished black turban sat upon a camel in the center of the procession. The man removed his turban and laid it on the pommel of his saddle. Salman was astonished to see a fully armed soldier riding alongside the man. Salman approached a local shepherd and asked about the procession. He was told that this man was Muhammad, the Prophet and Messenger of God, and the man next to him was Usama bin Zayd, his servant.

"He follows the Prophet, peace be upon him, to demonstrate his humbleness," the local explained. Salman was astounded by the peacefulness of the spectacle and pleasant sight before him and thought to himself, 'no wonder this man, with all these fine traits, is victorious everywhere he travels.' Salman then asked the shepherd what he knew of the conquest of Mecca and was told that the army was already occupying the city under the leadership of Khalid ibn al-Walid who had entered the city several days ago. Salman thanked the man and then turned to make haste to his master after hearing this news.

On his way, he saw the Qurayshi preparing for defence but signs of worry showed in their faces. He watched women, their hair flying wildly, provoking the men with songs while others yet threw wine in their horses' faces. Hammad, who had been inside the city looking for information, saw Salman approaching and together they hurried to the chapel for refuge and to stay close to the events unfolding around them. Sitting on the far side of the room, they watched people sitting with a glassy-eyed look of dread on their faces. A few hours later, they heard shouting from outside that the Messenger of God had arrived.

Hammad and Salman watched as the Prophet Muhammad entered the plaza outside the chapel, his camel held in tow by one of his comrades not far behind him. The Prophet then proceeded to each one of the chapel's three hundred and sixty idols and began to smash the iron molded around their feet with an iron rod to topple the statues over. With each one he felled, he announced, "The truth has come and the false has vanished, as the false will always vanish." They watched the calm desecration, stricken with awe, and beheld the Prophet as he walked up to the largest image set beside al-Ka'aba and destroyed it. They watched closely as the Prophet's men began to ransack the ruins of the chapel courtyard, secretly hoping they might come upon the earrings, but alas, they were disappointed when no earrings were found. The Prophet Muhammad ushered the people out of the chapel after the pillage, and sealed it shut. Then, he and his men made their way into the city.

However awestruck, Hammad and Salman could not help but feel a great letdown at this turn of events. They found themselves in a quandary as to what they should do next. Hammad sat restlessly and realized for the first time that his hopes were vanishing. He went up to the roof of the inn and sat alone, looking out over the city. His gaze wandered across the plains to the mountains on either side of the valley, his mood very troubled. Hammad thought of Hind and of his missing father, and blamed himself for these failures. Worried by his master's troubles, Salman decided to leave him be and instead rode through the city in search of more news.

Salman was passing a house where he saw a mule outfitted with an expensive saddle being tended by a small boy. Salman asked him who the owner of the mule was.

"This is the mule of Hassan ibn Thabit, the famous poet," replied the lad.

Salman remembered hearing about this poet who used to travel the world over to praise kings and receive patronage for his verse. He thought to himself, 'I think I have found what I have been looking for, this poet may have news about what happened to the earrings!'

"Is your master home?" Salman inquired.

"Yes," replied the boy, "would you like to see him?"

"I would," Salman smiled.

A few moments later, Salman was beckoned inside to meet the poet. When he entered, he saw a very old man with poor eyesight, gray hair, and a long beard who was sitting upon a cushion in a corner of the room. Joining him, Salman spoke with the old man about many different topics and listened to several of his tales before asking him about the earrings.

"I think they are in al-Hira," the poet remarked after a long, thoughtful pause. "I recall a Persian merchant who often brought goods to sell in Mecca who left with Mary's Earrings in his possession. As I recall, he sold them to King al-Nu'man of Iraq," continued the lyrist, "but I do not recall who the merchant was."

Salman excused himself hurriedly, bidding the poet farewell, and returned to his master.

"Rejoice, Master," he announced as he burst into the room, "I have good news, rejoice!"

"What could have you so elated, Salman?" asked Hammad. "Tell me the news!"

Salman explained everything to Hammad about the old poet and what he had to say. At once, Hammad stood up and got dressed saying, "Salman, let us both go back to him and listen to what he has to say!"

"With pleasure!" Salman replied.

Feeling hungry for the first time in a long time, Hammad ate some dates to satisfy the rumblings and left with Salman on foot. They soon reached the house of the poet Hassan. At the gate, Salman asked permission to enter and they were admitted only a moment later. Salman introduced Hammad to Hassan, explaining that he was

Salman's master, one of the princes of Iraq. Hammad approached the poet to kiss his hand but the man would not allow him to, he only stared at Hammad, recounting in his memory the princes of Iraq. Hassan did not recognize him.

"Please, would you tell me your name and your family's name?" asked Hassan.

"I am Hammad, the son of Emir Abdullah." Hammad replied.

"I do not remember an Emir by that name in the palace of King al-Nu'man," the poet reminisced, "or maybe my memory has dimmed. As for King al-Nu'man, he was defeated by treachery over twenty years ago and all his friends have been scattered." Hassan shook his head softly, and added, "That king was truly noble, and his memory honors the Persian Empire."

"Did you see him often," asked Hammad.

"I would visit several times before the end of every year," he said, "I used to ride my camel from here to Syria, and once there, I would go to al-Balqa and see King Jabalah and his cousin, King al-Harith, then I would leave for Iraq and enter the audience of King al-Nu'man and receive expensive prizes and gold from him. The Sons of Ghassan were generous too, but now that I am in attendance to the Prophet, peace be upon him, I no longer have need to travel."

"You said, Sir, that the earrings were sold to King al-Nu'man," Salman remarked. "What happened to them after his death?"

"I do not know," said the poet with a shrug of his shoulders, "perhaps they are in the possession of those who murdered him. If that is what happened they must still be in the treasuries of al-Hira in Iraq."

The entire time, Hassan addressed Salman, but his eyes were fixated upon Hammad, watching his every movement, scrutinizing him as if he had seen someone like Hammad before. Hammad did not notice the attention, lost in his own anxieties. Hassan could see that Hammad was uneasy and anxious to leave.

"You looked disturbed, young prince," he commented.

Hammad looked up as if having just awoken from a daze, and nodded, "I would like to leave as soon as I can to continue my search for the earrings."

"Are you passing through Yathrib?" Hassan inquired. "Because if you are I had planned on going there tomorrow myself, how do you feel about going in my company?"

"With pleasure," answered Hammad, "we would be honored to travel with you."

"Do not mention it," replied Hassan. "Bring your possessions here to the house and we will stay here tonight, and then we will all leave together on the morrow."

The Reunion

They lodged that night in the home of the poet Hassan. In the morning, they all left for the city of Yathrib and while on route were entertained by Hassan, who sang poems praising both kings of Ghassan.

"What do you think of King al-Harith?" asked Hammad.

"He was a generous man," the poet answered, "but an envious one, too."

"And what of King Jabalah?" Hammad continued.

"He is a man of great prestige and magnanimity," Hassan announced without delay, "and has not a jealous bone in his body."

"Does one king hold more authority than the other?" asked Hammad.

"King Jabalah is of higher rank and more respected," the poet reflected, "but King al-Harith is dead now, as I have recently learned, so I cannot imagine the matter of authority being an issue."

Hammad and Salman exchanged shocked looks.

"Who do you think will take his place on the throne?" asked Hammad.

Hassan thought for a moment and then replied, "I do not think there is anyone worthy of it. It is likely that the tribes of Ghassan will come together under the banner of King Jabalah."

This news should have elated Hammad but for the futile search for the earrings, which were still no closer to being found. They arrived at Yathrib the next morning and saw all the people rejoicing and praying to God. Making their way through the commotion was taxing, and as soon as the poet arrived at his house he wanted nothing else but to rest and relax, and he invited his guests to join him. They talked over refreshments for much of the rest of the day.

"I remember something that might concern you," Hassan said to Salman, "that I forgot to tell you before."

"What might that be?" asked Salman.

"Do you recall our conversation yesterday?" Hassan asked. "I mentioned the battle of Mu'tah, I believe."

"No, Sir, not too well," answered Salman.

"It happened that the Prophet Muhammad sent some of his men to fight the tribes of Ghassan last year, those soldiers fought in Mu'tah, not far from the Holy City. I regret not mentioning that the soldiers captured a man during that attack who was brought to us. I knew that it was a mistake to capture him, since the man is Iraqi and not from Ghassan as our soldiers believed, so he has stayed here as my guest instead of as a prisoner," explained Hassan. "Seeing that you are from Iraq as well, I thought you might be glad to see your countryman."

Hassan gave the servant orders to call the Iraqi guest. The servant returned a few moments later followed by a middle-aged man wrapped in a cloak. As soon as Salman saw the man he felt his heart drop. This man looked like his master Abdullah, but his face bore a desolation unlike any Salman had seen before. Abdullah once had a long, proud moustache and beard but this man standing before him had very little facial hair. Salman considered him very carefully before cautiously asking, "Master Abdullah?" Hammad and Salman still had their heads and faces covered, as was the usual custom while traveling, therefore it was no small wonder that Abdullah did not recognize them.

Hearing his father's name, Hammad's preoccupation vanished as he turned his attention to see his father before him, alive and well. Hammad jumped to his feet and clasped his father tightly and kissed him. Salman kissed Abdullah's hand and rejoiced for the reunited father and son. Merriment reigned as they bantered back and forth, and the poet Hassan could not have been happier, overjoyed that father and son were reunited through him.

As they laughed and talked, they each enjoyed a demitasse of bitter coffee and retold their stories to one another. Hammad related his story about the lion and the loss of his horse and their long search for Abdullah all the way to Mecca and back. He told his father about the quest for the earrings and that perhaps they were in Iraq, and he indicated that a search may yet find them. Abdullah listened in astonishment to all the stories and sat transfixed as Hammad related everything that had happened during his absence. Silently he did not approve of everything he heard.

Abdullah then told them exactly what had happened to him during his travels with Abu Sufyan, and his abduction by the Muslim soldiers outside of Mu'tah, and his imprisonment during the siege. He told the story of how three thousand Muslims, who had arrived outside Mu'tah to attack Ghassan, had been very successful in their campaign. While morale was low from the start, the Muslim army was inspired by the men who led them. Even though three of the generals died in the battle, the last, Khalid ibn al-Walid was a great fighter and general, and brought them victory and gains of considerable proportion. Many tribes, Abdullah told them, along with the Romans, prepared to reinforce Ghassan for the assault. The Ghassani force massed in the city of Jerusalem and were two hundred thousand strong against what was left of the three thousand Muslims. After the victory, however, the Muslims refused to stay and occupy, and left for their own country. At last, Abdullah told them how he had become ill and lost most of his hair from despair and how, through the graciousness of the poet Hassan, he was brought to Yathrib for solace.

Palm Sunday

After they had exchanged their stories, they all rejoiced and shared their happiness at everyone's well-being.

"Where is my horse now?" asked Hammad.

"He is stabled here," Abdullah answered. "Would you like to see him?"

"Yes, I would," came Hammad's eager reply.

They left for an orchard adjacent to the house. The stallion was tied to a palm tree and recognized Hammad's whistle and began to whinny as his master approached. Hammad greeted his horse and touched his forehead and kissed him between the eyes, then father and son returned to the house with cheer filling their hearts. Hammad still showed some anxiety, however, so once they had made themselves comfortable, Abdullah asked, "Do you still intend to wed Hind?"

"Yes, father," Hammad replied, "I do not think I could give her up."

"Did you forget about our vow?" asked Abdullah.

"What vow?" asked Hammad.

"The vow of Palm Sunday, when your hair is to be cut," said Abdullah.

"What has that to do with the wedding?" Hammad asked. "That was over a year ago."

"It has a great deal to do with the wedding and I will tell you a story after we honor our vow that will make you aware of some of the realities you will face with the matters of marriage," Abdullah reminded Hammad.

Hammad feared yet another obstacle that might come between him and his beloved Hind.

"Would this secret keep us apart?" ask Hammad.

"I cannot disclose the secret now," Abdullah explained yet again, "but after the ceremony on Palm Sunday everything will be revealed to you."

"It will be a long time before Palm Sunday arrives," Hammad complained, "can't we perform the vow sooner?"

"No, my son," Abdullah said with finality, "we have to carry out the vow religiously exact as we swore to God we would!"

Hammad was in a quandary, afraid that this secret would interfere with his plans to wed Hind. He had hoped his father would help him search for the earrings but now he had his doubts after hearing his father's adamant reply. Abdullah warned him not to do anything before Palm Sunday. He remained silent, but a thought occurred to him, perhaps he could ask Salman if he knew anything about the vow. That evening he met Salman alone and asked him bluntly if he had any knowledge of Palm Sunday's vow.

"Your father is the only human alive who knows the secret he carries. I have been in the service of your father since I was a small boy and not once has he revealed anything about the secret. Though I have had on many occasions as great a desire to know as you do, we will just have to wait until Palm Sunday," Salman said.

As they talked, Abdullah walked up to them and suggested they prepare for their return to Syria. In the morning they were ready to set out and said good-bye to their host, Hassan the poet. Being of a generous nature, Hassan provided them with a guide to lead them home. They arrived in Busra a few weeks later and decided to stay at Bahira Monastery. Returning to the monastery brought back bittersweet memories for Hammad, memories of his first meeting with Hind and of the unexpected arrival of Tha'labah. He ached to see her, but his heart was heavy with despair and worry at the thought of facing her without the earrings.

The Stream Palace

Let us leave Abdullah, Hammad, and Salman content and reunited for now, and return our thoughts to the Stream Palace to learn what happened after Hammad's departure.

Hind had bid Hammad farewell, her heart solicitous toward him, for she knew that his mission to retrieve the earrings would bring him no end of danger. At first her confidence in his bravery and wise intuition put her anxieties at ease, and she then learned that the fighting had moved toward Mu'tah, not far from Jerusalem. She was grateful for the knowledge that Hammad's journey would be out of harm's way. Even so, when the war ended and calm once again returned to Balqa, Queen Saada noticed depression and fear in her daughter's face again. Hind could not pin-point it, but she felt an uneasiness, a sensation of impending trouble. Queen Saada tried to console Hind with words of encouragement, but they had little effect.

A Muslim caravan passed through bringing news of the fall of Mecca and bringing Hind a whole new set of fears. She secluded herself in the palace, worried that if she were to venture out she would only find more bad news about Hammad. Word also came bringing the news of the death of her uncle, King al-Harith, which brought Hind and her mother great sorrow but also eased Hind's mind some knowing that the authority of Tha'labah had been substantially weakened. Even that was little solace for Hind, for she grieved deeply over Hammad's absence and sought quiet solitude. Whenever she was alone Hind would idly spin the bracelets on her wrists with tears running down her cheeks, recalling Hammad with unfettered admiration. Queen Saada was very concerned with the condition of her daughter and was beginning to regret the plan she and her husband had imposed on Hammad, and wished for Hammad to return even in failure. The death of King al-Harith had now made the wedding of Hammad to Hind possible without benefit of an endowment.

King Jabalah, however, was indisposed at al-Balqa during the fighting in Mu'tah and too occupied with the war efforts to think of Hammad and Hind. The news of the withdrawal of the Muslim force and the death of his cousin had left King Jabalah more pressed with the serious job of uniting all the tribes of Syria together under his flag. He knew that Tha'labah did not have the diligence of his father, and all of the tribesmen had an extreme hatred for his ruthlessness. Tha'labah reacted with vindictive hatred. Tha'labah spoke unjustly about King Jabalah wherever he traveled, opening King Jabalah's eyes to Tha'labah's true nature. Tha'labah's personality became increasingly ugly as he continued to smear the good name of his uncle, his queen, and his cousin, degrading them every chance he could. King Jabalah felt regret for what he had done to Hammad, he was sincerely sorry for sending the noble young man on such a risky undertaking. The king decided in his heart to wed his daughter to Hammad whether he succeeded or not in acquiring the earrings.

Hind and the Moon

Hind continued to grieve, and her depression would not yield. A year had passed without word of Hammad. She thought he was dead, or at the very least, had failed to get the earrings, so in abject disappointment had chosen not to return.

Late one evening, Hind entered her room and locked the door, and sat by the window that overlooked the park. She leaned against a cushion and cradled her face in the palms of her hands. Just then, the full moon broke from behind the hills with its light spilling over the valleys and mountains. She contemplated the hues of silver over the plains and shadows in the orchards, she looked at the park and saw how the shadows of the trees elongated the branches which then spread and fell upon the various plants of the garden, and she caught an aroma of perfume from plants unseen. The night was calm, the birds were safely in their nests, and the winds eased to a caressing breeze now and then. Hearing only the sound of the rippling streams running through the orchards and the croaking of the frogs, Hind looked up at the moon, now in full view, only to be reminded of her sweetheart. The warm feeling brought a tremor of dejection to her heart after having been delighted with the sights and sounds of the night. She began to cry and then started to sob uncontrollably. Her mother heard her from the hall and knocked on her door, but Hind would not grant her entry. Queen Saada urged her daughter to let her in, so Hind eventually opened the door slowly and her arms reached out for the safe refuge of her mother's embrace.

"What are you crying for, my child?" the queen asked. "Why did you not come to me, do you not know that my heart is breaking for you?"

Hind did not reply but flashed her mother an accusing glance. Queen Saada ignored the stare and asked again, "Why are you so secretive with me?"

Hind looked at her mother with tears in her eyes, and Queen Saada wiped them away with a small cloth. Hind walked away from her mother to the open window and sighed deeply, looking out over the gardens again.

Queen Saada walked over to Hind and stood between her and the window, taking hold of her hand, "Speak, Hind, what makes you cry? You are breaking my heart, and I have no endurance left to hear you cry, do you not know how fragile the heart of a mother is?"

Looking in her mother's eyes, Hind said, "Yes, Mama, I know the heart of a mother, but a mother does not always know the heart of a daughter."

"Who told you that, Hind," asked Queen Saada, shocked, "that I do not know your heart?"

"If you had known my heart, you would not have brought this misery to it," said Hind.

"Then tell me about your heart, my child," Queen Saada returned, "since you have uncovered the obscurities of its secrets."

"Then you knew all along why my heart aches but you would not pity it!" Hind exclaimed. "May God forgive you and my father!"

"Hind!" cried an admonished Queen Saada. "How can you say that we would not pity your heart? All that has happened was of your own consent, there is pride in that for you! And now," she continued, "this matter has changed because of the death of King al-Harith and the shame of Tha'labah. There is nothing, no one, in Hammad's way, whether he brings the earrings back or not."

"This would be our destiny were we to see him again, but if he cannot retrieve the earrings," Hind cried, "he will not return to us!"

"Rely on God," said her mother, "and let us pray to Him to send Hammad back safely."

Hind listened to her mother's wise words and realized that she spoke the truth, but she still wished to be sure of her father's stance.

"I am certain of your consent but what of my father's?" asked Hind.

"Your father is more desirous of this union than ever because of his loathing for Tha'labah's slanderous words. They have only shown your father too clearly how gentle and trustworthy Hammad is compared to your dishonorable cousin, so cheer up and put your faith in God for his safe return to us."

The queen's words worked their way into Hind's heart and soothed her soul, and the princess finally went to bed to get some much needed rest.

The Good News

Hind woke from a restful night's sleep, but her doubts crept back and she wished that she had not awoken except to the soothing sound of Hammad's voice. She lay back in bed, trying to fall asleep again, but could not shake her depressing thoughts. Later that morning her mother came to visit, showing great concern when she found Hind still in bed. She asked what ailed her daughter and Hind pleaded laziness. Queen Saada settled herself in a chair next to her daughter's bed, and they chatted cheerfully in an attempt to raise Hind's spirits.

Around the noon hour, they heard a voice calling out in the courtyard asking for vows for Bahira. The voice made Hind's heart skip a beat and she bounded out of bed, her mother close behind. Remembering Salman's first visit, Hind and her mother hurried to the window and saw the monk on his horse. Hind's senses reeled and she thought she was dreaming. Salman was the last person she expected to see and she greeted him from her window, calling on him to enter the palace. Queen Saada left the room to meet him but Hind stayed behind in her room, unable to stand on her trembling legs. She listened to the fall of his footsteps on the stone as he entered the palace with her mother, and she summoned all her strength to stand up for Salman when he arrived in the room. He greeted her, and smiled broadly, and attempted to kiss her hand, but she would not allow him to do so in order to hide her shaking. In a quivering voice she asked, "What news have you brought me?"

"I have good news, Princess!" he replied. "But first, how are you?"

"We are all well, thank you," she answered, "but how is Hammad? Where is he?"

"He is likewise well," Salman answered. "I left him at Bahira Monastery, most impatiently waiting for word from you."

"He is in good health?" Hind asked, reassuring herself.

"Yes," Salman repeated, "and he had a joyful reunion with his father in Yathrib."

Hind knelt down and took Salman's hand to kiss it. "Thank God for his safety," she praised, her face radiant and placid.

"Why did Hammad not accompany you?" asked Queen Saada.

"He remained in the monastery," Salman explained. "I fear he feels too humble to meet with you."

"What is he timid about?" the queen asked. "We want nothing of him except his safety!"

"And what of the earrings?" Salman asked.

"There is no need to be concerned with the earrings now," Queen Saada answered, "since the reason for their endowment is a thing of the past."

"We have failed in our efforts to find them," Salman went on, and he told them the tale of their ordeal in Mecca and of their chance reunion with Abdullah. He also told them of Hammad's intention to continue their search in Iraq.

"Forget about the earrings," said Hind, "we can do without them!"

Salman, surprised at the sudden change, wondered if King Jabalah was of the same mind.

"Is my master, King Jabalah, well?" he asked.

"Very much so," Queen Saada replied. "He waits impatiently for his son-in-law's arrival."

The words "son-in-law" satisfied Salman's curiosity, and he was glad for her consent. "Is his judgment also indifferent toward the earrings?"

"He wants nothing except the safety of our child, Hammad," she said. "Summon him to us."

"My master wishes that with all his heart," Salman said with a smile, "so allow us a short time to bring him to you. He will arrive as swiftly as he can."

The queen nodded and smiled, adding, "We all wish his presence when Hind's father is here so that we may all celebrate the happiness of Hammad's return. It would also please us for his father to be in his company so that our joy will be complete."

Salman was cheered by Queen Saada's words but pondered silently. Hind noticed the change in him and asked, "What is the matter, Salman? What could trouble you so? Is there something that would stop him from coming?"

"No, my Mistress," Salman reassured her, "he is extremely anxious to be with you, but…"

Hind exchanged looks with the queen and hung on Salman's last word. "What makes you hesitate, Salman?" asked Hind. "You make us anxious!"

"Well, you see," Salman continued apologetically, "Hammad's engagement to Hind was made in the absence of his father, and so without his father's knowledge. When my Master heard the news, his joy was boundless, but he has asked Hammad to hold off on the wedding plans until after Palm Sunday."

"What has Palm Sunday to do with the wedding?" asked the queen.

"The details are not mine to know," acknowledged Salman, "but that my Master and Hammad have made a vow that Hammad's hair be cut on that day. Hammad will also be told something of great importance, but I do not know any more than this."

The color drained from Hind's face and she silently prayed for God's help in this unexpected turn of events.

"That does not matter," said Queen Saada, "there is no hurry concerning the wedding plans. Call Hammad to come and meet with his father-in-law. He will be glad to see Hammad."

"Praise God for your grace," said Salman. "I will hasten him to you. He will feel blessed to rejoin you. Just appoint the time, and we will be here with his father."

"I would like you to tell him to come here alone straight away," interjected Hind, "and then also when my father comes so that Hammad may bring his father too."

"I will leave now to return with my master on the morrow," said Salman, taking his leave to return to Hammad at Bahira.

Hammad greeted Salman on his return and strained to read some news on his servant's face, but Salman kept his joy well hidden. "Well?" Hammad asked with vexation.

"Cheer up, Master," said Salman, "God has removed all the obstacles from our path!"

"How is Hind?" Hammad asked, "Is she glad that I am back? Does she know that we could not find the earrings?"

After a boisterous laugh, Salman struggled to say, "The earrings are no longer required as an endowment. The situation has changed with the death of King al-Harith. You are free to marry tomorrow if you wished, if it were possible. As for Hind, you know her heart."

"Did she ask to meet me?" asked Hammad.

"Yes, she did," Salman answered, "and she asked that you bring your father with you when her father is present so they may be introduced to each other."

"There is no way that father would consent to join us!" cried Hammad.

"I do not know," said Salman, "but I did explain this to my mistress Hind."

"How did you explain it?" asked Hammad.

"I referred to it in a most pleasing manner," Salman answered, "explaining that my master Abdullah was joyous after hearing of the engagement, but that he wished to fulfill your vow before the wedding."

"I fear some misunderstanding on Hind's part," Hammad said, cautiously.

"I cannot say for sure," Salman repeated. "I am taking you to her tomorrow. That will be the time to understand one another."

Hind and Hammad

Hammad spoke to his father about Hind that evening and explained that the death of King al-Harith had removed all obstacles barring the marriage, even the earrings no longer mattered. Abdullah remained silent.

"Does this news not please you, father?" Hammad asked.

"I am happy for your happiness, but I still urge you to hold off in your excitement until after Palm Sunday," Abdullah answered wearily.

"Father, I promise to do nothing before the day of our vow, but I am going to Stream Palace tomorrow to see Hind and her mother for some peace of mind," Hammad said. "I think they would be pleased to meet you."

"I will meet them, but after Palm Sunday," Abdullah reaffirmed, "you can go to see them, but do not arrange anything yet!"

"Yes father," Hammad answered. "I understand."

The next morning, Hammad mounted his horse and left for the Stream Palace with Salman at his side. Hind spent a sleepless night in joyful anticipation of Hammad's arrival and only fell asleep toward dawn. She awoke with a start to see that the sun had risen and for one moment thought that Hammad might have come and gone while she was asleep. Hind luxuriated in a perfumed bath for most of the morning, and then returned to her room to look out her window down the road to Busra. She tired of standing, and sat with her eyes fixed at the horizon to watch for Hammad's approach. She scrutinized everything that looked like a moving object and any noise that might mark a horse's gallop or whinny. Meanwhile, Queen Saada was busy with the servants preparing the food for the guests. When she had completed her instructions, the queen turned her steps toward Hind's room and saw her daughter sitting alone, staring out the window. Hind gave her mother a radiant smile.

"Why are you sitting alone, my daughter?" the queen asked, "I think you wish Hammad would change his mind about coming."

Hind laughed at the joke but said nothing, her attention transfixed on the horizon.

"Let us go to the park to enjoy the fragrance of the flowers," the queen suggested, "staying here is wearisome."

Taking Hind by the hand, she led her daughter to the gardens where they strolled leisurely until they came to the park. They walked among the trees in the orchard, Hind stealing a backward glance from time to time in the hope that she might catch a glimpse of Hammad's arrival. Her mother urged her on through the park with glib conversation. Strolling through the flowerbeds, Hind finally heard the whinny of horses and her heart swelled and beat rapidly with pride.

"Let us stay here, my child," Queen Saada suggested. "Hammad will find us in the park."

Hind did not reply, her eyes were transfixed on the gate, her impatience beginning to show. She waited only a moment more before she saw him striding toward her, tall and proud. He wore a sword under a jacket laced with a satin cord. He was handsome, the beating of her heart intensified and her face paled and then flushed a deep crimson. She stood frozen and mesmerized as the queen approached Hammad to greet him. Hind stayed in the background, too painfully shy to approach him. Hammad hurried toward her, his face beaming, and stretched his hands out to greet her. She gently extended her hand and placed it in his palms, lowering her head to obscure the smile that lit her face at his touch.

"How are you, Hind?" he asked, lowering his eyes. "I have failed in my mission."

"We are not concerned with that now," she answered, "our only desire is that you are safe, and so you are, thank God."

With tears rolling down her cheeks, Hind turned to sit on a stone bench under the shade of a lovely tree and Hammad sat next to her, the queen resting on the next bench over. After a moment of silence, Queen Saada lamented over Hammad's absence and praised God for his safe return.

"I did not mind the mission," he explained. "I do not consider my trials extraordinary, nor the hardships unbearable. Yet my journey was unsuccessful, even though I was not idle. I feel that the cause of my failure is beyond our providence. The earrings disappeared a half century ago in the hands of Persian merchants. I intend to pick up the search for them in Iraq…"

"No! No! No!" Hind interrupted him. "They are unnecessary now, I can do without them. There is no need to subject yourself to any more hardships for my sake!"

"I see the traces of your journey on your clothes, Hammad," the queen observed. "Would you like to wash and change? Let us return to the palace and forget about the earrings."

"I can change my clothes at any time, but sitting here beneath this tree with the gentle whisper of the stream gives me all the comfort I need," he answered. "I do not hide the fact that I did not expect this assembly after all the trouble that has crossed my path. I will never forget my days in Mecca, the memories will be with me all my life.

"Tell me what happened," Hind urged.

"I cannot speak of what I saw," he said, shaking his head, "so let us be content knowing that between the absence of my father, the occupation of Mecca, and the disappearance of the earrings, I was in a very difficult position."

Queen Saada smiled, and added, "We are very glad that you were reunited with your father. We hope he is well. Does he plan to visit? I would like to introduce him to King Jabalah."

Hammad's thoughts returned to his father's warning about the vow, and he said to himself, 'There is yet another obstacle in my path, and no one but my father knows what it is.' Out loud, he said to the queen, "My father will be very pleased to meet King Jabalah, but he is preoccupied at the moment and looks forward to an opportunity to enjoy your hospitality."

King Jabalah

During their conversation, a servant announced that King Jabalah had arrived in the courtyard. The news surprised everyone. They continued to talk merrily as they retired to the reception hall to greet the king, even though Hammad was still anxious that his failure to find the earrings would harm their relationship. Hind, on the other hand, expected her father to show deep affection for Hammad since her mother had given her that impression. Queen Saada was the only one not surprised at his arrival since she is the one who had sent a messenger to inform the king of Hammad's safe return and forthcoming visit. Upon returning to the palace Queen Saada, Hind, and Hammad entered the reception hall and seated themselves, and all the servants followed suit to wait to greet the king.

King Jabalah and his horsemen dismounted and servants rushed over to tend to the horses. The king's travelling robes here covered in dust and his sword hung from his side. His family was the first thing his eyes fell upon as he entered the hall and he regarded them warmly. His eyes then fell upon Hammad. Hammad stepped forward and then, being overly cautious, took a step back and waited for the king's acknowledgement. King Jabalah did not hesitate and proudly strode straight over to Hammad, saluted him, shook his hand, and kissed him as a father would. Meanwhile, the members of the audience hall stood watching them, wondering who this young man was to be greeted like family.

"It pleases us, Hammad," the king said, "that you have returned safely from your journey. You have been away from us for some time, tell us of your travels."

Humbled by the king's familiarity, Hammad retold the story of his flight from Bahira through the land of the beasts, of the loss of his father and the despair in the search for him, and of the journey to Mecca into the heart of the land of the Muslims. As he carried on, Hammad revealed the treachery of the king's cousin Tha'labah and the hand he played in orchestrating Hammad's troubles. As last he came to the story of his love for Hind and his regret that they had been kept apart for so long.

"And all because of that race between you and Tha'labah," the king commented, leaning back in his chair. "I see now that he got everything that he deserved."

The audience was listening to this exchange in awed silence, fearing an outburst of anger when Hammad started to speak of Tha'labah. They rejoiced, however, at the king's words of scorn for the treacherous prince.

King Jabalah turned to his wife and announced, "Do offer us some refreshments, we shall drink of good cheer and celebrate the safe return of our son-in-law!"

"Shall we sit together at the table and have our food and drink brought to us all at once?" Queen Saada asked.

"Very good!" the king answered.

The queen clapped her hands and a boy immediately came to her side. "Has everything been prepared?" she asked.

"Yes, mistress," the boy nodded.

King Jabalah rose and led the way, everyone following him into the dining room where the tables had been set with lavish dishes served in bowls made of gold and silver. They sat down together and enjoyed the food and wine and pleasing conversation. After they had finished, King Jabalah approached Hammad and bade him to follow.

Alone now, they walked together through the park and King Jabalah began the conversation, "Do you understand, Hammad, that you hold the position of my son and that it has been ordained by God that you be my son-in-law? Do you also know that I am proud of you? I leave the details of your wedding to you because Hind is my only child. You will live among us afterward, and if you become well versed in politics you will become king after my death."

They stopped walking and Hammad answered, "This is a great honour for which words do not suffice to express my gratitude and appreciation. Your condition is hardly a condition at all, and I thank you, my king. But the time of the wedding cannot yet be decided, allow me to tell you why."

"Yes," the king assented, "your servant also suggested as much. What is the reason?"

"My father made a vow that if I lived, my hair would not be cut until my twenty-first birthday, and he chose Palm Sunday as the day to consummate the vow. That vow was broken a year and a half ago due to the circumstances which bring us together here today. Because of this, we are obligated to wait until Palm Sunday. My father also explained to me that there is a story which he must relate to me on that day. He has urged me with great conviction to hold off until that day."

With an astonished look King Jabalah replied, "There is no objection from me to delay the wedding until Easter, but I grant you that this is a strange secret to withhold in such a way. Do you know anything about it?"

"No, father," Hammad answered. "I know nothing about it. My father is the only living soul on this earth that knows the secret."

"Well, we shall wait for Palm Sunday then. It is not long now, at any rate," said King Jabalah.

They returned to the hall where Queen Saada and Hind were sitting engaged in conversation. They enjoyed one another's company until the end of the day. Before dusk, Hammad asked them for their leave to depart, "My father may worry about my tardiness."

"Do what is necessary," the king said, "and be assured that whenever you wish this is your home now as well."

Hammad thanked him and bade everyone good evening. He and Salman arrived at the monastery late that night, and he told his father all about the visit, hoping to make him happy. Sadly, it did not.

The Palm Sunday Vow

Abdullah became more and more perturbed as Palm Sunday approached. He knew that the monastery would be crowded, and he wished to be alone with Hammad to tell him the story, so he visited the abbot to explain his situation and intentions.

"What room would you like?" asked the abbot.

"We would prefer to have the Bahira hermitage, if we could," replied Abdullah.

"Many pilgrims usually visit the hermitage on a day like Palm Sunday," the abbot said.

"We would only be there a few hours," Abdullah explained. "We could come early and they could visit after we leave, perhaps."

"As you wish," the abbot nodded.

"I once knew an old monk who was one of Bahira's disciples," mentioned Abdullah, "is he still here?"

"Yes, he is still here with us," answered the abbot. "He is very old now, and seldom leaves his room."

"Do you think he would join us on Palm Sunday?" Abdullah inquired. "I was hoping that he would accompany us to the hermitage to shear the hair of my son."

"Let us go now and ask him," offered the abbot.

The abbot led Abdullah to a closed door, and then knocked softly. They waited to give the elderly monk time to get up and open it. The door was slowly opened a moment later by a wizened old man. His hair, beard, moustache, and eyebrows were all bushes of gray, and his skin had been mottled with signs of advanced age. He stood hunched over, straining to see, and he held the door tightly with a trembling hand while the other clutched a rod for support. The old man lifted his eyes and stared at his visitors. He recognized the monk by his clothes, but did not show any sign of recognition toward Abdullah. The old monk stared at him for a long time, peering through the hair of his eyebrows that had fallen to cover his eyes. The monk went to brush his brows back with a gnarled hand as Abdullah bent down to kiss it in greeting, when something kindled the old man's memory because he suddenly blurted out, "Welcome, my son, Emir Abdullah! Son of my dear mother country, come my son, do enter!"

A very shocked Abdullah and the abbot entered and sat on a cushion, not daring to open the conversation as a respectful gesture to the old age of the monk. After a short time, however, the abbot asked, "Your son, Abdullah, requests your presence at a ceremony to shear the hair of his son in accordance with a vow he made over twenty years ago."

The monk thought seriously then asked Abdullah, "What is your son's name?"

"His name is Hammad." Abdullah replied.

"Yes," the monk nodded, "I remember now, I met him nearly two years ago. He told me then that he came for his haircut. Have you not made good this vow yet?"

"We could not," Abdullah answered gravely, "for many serious circumstances separated us, but now we are reunited and have come to make good on the vow by your hand."

"I am too old to perform the duties during the prayers," the monk said.

"The duties could be performed by a priest," Abdullah suggested, "and you perform the prayers. Afterward, I was hoping that you, Hammad, and I could be alone for a story I must narrate to you both."

"Very well, my son," said the monk, "when would you like to perform the vow?"

"On the morning of Palm Sunday," answered Abdullah.

"Then, until we meet again in the hermitage," said the monk, turning his attention to his string of beads.

Knowing that the audience was over, Abdullah stood up and said farewell to the monk and the abbot. Abdullah returned to his room and waited for Hammad to return from the Stream Palace, where he been visiting several times a week to enjoy the company of Hind, passing the days with her and her mother while feeling that the angel of happiness was guarding him.

Hammad's joy permeated his soul, especially after King Jabalah shared his vision of what the future would hold. He eagerly awaited the arrival of Palm Sunday so that he and Hind might finally be united. His preoccupation with Hind, however, would not let Hammad shake the looming presence of the vow that prevented his father from travelling to meet King Jabalah. Hammad returned early in the evening with Salman and went straight to his room to find Abdullah already there.

"You are aware, aren't you, that Palm Sunday approaches quickly?" asked Abdullah.

"Yes, father," Hammad answered. "I am ready to make my vow."

"Then consider the vow accepted," Abdullah announced. "I have spoken with the old monk staying in Bahira hermitage, do you remember him?"

"Yes, I do," Hammad answered. "I remember sitting with him once and he told me the story of his teacher, the monk Bahira."

"He will be performing the prayers for our ceremony," Abdullah explained, "and I have asked him to join us afterward to hear the story that I have to tell you."

Salman stood near the door, adjusting his turban by pretending that the ikal had come loose, and paid attention to what Abdullah was saying to Hammad. He walked up to the two men and humbly asked, "Do you think your servant Salman is worthy of hearing this secret too?"

"Yes," said Abdullah with a smile, "you will be with us as well."

When Palm Sunday arrived, Abdullah woke Hammad and Salman before sunrise and led them to the hermitage. The room was softly illuminated by candles, and they found the old monk and the priest, along with a diocesan, already waiting for them. Since the entire assembly had gathered, they began the prayers, burned incense, and loosened Hammad's hair. It had grown long enough to fall past his shoulders and down to his wrists. The old monk started to walk around the monastery, and the others followed him in a solemn procession until the prayers were finished. He then read a chapter from the gospel before he finally yielded to fatigue and sat down to rest on a stone bench. Hammad knelt before him, and the priest handed the old monk a pair of scissors. With a trembling hand, he snipped a single lock of Hammad's hair and uttered a blessing that indicated the vow had been consummated. The priest then completed the ceremony by shearing the rest of Hammad's hair in the sight of the old monk and the diocesan.

After the ceremony, Abdullah motioned to the monk that the time for solitude had arrived. The monk dismissed the priest and the diocesan which left only Hammad, Salman, and the old monk behind with Abdullah. All the candles had expired and the only light was cast by the oil lamps that hung among the icons. Abdullah asked Salman to close the stone door, and as it slowly slid shut the light grew faint, offering everyone a feeling of being spiritually and bodily separated from the living world within this holy place. Hammad's heart thumped loudly within his chest as he prepared to hear the secret that had loomed over his entire life.

Abdullah removed his cloak and untied a small bundle from which he pulled out a lace robe that he had kept and treasured all these years. Kissing it he placed it around his shoulders and spread a mat of leather on the stone floor in front of the monk and sat down. Hammad and Salman followed his example, silently watching Abdullah's movements in nervous expectation at what they were all about to hear.

Uncovering the Secret

When they were all settled, Abdullah turned to the monk and said, "Father, we sit together in this house of God gathered for a holy purpose known only to God and myself. I will share a story with you that has been entrusted to me for over twenty years and I hope you will listen to me without interruption until its end. I must ask you to promise to keep this story secret from all on this earth. Will you accept this pledge?"

"Yes, Sir," replied the monk. "Your secret will not go beyond the walls of this hermitage."

"Would you lead us in the Lord's Prayer before I divulge the secret?" Abdullah requested. "We will each take the oath secrecy together."

The monk began the prayer, "Our Father, who art in heaven," and when he had finished each of them pledged on the cross to keep one's own council concerning what they were about to hear. They all looked at Abdullah in great expectation of what would come next, humbled by the respectful manner in his posture, as if he were under a great influence.

Abdullah, with an air of heavy responsibility, turned his attention to Hammad and addressed him, "Hear now my son, that the Arabian world can trace their origin to two great men. One, called Ishmael, inhabited Hejaz and ruled the surrounding lands. The other, named Qahtan, settled in Yemen and ruled its surrounding lands. From Qahtan descended many historic nations who dwelled in Yemen until the flood of Ma'arib came and scattered the people to far-away lands." He paused and asked, "Do you know about the flood of Ma'arib, my son?"

"No, father," replied Hammad, "I do not."

"Yemen and all of the Arabian Peninsula," Abdullah explained, "is bountiful with rivers and spring-fed streams. The people rely upon rains to fill these rivers and thus irrigate their trees and crops. The rain water runs off and nourishes the valley and slowly the streams converge to form widening rivers. During the summer's heat, all the water dries up and the land becomes arid. To address this problem, the tribes built dams of granite blocks that spanned the width of the valleys to impede the run-off in the hopes that the water would rise to the top of the dam and overflow into their constructed channels, thereby irrigating the surface of the land. One of these dams was constructed in Yemen and was called the Ma'arib Dam. It was left in ruins by years of neglect, and in truth most of the people left before the collapse of the dam. But collapse it finally did, and the remaining tribes escaped and migrated to other areas of the land. This tragedy occurred over four hundred years ago."

The Kings of al-Hira

"The people who fled Yemen divided into three tribes. One group immigrated to Iraq, and they are our forefathers named after Lakhum. Another tribe immigrated to Syria and called themselves Ghassan. The third founded their home between the mountains Aja and Salma, and are known as Najd."

Hammad was pleased to hear that there a relationship between his people and the Ghassani and waited for his father to continue.

"Our ancestors continued to rule Iraq under the governance of Persia much as it is today," Abdullah went on, "and made the city of al-Hira their capital. Our kings bear the name of al-Mundhir, and one of our kings waged a war against Ghassan. This, my son, is the cause of enmity between our people and why I have not yet met King Jabalah. The king I speak of was the last great king of the Lakhmids, King al-Nu'man III ibn al-Mundhir, the son of al-Mundhir IV ibn al-Mundhir."

"Do you mean Abu Qabus?" asked the monk.

"Yes, I do," Abdullah replied. "Abu Qabus was the nickname for King al-Nu'man III, the same that was imprisoned by Khosrau Parvez."

"King Khosrau allowed him to die in that prison," lamented the monk, "setting upon us the great war of Dhi Qar which stained the earth with blood. I witnessed it in my youth."

The Capture of King al-Nu'man III

Abdullah sighed and resettled himself, straightening the sleeves of his robe at the shoulder before saying, "Having given you the background for the story, heed me now so that I may bridge the connection between us King al-Nu'man III."

He rubbed tears from his cheeks and continued, "I need not give you a long dissertation on King al-Nu'man for all of you are well informed regarding him with the exception perhaps of Hammad, but we all know that he was a brave and truthful man and brought the return of Christianity to the kingdom. His ancestors converted from heathenism and you might fail to understand or question the substance of my story if I do not tell you everything.

"King al-Nu'man was one of twelve brothers who all desired the throne and each boasted the allegiance of their party to help them seize it. At the time, I must remind you, Iraq was still under the administration of Persia. King al-Nu'man took over the throne with the help of a faithful party led by an influential man named Adi ibn Zayd who had a strong friendship with the King of Persia, Khosrau II Parvez.

"One of al-Nu'man's brothers was named Merina. This brother provoked King al-Nu'man with slander about Adi, and cunningly deceived his brother by telling him that Adi was taking all the credit for al-Nu'man's ascent to the throne and that he, King al-Nu'man, actually took orders from Adi. King al-Nu'man, believing Merina, arrested Adi and jailed him. Upon hearing this news from a friend, King Khosrau wrote to King al-Nu'man to free the aide. Unfortunately Adi had already been executed before the letter arrived, so King al-Nu'man had no other recourse but to inform his emperor that the aide Adi ibn Zayd was dead. Now, Adi had a son named Zaid who went to Persia to seek the help of King Khosrau in avenging his father's death. Their trickery was devious and knew no bounds, Zaid would stop at nothing to ruin King al-Nu'man.

"The kings of Persia had a history of frequently requesting women from the kingdoms under their rule, however, they often avoided the Arabian lands due to how vehemently the Arabs would defend their wives and daughters. Zaid shrewdly motivated King Khosrau to demand women from King al-Nu'man, enticing the Persian king with promises that the women of Arabia were far more beautiful and worthy. So King Khosrau sent one of his attendants with Zaid in search of Arabian women. In a state of manic resentment, King al-Nu'man sneered, 'Are there none among the bovine Persians who can satisfy Parvez?' Zaid's companion then asked 'What does the word 'bovine' mean?' Still outraged, King al-Nu'man spat, 'It means cattle!'

"Upon their return to King Khosrau, Zaid related everything that King al-Nu'man had said and explained what he had meant by his remarks. The insult slighted King Khosrau's prestige and the king of Persia became greatly outraged. King al-Nu'man received a note from King Khosrau summoning him to Persia. King al-Nu'man had fully expected this repercussion, and knew that his remark was the reason for the call. He also knew that King Khosrau meant to have him put to death. So King al-Nu'man bore his arms, gathered his family, and fled."

Abdullah paused for a moment, gathering his thoughts. "I was an attendant in the service of King al-Nu'man for many years and felt both quiescent and inspired when I was in his company. 'What would you do, Abdullah?' he asked me. I told him I was an attendant of his and would follow him as he pleased. 'There is danger for you, my friend,' he told me. I told him that my life was no dearer to me than the life of my master. King al-Nu'man then blessed me, and I followed him faithfully from that day on. We traveled to Najd, where his wife had been born, and asked for protection.

"Najd is nestled between two mountains, the Aja and Salma, but when faced with the wrath of the King of Persia the community could not in all good conscience protect King al-Nu'man. He beseeched other tribes who were also fearful, until he met Banu

Hanifa of the Bakr tribe. Although he was the greatest hero and horseman and the bravest of men at the time, even Hanifa too was afraid to harbor King al-Nu'man. Instead, Hanifa suggested that the king go to King Khosrau with many gifts and ask for his pardon. 'If he does not forgive you,' Hanifa reasoned, 'death would be much more preferable than the troublesome Persian curse.' King al-Nu'man bravely approved of the idea but asked what would happen to his family. 'They are under my protection,' announced Hanifa. 'The Persians would have to touch my daughters first before I would allow them to capture yours.' King al-Nu'man accepted this pledge, relieved that his family would be safe but lamented still for his own future.

"I wanted to prevent him from going, but dared not speak for I saw his face draw an ashen hue. At times his pallor looked gray, and at others his face turned red with rage as he pulled at his moustache resolutely. Thinking deeply one day, the king said to Hanifa, 'I shall see that gifts are sent to Parvez before I go. If he accepts them, it will mean that he does not intend to harm me.' Hanifa agreed and the gifts were sent and accepted. But that was just a trap to fool my king.

"My master, King al-Nu'man, set off for Persia and I accompanied him. We arrived at al-Mada'in, the capital of Persia, where we were met by Zaid who affirmed for King al-Nu'man that the acceptance of the gifts was just a trick to get him there. My master simply replied that he had expected this fate. King al-Nu'man then appeared before King Khosrau who imprisoned him in chains. My king had lost heart and the will to live, but I continued to visit him in the prison hoping he might eventually be freed."

The Secret

Abdullah took a breath, then continued, "I visited my king one morning and noticed how his physical condition had changed. He had taken on a dark, foreboding pallor as though he feared what was soon to come. I will remember that day until my last. I stood waiting for his orders and he beckoned me closer, and said only, 'Abdullah.'

'At your order, Sir,' I answered.

'I must ask you to carry the burden of a secret,' he said to me, adding solemnly, 'that you must protect with your life.'

'With my life,' I promised him. He stretched out his hand and gave me this lace robe."

Abdullah paused and removed the robe from his shoulders and spread it out in front of him.

"I accepted the robe and then the king pulled the royal ring from his finger and handed it to me as well. The ring bore his name and title," Abdullah explained as he then pulled the ring from his own finger and placed it on the robe. Everyone looked in stunned silence. A change in Abdullah's countenance took place and with a choked voice that trembled he continued.

"As I accepted the ring, King al-Nu'man said to me, 'Hear me, Abdullah. I am to be held in this prison until the day of my death so that the kingdom of Iraq will pass through the hands of our tribe into the hands of another and weaken the power of al-Hira. You know that I have a wife in Banu Hanifa's protection. She is heavy with child and soon will give birth. Go to her with this ring and robe and tell her that if she delivers a boy my wish is for you, Abdullah, to raise him and to train him in the art of warfare. Take heed against cutting his hair or telling him about his heritage before his twenty-first birthday lest it draw the wrong attention, and when he reaches that age, travel to Bahira Monastery and have his hair shorn. Tell him of his history and present him with this legacy from me. Adorn him with this lace robe and this ring.'

Abdullah then stood up and draped the robe around Hammad's shoulders and slipped the ring on his finger. He extended his hand out to Hammad, who clasped it proudly, and led the young prince to sit at the head of the assembly. Hammad sat down and Abdullah seated himself next to Salman. The monk, though feeble and tired, stood up and raised his hand above Hammad's head, blessed him with a prayer, and kissed him on the head. Hammad was euphoric – his happiness was now complete! He was a king about to wed a queen and inherit the Kingdom of Ghassan.

Abdullah's astuteness could see the pleasure running away in Hammad's mind and announced that he had not finished the story yet. "Will you not hear it to its conclusion?" he asked. Abdullah then reached into his pocket and brought out a sealed silver box which he handed to Hammad and said, "My master, King al-Nu'man, gave this box to me and made me swear an oath that I would deliver this to you at the end of my narration so that you might open it in this monastery and read the contents of the letter. But before you open it, I wish to tell you that your father died in prison of the plague. When I returned to your mother you had not yet been born, and she most regrettably died shortly after you arrived. King Khosrau endeavored to seize all of your father's possessions from Banu Hanifa, but failed because the chief defeated Parvez after a lengthy campaign."

Hammad carefully opened the silver box with a small knife and took out a meticulously folded piece of thin leather on which the last commandment of King al-Nu'man III was written. Hammad handed it to Abdullah who read the following words aloud:

> From al-Nu'man, who is in the other world, to his Son, who is in the living world, I write this letter while I still exist, while you are in the unborn world, and you will read it while you exist and when I am in the world no longer. If you read this after you have made good your vow and know your true heritage, then

know that my bones call unto you from the grave and ask you in the name of your grandfathers not to approach a woman or drink a liquor until you have avenged yourself for me on the Persian kings. If you have done that then blessed be you and your offspring. If you choose not to, then the remains of my body will tremble in anger and my soul will feel the pain as I watch your every move from the gates of eternity and wait for the Day of Judgment to bring us face to face.

Hammad's knees began to shake as Abdullah came to the end of the letter and the weight of its words took hold of him. He despaired as he realized that all of his efforts had been in vain, but on the other hand he felt a stirring devotion and a readiness to avenge his father's death yet also realized the enormity of the undertaking so he just sat awe-struck. Abdullah watched Hammad closely, waiting for him to speak, but the young king remained silent.

Abdullah pitied Hammad's confusion and said, "That, Sir, is the long-awaited secret that I have carried with me for all this time, it has been a burden for over twenty years. I was afraid of expiring before I could tell you. When we were separated, my fears only worsened."

"You have endured this burden for too long, father," Hammad finally said, "but now I must accept the responsibility of this secret. I pray that I succeed in fulfilling my father's dying wish and for God to help me and guide me."

Abdullah asked the monk to conclude their meeting with prayers. The monk offered prayers to God and beseeched Him to help these men protect what had transpired and to keep it a secret. They all departed, except for Hammad, who remained behind the entire day and passed a sleepless night in the hermitage. His innermost thoughts were a swirling vortex that left him bewildered as to what he must do.

Before dawn, Hammad left for the wilds of the forests to be alone with his thoughts without the benefit of Abdullah's or Salman's advice. He rode aimlessly, resting only after he became terribly fatigued. Late in the afternoon he became aware of his surroundings and noticed that he was in a valley with mountains looming along either side of him. He looked back in the direction that he had come from and saw that Busra and the monastery were out of sight. Looking skyward, he noticed that it was nearly dusk, so he stopped to gather his bearings and decide if he should he stay for a while or if he should return to Busra. Hammad surveyed the valley and eyed the mountains rising high on both sides, then dismounted and pulled his horse behind him, trudging up the mountainside in an effort to determine Busra's direction.

Hammad glanced at the other mountain and in between a group of rocks he thought he saw a shadowy creature peering out at him, a creature that appeared to be half-man and half-beast by the length of his hair and the nakedness of his body. Hammad stood still, curious to find out what this creature would do. Having been spotted, the creature criss-crossed through a copse of trees and then darted into a cave and disappeared from sight. Hammad's curiosity overwhelmed him and he wanted to know more about the fleeting figure. He mounted his horse and wandered up the other mountain until he neared the cave, but he heard no sound from within. Suddenly, Hammad heard a rumbling sound and he looked up to see a huge boulder plummeting toward him. He swiftly maneuvered his horse out of the way and continued on his path to the cave. Another boulder came hurtling down at him and Hammad yelled, "Do not cast another rock at me for I have no intention of leaving!"

The only sound he heard was his own voice echoing back at him which had a ghoulish quality created by this dark hollow in the earth. He felt for his sword and dagger at his side and crouched low in the saddle to peer inside but there was nothing but darkness. He dismounted and fastened the reins to a stone and then called out loudly, "Who is inside? Come out and fear not!" His trembling innards belied his brave voice and he prayed that the calm he exhibited would hold true.

There was compete silence, not a sound from a living creature nor a ripple of water save the intermittent snort of his horse. Before he could enter the cave, however, a shadow emerged from the dark recess. Hammad nervously clutched for his sword but the creature had reached him first, and was not a creature at all! He was a very old man clothed only by the gray hair on his head which had blessedly grown to reach his feet. His posture was straight, his movements alert and eyesight sharp, though the skin on his face had shrunken and the nails on his hands and feet were very long and curved. Hammad expressed awe at the sight before him, he would have taken the man for a goblin were it not for the cross in his hand.

Hammad recognized that the cross meant that this man was a hermit who had withdrawn from the outside world, seeking only to live in solitude with the profound devotion of worship. Hammad's anxieties eased and he courteously walked toward the hermit and attempted to kiss the cross. The hermit obliged and held the cross out. Hammad then addressed the hermit, asking to be sure. The monk moved his head in affirmation.

"Holy man, would you permit me to tell you what is on my conscience, as a confession?" Hammad asked. "Would you advise me accordingly as to what the Holy Ghost reveals unto you?"

The hermit made a sign indicating that he was not allowed to speak. He had taken a vow as a hermit that he would endure a week of silence after every week of communication. The hermit indicated to Hammad by drawing in the dirt that this evening was the end of his quiescence.

Hammad suggested that he would be pleased to return on the morrow to speak with the hermit, should the man agree. For now, Hammad might still be able to find his way home before nightfall.

"Shall I bring you some food from Busra when I return?" he asked the hermit, who signed a resolute 'no' and showed Hammad that he lived only off of herbs.

"But I see that the land is barren," said Hammad, looking around, "there are no herbs here."

The hermit gestured over the mountain suggesting that there was fertile land excellent for gathering herbs on the other side.

"Why did you throw stones at me while I was approaching?" asked Hammad.

The hermit only shook his head.

"Could you direct me back to Bahira Monastery?" Hammad inquired.

The hermit nodded and showed Hammad a more direct route back, and Hammad bid him farewell and kissed the cross once more. He cautiously led his horse to the road, mounted, and left for the monastery. Abdullah and Salman were waiting anxiously for him to return.

"Where have you been?" asked Abdullah impatiently. "We have been worried about you."

Hammad could not find the words to explain where he had been and decided to wait until he had seen the hermit again before he confided in the two. Instead, he said to them, "I dismounted for a rest and lost my bearings. It took me some time to find my way back."

"What made you go alone?" asked Abdullah.

"I needed some fresh air," replied Hammad, wearily.

Abdullah sensed his nervousness, and not wishing to discourage him or add to his anxieties, he said, "Sir, I see that you are troubled by what I have shared with you. I know that it is a lot to hear at once. Be mindful, however, that while there is nothing that demands your immediate devotion, neither can we tarry."

Hammad said nothing and Salman realized that there must be words in his master's soul which he would not confess openly, so Salman left the room to leave father and son alone. Abdullah, who watched Salman's exit, turned to Hammad and asked, "Why do you not tell me what is on your mind, am I not your partner and aide in this affair?"

"Yes," said Hammad, "you have always been my father, but I am worried and too embarrassed to tell you the truth. I am in need of an impartial adviser and our situation, as you know, is both complicated and dangerous."

"Let us go to the old monk, then," suggested Abdullah, "perhaps he can counsel us."

"Then let us go now," said Hammad.

They made their way to the old monk's room and knocked on his door. Hearing him beckon from within, they entered and saw the monk leaning over, but as soon as he saw them he straightened up and welcomed them.

"Sir, you are a partner to our secret and you know what is in our hearts," Abdullah said, then asked "would you be our mentor?"

"That is a very difficult and delicate burden," replied the monk, "and I realized the severity of your situation from the moment I witnessed it, but I have no advice to offer you." The monk was silent for a moment, then said suddenly, "Maybe you should seek the Hermit of Hauran. He dwells in a cave not far from here and may be able to give you the guidance you seek."

Hammad was surprised to hear the name of the hermit and asked, "You think he would be willing to do that for us?"

"Yes," answered the monk, "he is a learned man who has found enlightenment."

"Do you know this hermit?" Abdullah asked Hammad, seeing the recognition in his face.

"I confess to you," replied Hammad, "that I met him today and attempted to consult with him, but he could not talk since he seemed under a vow of silence. We can both visit to him tomorrow, as the week of silence is at an end."

"We will go tomorrow," said Abdullah, adding, "Would you accompany us to the hermit's cave, father?"

"Would I to God if I could," said the monk, "but I am an old man and unable to travel through that rocky terrain."

The Hermit of Hauran

Hammad and Abdullah rose early the next day to make their way to the hermit's cave and asked Salman to join them. Hammad led them through the hills to the cave where he had met the hermit on the mountainside.

"This is it," Hammad announced, "and it seems that the hermit is waiting for us."

The hermit stood at the cave's entrance, watching the party make their way toward him. Abdullah felt admiration for the hermit as soon as their eyes met. The hermit walked up to greet them as they dismounted their horses. He welcomed them and scrutinized their faces with his deep-set, alert eyes.

"Hail, pious worshipper, and welcome," replied Hammad. "As promised, I have returned. This is my father Abdullah, and my friend Salman."

Abdullah looked deeply into the hermit's face and felt that he had seen the man before, but he could not remember from where or when. The naked hermit was busy preparing stones for them to sit on, his body moved agilely back and forth, though they were reticent to look directly at him. When he was finished, they kissed his cross and sat down while he offered them blessings. At last, the hermit sat down on the rocky earth and gathered all of his hair and beard and smoothed it against his body. He excused himself for being unable to offer more comfortable accommodations.

"We have come for your council," Abdullah replied, "not for better accommodations. You are one of God's men, to have your regard is a greater blessing than fine furniture." Abdullah was still bothered by the fact that he could not remember where he had seen the hermit before.

"I thank you for thinking well of me. Tell me what is on your mind and I will try to help you," offered the hermit.

"We are Christians and believe in the sanctity of confession. We came to tell you our secret and to ask for your council, in the solemn belief that you are a trustworthy mentor," Abdullah explained.

"Speak, my son, and fear not, your confession is safe with me," said the hermit.

"It seems to me that you are from Iraq," Abdullah remarked cautiously.

"Yes, my son, I am," the hermit answered.

"Then, being from Iraq, you must know of King al-Nu'man III," Abdullah continued.

With surprise showing on his face, the hermit's eyes brightened and his eyebrows knit together as he replied, "Yes, I do."

Bewildered by the look on his face, Abdullah asked, "Did you know him well?"

"I knew him as you know your son," answered the hermit, his hand clutching his beard, his voice trembling with sorrow.

"I see then, Sir, that you may have taken part in our story from the start," said Abdullah, as tears welled up in his eyes.

Rubbing the tears from his eyes, the hermit said, "The mention of King al-Nu'man does stir my memories. What is your concern with him, or is it just a matter of happenstance that you mention his name?" asked the hermit.

"He is the core of our story, may god have mercy on him," Abdullah answered.

"Speak of what you know of King al-Nu'man, for I sense a deep familiarity as you make mention of his name," asked the hermit.

"If you are interested in what I know about King al-Nu'man then take a good look at this young man," said Abdullah, "do you have any idea who he is?"

The hermit stared at Hammad's face for a long while and then exclaimed, "He is the son of King al-Nu'man, without a doubt!" He embraced and kissed Hammad, and they all wept with happiness.

Abdullah said to the hermit just to be sure, "How do you know that this is the son of King al-Nu'man? The king was of a mild complexion, while Hammad is brown and dark."

"That does not matter," replied the hermit, "he bears the same facial features. It was for the king that I left the world and came to these mountains."

Abdullah was surprised and did not fully understand what the hermit meant by his last remark. "Do you know who I am?" he asked.

"Are you not the friend of King al-Nu'man who shared his troubles and served as his steward? Abdullah, that is your name, is it not?" asked the hermit.

Very perplexed, Abdullah looked at the hermit and said, "You have long been privy to our secret. Please, tell us who you are."

The hermit sighed, then answered, "I am the priest who converted King al-Nu'man to Christianity after his forefathers had reverted back to heathenism."

Abdullah was shocked by this declaration, as if he had been woken from a deep sleep, and exclaimed, "Then you are the priest Ya'cob of Losham!"

"Yes, I am," the hermit replied. "I used to live in the Der Hind al-Kubra Monastery and very often attended King al-Nu'man. He confided all his secrets to me. I left Iraq and went to Persia to visit him in the prison. Do you not remember seeing me there?"

"I do very well, now," replied Abdullah, "that is why I kept studying your face, believing that I had seen you before."

Ya'cob then told them all that he knew about the death of King al-Nu'man and his telling held true to all that Abdullah had known. Ya'cob then explained to them that before King al-Nu'man died, he told Ya'cob about the legacy he would leave to his son.

"The death of al-Nu'man ibn al-Mundhir at the hands of Khosrau Parvez made me detest the workings of the world and seek solitude in these mountains," said the hermit.

Abdullah regarded the hermit, and asked, seeing his deep benevolence, "For all these years you have known our story. What advice would you give us concerning Hammad's vengeance?"

The hermit stroked his beard and looked at Abdullah and said, "It is up to God to do the avenging. As you will soon learn from the story I am about to tell you, God has been hard at work. The son of Khosrau Parvez, the one who was called Sha'rya, conspired against his father and had him jailed and later slain. Do you know what happened to the family of the king after his death?"

"No," said Abdullah, "what happened?"

"Parvez had eighteen sons and the one called Sha'rya killed his seventeen brothers as well. As a result of the strong rebuke by his two sisters, Sha'rya rejected the crown and become melancholy until remorse killed him – and what is more," the hermit added, "there were strong rumors that an epidemic spread throughout Persia and destroyed the rest of the royal family. Could you enact any greater revenge than that?"

The three were all shocked to hear such a dreadful a story, especially Hammad, but he also felt as though a heavy burden had been lifted from his shoulders. Salman, who had sat silently through the whole story, stood up and kissed the hermit's hand and said, "You have brought peace to our hearts with this news, but we will not be consoled until we conquer those heathens!"

Ya'cob looked at him, smiled and said, "That is also the work of God, my son, and you will soon hear about the destruction of the Persian Empire. Then none will be left to avenge."

They did not understand the significance of his words, so Abdullah asked, "Are you saying that some revelation has been given to you by God? I have always believed that hermits are honored by our Lord with premonitions that others are not privileged to have."

"I am referring to something that needs no divination, my son, it is apparent to every sensible man. Do you not see the trouble the Persians face and the critical condition their empire currently finds itself in? They have had five kings within the last five years and each

192 | Jurji Zaidan

one of them turned out to be a tyrant. The most weak-minded of them all is Yazdegerd III, who happens to be ruling now. The Persian Empire will soon collapse because of their latest ruler! It seems to me that the age of the empire cannot sustain such weakness, and her fate is nigh at hand, just as the Roman Empire hangs in the balance," Ya'cob concluded sadly.

"But the fate of an empire is decided by the rise of another," said Abdullah. "What empire will take the place of those two?"

"The Prophet Muhammad is going to destroy these evil empires and impose his law instead," replied the hermit. "If not very soon, it will happen in time."

"I have seen with my own eyes," said Hammad, "how the Prophet struck at Mecca and conquered it with a host followers and attendants."

"Well then! You see?" Ya'cob exclaimed, "There is no rush for you to risk your life to avenge your father. You have seen how the murderer of King al-Nu'man has been killed already with his children following him quickly to the grave, and the Prophet Muhammad will soon destroy the rest of their empire, God willing."

Hammad felt a chill run down his spine hearing the cold resolution in the hermit's words and his desire for revenge completely diminished. His thoughts returned to Hind and he wished he could leave to take care of other matters. Abdullah noticed Hammad's restlessness, so he thanked the hermit Ya'cob for his courtesy and they all gave him a hearty farewell.

When they reached the monastery they stopped to tell the old monk about their audience with Ya'cob and what he had told them. After they had finished the monk sat quietly for a moment before saying, "I heard from a merchant who passed through two days ago that the Prophet had died after he conquered all of the Arabian Peninsula, and now all the tribes of Yemen, Hejaz, Najd, and Amman have become his followers. They are now marching not only into Syria, but into Iraq as well."

"Are you sure that they are invading Iraq?" Abdullah asked.

"Yes, I am," said the monk, "and if they are not completely victorious in Iraq, they will at least do great harm to Persia and put her in a difficult position indeed."

"Is that so," Abdullah remarked. "We did not think that the Muslims would invade Syria and Iraq so soon. This is very strange, as a matter of fact."

"I did not expect it either," said Hammad, "even though I have seen their power."

"Yes, my son," said the monk. "There are among the Prophet's followers some who have performed miracles. These generals are, in fact, responsible for their victories everywhere. The man who succeeded the Prophet is known as Caliph Abu Bakr. The merchant who spoke of this also told me a story that would astonish all those who were in league with the Roman and Persian rulers."

"What is it?" asked Abdullah.

"The merchant told me that Caliph Abu Bakr, shortly before the Prophet departed this world, had left with the army to conquer Syria under the leadership of general Usama bin Zayd. Usama, though only a young man, rode a horse among the troops, but Abu Bakr, who would become the Prophet's successor, walked among them. Usama showed embarrassment and asked Abu Bakr to ride since he was the elder, but Abu Bakr refused to ride and explained that walking demonstrated that their rulers wanted to serve and not receive positions as others do. And do you know what is more?" asked the monk.

"No," said Abdullah, "tell us all you know."

"Abu Bakr, before his return, directed his soldiers after their discharge to live by the following principles: to commit no treason, to take not the harvest of others, to commit no atrocity, to kill no child, to slay no woman or old man, to burn no palm tree, to fell no fruit-bearing tree, and to not kill any lamb nor cow nor camel. These were the doctrines given to the Muslim soldiers," the monk regaled. He added sorrowfully, "You know, Christianity asks us to live in much the same way, but our Roman rulers have rejected the spirit of Christianity in their hearts."

Both Abdullah and Hammad listened to his tale with rapt attention and were greatly impressed with what the monk had told them. "There is no surprise as to why these people are victorious wherever they go," Abdullah remarked.

Hammad turned to his father and said, "Would you ask the monk about my marriage?"

Abdullah addressed Ya'cob, "Do you think Hammad can marry now, or is he still bound by his father's wish for revenge?"

"It seems to me that the hermit has liberated you from this debt, not to mention that it is a Christian virtue to abandon vengeance and embrace forgiveness," he offered, "for our doctrine commands us to love our enemy and bless those who curse us." Hammad was relieved to hear this verdict and said nothing. Their conversation was at an end, so they took their leave after thanking the monk for his welcome advice.

As they made their way back to their room, Hammad turned and hesitantly asked Abdullah, "Will you join me now in al-Balqa to meet with King Jabalah? We have completed the vow and the time has come to honor him with your presence. The origin of my birth has been uncovered."

"I suggest, Sir, that you keep it covered for now to see what time will tell," replied Abdullah.

Hammad said nothing. Their conversation had brought them to the door of their room. Salman had stayed a few paces away to give them a chance to speak alone. Hammad summoned him over and the servant responded by saying, "I would like to go to Iraq, Sir, to see what is happening, do I have your permission to leave?"

"Let him go," said Abdullah to Hammad, "Salman has been a loyal servant and his services are no longer needed, everything is settled."

"Go in peace my friend," replied Hammad, "and keep us advised of the news."

Salman left early the following morning. When they were alone, Hammad said to Abdullah, "It is time to go to King Jabalah. We could visit the Stream Palace first."

"We should visit al-Balqa first," Abdullah advised. "Not until the introduction will I have the right to visit the palace."

"Then I will go ahead and make the arrangements for your audience with King Jabalah," replied Hammad.

"Very well, my son," Abdullah nodded.

The Robe and the Ring

Hind had been restlessly waiting for Palm Sunday. She expected to see Hammad that very day. Three days had passed already, however, and he had not made an appearance. His absence stirred her anxieties and she began to worry. On the fourth day, Hind got out of bed early in the morning, dressed, and left for the park. While she gathered flowers, her eyes wandered frequently toward the path that Hammad would have to take to reach her. She sat down on a stone bench deep in thought, and watched closely until she saw a horseman coming from afar. She instinctively knew that it was Hammad, she recognized his traveling clothes and the horse he rode.

Filled with excitement, she ran to her mother to tell her that Hammad was coming. They both left for the reception room and patiently waited for a servant to announce his arrival. Queen Saada went out to receive Hammad and welcome him home. Hammad kissed her hand and entered the palace. Hammad felt a flush course through his whole body when he set eyes on Hind, awestruck by her beauty. After greeting her warmly, they all retired to the reception room and Hind silently regarded the change in his countenance, able to take in more of his features now since his haircut.

"You have had your hair cut, my son," praised Queen Saada, "may God accept your vow." She was surprised to see he had come alone, and asked about his father.

"Yes, I have," Hammad proclaimed with a smile. "My hair was shorn on Palm Sunday in the hermitage of Bahira Monastery. My father intended to come, but we assumed that it would be proper for me to come ahead to arrange a meeting with King Jabalah prior to his arrival. If my father-in-law is here, we can arrange the time of meeting then I will send for my father."

"Did you hear the story, then?" the queen inquired.

"Yes, I have been told everything," Hammad answered, offering nothing more.

The queen did not impose any further questions on him and changed the subject by asking if he would like to go outside and enjoy the beauty of the park. He admitted that he would like to very much, so he left with Hind through a small narrow door that led directly into the park, and the queen stayed behind to give the servants instructions for dinner. They strolled through the groves of fruit-laden trees down to the banks of the stream. Hind could not believe that she was alone with Hammad until she looked at him, her vivid brown eyes flashing whenever the sun's light broke through the leaves of the trees.

"What made you hurry to visit us," she jested, "is it not customary for your love to delay until next Easter?"

Realizing that she was joking and having fun at his expense, Hammad replied coyly, "We are reserving Easter for the day to confer with your father regarding our wedding plans. Perhaps you want to put off the wedding to a later date?"

"If I had known you would answer me in that manner," she said with a blush, "I would not have asked you the question!" Her demure admission only added more to his love and admiration for her.

"I never imagined that the mention of our marriage would distress you," Hammad replied, looking deeply into her eyes. "All this time our effort was to be free to wed, and here we are, are we not?" He waited for her to answer but she turned her face away from him and strolled toward an orange tree to pick some flowers growing nearby. Hammad followed her, asking, "Why are you turning away from me, Hind? Do you mean to rid yourself of me so soon? You do not yet know the whole story of my past, of my family!"

Hammad was trying to pique her curiosity with his questioning, or to attract her attention perhaps, but she did not respond and instead feigned disinterest in the vow and the secret. He turned her around so they were face to face and held her hands, asking, "Why haven't you asked me yet about the secret?"

Hind looked down at his strong hands gently wrapped around hers, and replied, "It seemed as though the secret were too precious to you, that you cannot speak of it or you would have."

"Nothing is so precious that I cannot share it with you, my sweetheart," Hammad declared. He freed one of his hands and reached into his pocket to reveal his father's ring.

"This is our secret," he said, giving her the ring.

"Will you read what is engraved in it?" Hind asked, "I cannot read the writing."

"It says," Hammad revealed, "al-Nu'man III, son of al-Mundhir."

"What does that mean?" she asked.

"It means that I am related to the former owner of this ring," Hammad hinted.

"Are you related to King al-Nu'man?" Hind gasped.

"He was my father," Hammad answered proudly. He read the expression of awe on her face, mixed with gladness and admiration and pride. She tried unsuccessfully to force herself not to show surprise as well.

"Who told you of your relationship to King al-Nu'man?" she asked.

"That," Hammad said, "is a very long story that I will tell you later. And, if you are not convinced by the ring, I have brought this," and he revealed the lace robe he wore beneath his cloak. There was no question in Hind's mind that Hammad was the heir of King al-Nu'man.

At the sound of footsteps, Hammad slipped the ring back into his pocket. A moment later, Queen Saada entered the grove, her face flushed with excitement. Hammad and Hind looked at each other curiously.

"I apologize for taking so long to join you. I was delayed by a messenger from King Jabalah. He sends a note," and she explained, handing a folded parchment to Hind for her to read.

Hind read the following,

Have you heard anything from our son Hammad? Did he make good on his vow? I would like to see him before I leave to visit the Emperor. The Emperor has sent one of his apostles, calling me to his court. I will tell you all about it when I see you next.

Hind finished reading the message and looked up at her mother.

"Hind, write to him right away," said Queen Saada, "and tell him Hammad has come and made good his vow."

"I will return to my father and bring him here tomorrow to have the honor of meeting King Jabalah," said Hammad.

"A worthy idea," replied the queen.

And so they all retired to the dining room to enjoy a midday meal. After they had finished eating, Hind wrote to King Jabalah, asking him to be at the palace the next morning, and Hammad left for the monastery to make preparations for the following day.

The Secret Revealed

A change had taken place in Hind's mood after she had learned the secret from Hammad. Queen Saada took notice and questioned her daughter again and again until she too knew the secret. Queen Saada was overwhelmed by the news and urged Hind to confide in her father.

When King Jabalah arrived the next morning, Hind told him the secret and thought he would be glad to hear it. On the contrary, however, he became disagreeable and ill-humoured after he learned of Hammad's royal ties. Hind regretted having told him, fearing that some injustice might come out of it. King Jabalah was very depressed after he learned about Hammad and was constantly in deep thought. He had no son and he knew that Hammad would one day take his place, and so he feared that his beloved Ghassan would lose their kingdom to another, and the rule of his people would come to an end. He then thought perhaps he would rather marry his daughter to her cousin Tha'labah, after all, he would keep the name alive rather than deliver this kingdom into the hands of another, of the enemy's no less! He quickly dismissed the idea, realizing its zealous, vindictive nature. Hind watched her father's mood with a depressed spirit, regretting over and over that she had told him Hammad's secret. Not only was her father miserable, but she had betrayed Hammad's confidence.

As the turmoil simmered within the palace walls, they heard the clattering of harnesses and the whinnying of horses. Hammad had arrived accompanied by another horseman. They dismounted and approached the waiting king to greet him. After Hammad had introduced his father, the king led them to the reception room where they sat and conversed about everything except for the vow and Hammad's secret.

"You told us in your note," Queen Saada said to the king, "that Emperor Heraclius has bid you to see him. What did he call you for?"

"His communication announced political trouble," King Jabalah replied. "He wishes to prepare for war."

Surprise at the news jolted them all upright in their seats. Hammad struggled with the fear that another obstacle had come between him and his beloved.

"What sort of political trouble, father?" Hammad asked the king.

"We have had contact with our informants," said the king. "They tell us that the Muslims of Hejaz, who only a few years ago came to conquer us, have arrived once again more powerful than before and fully prepared to meet us. We have informed the Emperor of their activities, so we must meet with him to oversee the mobilization of our forces."

"But we heard that the Muslim army had been sent into Iraq to battle the Persians, not to Syria," said Abdullah, dismayed.

"That was a different battalion which marched into Iraq last year. This time around they are intent on destroying us," said King Jabalah.

"Do you think your absence will be a long one?" asked Hammad.

"It is difficult to say," the king replied.

"Then we will go in your attendance," said Hammad.

"I see no need for that," said King Jabalah. "It would be best if you stayed in Busra until I return. That said, the queen and my daughter will accompany me, for I fear the enemy might strike here as well."

Hind's heart dropped and tears filled her eyes as she listened to her father's words. Hammad felt the same alarm, and feared losing her after all the hardships he had overcome, but Abdullah was suspicious. Something had happened to bring on this flight. He wondered if Hammad had slipped the secret to Hind and if she, in turn, had been coerced into confiding the secret to them. This could cause the king's sudden change in attitude. Abdullah glanced at Hammad and rebuked him with his eyes and a curt nod. Hammad suddenly realized his mistake, and even the queen realized that if she had not insisted that Hind tell her father, none of this would be happening.

Queen Saada turned to her husband, "Do you not see it better to take Hammad with us?"

"I think it wiser for him to stay here and I will explain my reason to you later," he answered in an elevated tone that clearly indicated he wished the subject closed.

Their dinner was served, so they promptly adjourned to the dining room and ate heartily. Meanwhile, the servants prepared for the departure of the king and his family. Abdullah felt badly about the situation that had marred his first meeting with King Jabalah, and wanted to urge Hammad to give up his love, so he suggested to Hammad that they take their leave. Hammad agreed with great reluctance and bid the family goodbye. Hind sobbed woefully with Queen Saada at her side trying to console her. Hammad felt as though the world had come to an end as he and Abdullah started back for the monastery.

The Heartwarming Message

As they neared the monastery, Abdullah asked Hammad, "Would you like to stay at the monastery or would you prefer to go back to Busra?'

"I would rather we returned to Busra," Hammad replied. "I think it will be safer after what we have just heard about the Muslim army."

"As you wish," said Abdullah, but they decided to lodge at the monastery for the night and start for Busra in the morning. As they prepared to leave, Abdullah decided to say good-bye to the monk while Hammad stayed behind to await his return. While he waited, Hammad saw a woman outside in the courtyard looking in his direction. He recognized her after a moment, she was the maiden who had accompanied Hind to the monastery the very first time they had met.

He hurried over to greet her and she said, "Do you know where I might find a jewelry merchant?"

"Yes," Hammad answered, smiling, "I am that merchant."

After he had identified himself, the servant girl handed him a handkerchief and departed without another word. He carefully unfolded the delicate cloth and found a note inside that read:

> *Do not be discouraged by what you witnessed yesterday*
> *with my father. Have patience.*

Hammad's heart warmed at the message from Hind, it was her way of reassuring him to ease his worries. He yearned to know where she was at that moment and remembered her father's duty in Homs to see the Roman emperor. He thought it would be wrong to assume that he had taken his family there, and supposed that they were most likely still in al-Balqa. Abdullah had returned from his talk with the monk of Bahira, so they both mounted their horses and rode to Busra.

Upon arrival, they leased a house near the stone-capped rampart. Hammad was still anxious about Hind, and blamed himself for disclosing the secret even though Abdullah advised him against telling it. Abdullah ignored Hammad's worrisome state of mind and tried to interest him in hunting instead. Hammad agreed, hoping that the hunt would give him a chance to roam around and perhaps learn some news about Hind or her father. They continued to go on these hunts for several months but learned nothing except of the preparations of the Romans to repel the Muslims who were now occupying the outlying villages of Syria.

The Fortress of Busra

"I see that there is nothing left to hunt in this barren land," said Hammad one day, while out on another of the hunting trips.

"Game is sometimes very scarce, especially with two armies to feed," said Abdullah. "If you want to find more game, we can go to Balqa."

"A change of scenery might do some good," Hammad agreed.

As they talked, they saw a sizable herd of gazelle gracefully loping across the wilderness the likes of which they had never seen before. Amazed at the magnitude of the spectacle before them, Hammad remarked, "The gazelle are coming in our direction! Have you ever seen anything like this, father?"

"The size of the herd suggests grave danger," said Abdullah, watching the herd closely.

"What could it be?" asked Hammad.

"Never before has so great a number of gazelle migrated together at once in these lands," Abdullah remarked. "Perhaps this is the first sign of the invasion march of the Muslim army heading toward Busra," he postulated. They decided to climb the hill and survey the distant plains. What they saw was a tremendous cloud of dust rising in the distance.

"It would appear that I was correct," said Abdullah.

"The army is already at Busra!" Hammad exclaimed, "I wish we had already left!"

"If we have to take refuge in this country, Busra is the best place," Abdullah reasoned. "It is the most heavily fortified city."

Hammad was greatly disturbed that the matter of Hind's well-being would have to wait yet again. Hammad and Abdullah took refuge within the walls of the city and awaited the marching army's arrival.

The Fall of Busra

The Romans opened the gates of the city and sent their soldiers, twelve thousand strong, to meet the Muslim forces. The bells of the city began to peal as the Romans moved forward, preceded by the clergy who were bearing crosses and incense burners. Abdullah and Hammad passed through the business district and saw people hurrying into the churches to say their prayers. The clergy ascended the crest of the rampart, holding their crosses and candles, sprinkling the soldiers with holy water. Hymns filled the streets and the crowds rallied for a sweeping victory by the Roman army.

The Muslims had an army of about four thousand soldiers, led by Sharhabeel ibn Hasanah, one of the Prophet's companions. Over the next few days, many skirmishes took place between the two armies and the Romans were largely victorious, a fact which did not astonish Abdullah since the Romans were far greater in number and superior in equipment. A particularly bloody battle was under way between the two armies that shook the Muslim soldiers, disorganizing their forces and routing their advance. As the swirling dust cleared away, a large detachment of horsemen was seen coming to the aid of the Muslims led by a tall, massively-built man holding a black flag. He was Khalid ibn al-Walid, and his well-timed charge turned the tides of the battle. The brilliant commander obtained a supreme victory over the Romans that day, sending them back behind the walls of Busra in retreat.

The following day, Khalid ibn al-Walid returned to the battlefield and challenged the Roman soldiers to fight him. They sent a battalion to face him and they battled all day long but returned defeated. As the third day dawned another Roman commander proceeded to engage Khalid's forces and likewise returned in shame.

"I have a feeling," remarked Abdullah to Hammad, "that the Romans will deliver the city into the hands of the enemy. There appears to be no strength among their leaders."

"Should we be worried?" asked Hammad.

"Yes," Abdullah nodded gravely, "for if we had known that the Romans would lose morale so swiftly, we would have been safer at the monastery. The Muslims have vowed not to harm those in churches."

"Stay here," Abdullah said to Hammad a moment later. "I will go to Romanus's estate this very evening to find out what is going on. He and I became friends after my arrest and subsequent acquittal by Emperor Heraclius, perhaps he will confide in me."

Hammad nodded in agreement and Abdullah left for Romanus's residence. He returned very quickly. When he entered the room he had a perplexed look on his face.

"What is it," asked Hammad, "what did you discover?"

"When I reached his house, the guard told me that Romanus was asleep but I have a suspicion that he has gone to surrender the city to the Muslims," Abdullah remarked.

"I believe he would do it!" replied Hammad with an anxious look on his face.

"We will find out about it tomorrow," said Abdullah, "there is nothing we can do now, so let us go to bed and get some rest."

A little after midnight they were awoken by a knocking at their door. They heard a voice saying, "Open the door, I am your servant Salman!"

Abdullah hurried to the door and opened it. Under the blanket of night, illuminated only by a lamp held in the caller's hand, stood a figure dressed like a traveler from Hejaz, an appearance that startled them, but the man repeated calmly, "Fear not, it is me, your servant Salman!" The man lifted his scarf to reveal his face. The two men breathed a sigh of relief and welcomed their servant home.

"Where have you been, Salman," Abdullah asked. "What news have you brought for us?"

"I come from the camp of Khalid ibn al-Walid, he will soon take over the city!" Salman explained. "This is one of his flags, erect it by your door and you will be secure."

"Be blessed," said Abdullah, closing the door behind them. "Tell us everything you saw."

"In short," replied Salman, "Romanus delivered the city to the Muslims after converting to their religion. He led Caliph Abu Bakr and about a hundred of the Caliph's men through an opening in the ramparts and armed them. I was one of them. We were ordered to kill the Roman generals who tried to take the city from Romanus. Soon you will hear about the massacre."

Salman also boasted about Khalid ibn al-Walid's bravery and cunning. Salman was of the mind that were it not for Khalid, the Romans would have won the war. As they talked, they heard the tumult in the streets, the shouting voices of the Muslim soldiers, and the crying and moaning of the women and children. They ran out on the balcony overlooking the street and saw bodies of the dead and injured. The soldiers were busy plundering and razing the city. The soldiers avoided the houses with the flag displayed outside, including the house of Abdullah and Hammad. Salman had to leave, and promised to find more information before departing for the camp of Khalid ibn al-Walid. He let them know that the Muslims had chosen Romanus to rule for them, and left to join the army as it began preparing to leave the city to invade another. Returning one last time to bid Abdullah and Hammad farewell, Salman told them that he was going with their troops to Yarmouk.

"Let us know," said Hammad to Salman, "if King Jabalah and his family are there."

"Yes, I will," said Salman.

The Muslim army in Yarmouk was thirty-six thousand strong, and their commander-in-chief was Khalid ibn al-Walid, who had gained renown for his astounding feats on the field of battle. As soon as they had set camp, Salman tried to make his way to the Roman encampment to ask about news of Jabalah and Hind. He ascended a hill at the bank of the river and stood on the ridge overlooking the Roman army. It was decorated with waving banners and crosses that glittered in the sunlight. He saw the camp of Ghassan separated from the Romans, with King Jabalah's flag soaring atop a large tent in the center. Salman wanted to go to see King Jabalah to find out how Hind was faring, but thought the Muslims would think evil of him.

Instead, Salman asked Khalid permission to act as a spy. He changed his costume to that of a Ghassani soldier and made his way into their midst, mingling with them once there. He met some people who knew him from al-Balqa, and they were under the impression that he had come with them. He asked about Hind and was told that she was with her mother in Damascus. He also learned that the Roman forces were vast, twenty banners in all, including those of the Armenians, Assyrians, and the Egyptians, almost two hundred and forty thousand men including the Christian Arabs. Salman was gravely concerned and feared the Romans would win the war this time, so he returned to the Muslim camp and decided he would return to his master before it was too late. It was late evening when Salman arrived back at the camp and reported the strength of the Roman forces to Khalid.

The following morning, the Muslims prepared for the battle and divided into thirty groups, each headed by a commander. Against all odds, the Muslims routed the Roman army, and within three days were the decisive victors. Salman was thinking of Hind and feared for King Jabalah's life, but discovered that the king had survived the battle. The Muslim army then packed up camp and made way for Damascus.

Surprising News

Hammad worried about Hind and waited for Salman's return, hopefully with some news. He heard the whinny of a horse outside. A mounted stranger came up to the door and asked, "Is this the house of Emir Abdullah?"

"Yes, it is," responded Hammad.

"Where is his son Hammad?" the man asked.

"I am Hammad," he answered suspiciously, "what do you want of me?"

"There is a merchant in the monastery who would like to see you," said the stranger.

"I will leave immediately," Hammad replied. The stranger bade him good-bye.

Hammad changed his clothing and a few minutes later was riding his horse toward the monastery. He met Abdullah on the way and excused himself, claiming that he would like to visit the monastery alone. He rode his horse hard, and when he reached the monastery he saw a horse that belonged to the Stream Palace stables. He entered and looked around carefully until he saw a woman who he recognized as one of Hind's maids. She greeted him by kissing his hand and led him to a room where she handed him a handkerchief. Enclosed in the handkerchief was a note that read:

> *My father has again picked up his friendship with that fox, Tha'labah. You know how I feel about that. The rat is once again demanding my hand in marriage, but I would rather die than wed him. I am now in Damascus, come soon before it is too late. Hind.*

Hammad turned to the woman and asked, "Where in Damascus is Hind?"

"She stays in a house near Mary's Church," she replied.

"Is Tha'labah in Damascus?" he asked.

"No," said the maid, "Tha'labah is in Homs with my master, King Jabalah."

"How did they come to be comrades again?" asked Hammad.

"They joined forces after their soldiers had been beaten in the battle of Yarmouk," she answered.

"What else happened?" Hammad continued.

"My master King Jabalah sent a note to his wife telling her that he would soon be in Damascus with Tha'labah, and that Hind and Tha'labah would be wed. This is the reason why Hind sends you this message of desperation."

Hammad was incensed and beyond provocation. "Very well," said Hammad, "tell her that I will be there as fast as my horse will carry me."

Bidding him good-bye, the maid left, and Hammad went to the monk's room to ask him to inform Emir Abdullah that he would be on his way to Damascus.

Hind in Damascus

While Hammad journeys to Damascus, swift as the wind on the back of his stallion, let us be mindful of what has happened with Hind since we saw her last at the Stream Palace, grimly discouraged and embarrassed.

Hind felt her heart drop the moment that Hammad took his leave, and she spent her time crying alone. Her father was preoccupied with issuing last minute instructions, but Queen Saada realized her daughter's woeful state and tried very hard to calm her. The following day, all of the royal occupants of the Stream Palace traveled to al-Balqa with the exception of the king. King Jabalah was headed for Homs to see Emperor Heraclius about the preparations for the coming battle. He found it necessary to reconcile with his nephew Tha'labah because Tha'labah could get him the extra men they desperately needed.

King Jabalah later learned of the arrival of the Muslims in Yarmouk and Busra, and fearing for the safety of his family, sent them to Damascus where they could reside with the wives of his friends. He then fought in the battle of Yarmouk where he and his men were defeated. Through the hardship of defeat, King Jabalah found common ground with Tha'labah once more, as often happens when common misfortune strikes two enemies. Tha'labah had actually become very passive after the death of his father. The tragedy humbled him and he now truly wished to marry Hind. King Jabalah still feared losing the crown to the prince of Iraq, and accepted Tha'labah's petition to be his daughter's betrothed once again.

Now certain that King Jabalah was willing to accept him as a son-in-law, Tha'labah asked his uncle when the wedding could take place. The king replied, "It will have to be after the war is ended."

"This war could last until eternity," said Tha'labah, "why not have the ceremony as soon as possible? The celebration will bring good cheer."

"Very well, we will do as you say," nodded King Jabalah.

He wrote a message to his wife and explained that he and Tha'labah had let the wounds between them heal and asked her to prepare Hind for the wedding, further explaining to her that he preferred Tha'labah to Hammad because he would keep the throne within Ghassan. When Queen Saada read the letter she sympathized with the sudden change of heart that had taken over her husband in the wake of the war, but then wrote a note to Hammad and signed Hind's name to it without letting her daughter know.

Back in Busra, Hammad had bid the monk good-bye and left for Damascus with a guide to show him the way. They set out as fast as possible along the path the guide suggested. Having traveled hard for two days, Hammad realized they had gone astray and worried that some trouble might befall them and delay the rest of his trip to Damascus. They wandered in the wilderness for another two days trying to find their way again. Nevertheless, even with the experience of the guide the two men had become utterly lost. Only by chance, once they had determined a path and followed it slowly, did they arrive at a point that they remembered and manage to finish the trip unhindered. They rode cautiously until they arrived on the outskirts of Damascus where they encountered a man looking around, intently seeking someone.

A flood of relief washed over Hammad as he recognized his father, who had come looking for him and arrived before Hammad, having not gotten himself lost on the way. Abdullah joined them and they rode on. Hammad was astonished to see that the city had surrendered to the enemy and the Muslims had been victorious once again. They furtively mingled through the crowded streets until they came to Mary's Church. The church had been closed during the siege and was still sealed. When Hammad and Abdullah walked up to the door and knocked on it, there was no answer, apparently the custodians were afraid to open up, fearing the invaders. Abdullah announced loudly, "We are Christians looking for someone living inside the church!" and they revealed the crosses that hung from their necks. The priest came out and informed them that it was unusual that someone might be residing in the church.

"Are you sure?" asked Hammad. "There is no one making use of your rooms presently?"

"No, Sir," said the priest, scrutinizing the two men, "only the family of King Jabalah of Ghassan and their servants have recently stayed here, but they left several days ago."

Trembling with shock, Hammad asked if he knew where they had gone.

"I do not know," said the priest, "but some men dispatched by King Jabalah came here and stayed a few hours before leaving."

"Did they leave before or after the siege?" Abdullah asked.

"I think they left before the siege," said the priest.

Hammad looked at Abdullah as if silently asking his opinion.

"I think," said Abdullah, "that King Jabalah sent for his family when he heard of the siege, and sent them somewhere safer." Addressing the priest, Abdullah then asked, "Would you show us the room that they occupied?"

The Information

"I would be happy to," said the priest, leading the way.

Abdullah and Hammad followed him through a door that opened into a narrow alley paved with large stones. They wandered through the alleyway and arrived at the door of a house that appeared unworthy of kings. As they walked in, however, they saw the elegance and beauty of it. They heard no sound save the quiet ripple of water in the courtyard over which the graceful, feathery branches of a willow hung and the aromatic scent of multicolored flowers permeated the air, offering an aura of tranquility.

Hammad stood still as though expecting to hear a voice. He walked to the front door, opened it, and entered. Climbing the stairs, he reached the gallery and walked its length until he came to a closed room. He strode over to the door and tried to open it but it was locked. The door had a window in it so Hammad craned his neck to peer inside, and from the corner of his eye he saw someone hiding in the room! Hammad called out and a female voice, trembling with fear, cried out, "There are no men in this place, if you are going to pillage, have pity on the women!"

Hammad's heart trembled at the sound of the baleful voice and thought he recognized it, so he replied, "Fear not, aunt, we are not the enemy! We do not want to hurt you, but we are seeking the family of King Jabalah."

Believing the sympathy in Hammad's voice, the woman approached the window to scrutinize his face. It was indeed Hind's maid, the same one who had brought the note to the monastery.

"Where have you been, Hammad, Sir?" she asked meekly, relieved to see him. "I have been fearing I may meet my fate waiting for you."

"Open the door," said Hammad.

The door opened quickly, and the maid took his hand to kiss it, and then she said, "King Jabalah and his family took their servants and left Damascus several days ago. I was asked to wait here for your arrival to give you their news. But a long time has passed since I sent for you, and I have stayed hidden here in despair during the siege."

"Tell me, aunt, where is Hind now?" asked Hammad.

"She left in the company of her mother and the servants before the siege," she answered.

"But where is she now?" he repeated.

"I think she is in Jerusalem," she said, "because it is further from danger than Damascus."

"What do you think we should we do, father?" asked Hammad, turning to Abdullah.

"I suggest that we start out for Jerusalem tonight," Abdullah advised.

Turning back to the servant, he asked, "What will you do?"

"I will leave as well," she said, "if I want to stay alive."

"That is true but a woman cannot travel alone," said Hammad.

"Actually, since I am a woman, I can go alone," she explained, "the Muslims are in the habit of protecting their women and if any of those Hejazi soldiers found me he would lead me to where I need to go. But this city is no longer safe."

"Then give my love to Hind if you should arrive ahead of me," said Hammad, "and tell her that I will see her soon."

Hammad and Abdullah left the woman and returned to wander through the streets. They came to a crossroad where they were stopped by a Muslim guard who detained them and brought them before his commanders. Some of the soldiers recognized them from Hejaz and knew that they were from Iraq. Their commander, who happened to be Khalid ibn al-Walid, asked Abdullah if he would serve as a guide to Iraq.

"With pleasure," said Abdullah, compelled to accept out of fear for Khalid's wrath. He turned to Hammad and said, "You should go on alone to the Holy City without fear, for we are now under the protection of our masters Khalid ibn al-Walid and Abu Ubaidah ibn al-Jarrah."

"Most certainly," said Abu Ubaidah, "I will send some of my men to guard your son on route. We may need his help there."

Bidding his father farewell, Hammad rode until he was out of sight. He arrived in the Holy City several days later and lodged at the monastery near the Church of the Resurrection. After a short rest, he ventured out and asked around the monastery for information about Hind and her family. He met no one who knew King Jabalah, but heard everybody talking about the fall of Damascus and their fears of the coming battle at the Holy City. When he was about to give up, Hammad approached the abbot of the monastery and asked him about the family of King Jabalah.

"They were here for a few days and left about a week ago," the abbot replied.

"Did they all go, the men and the women?" asked Hammad, dismayed by the news.

"Only the women were here originally," the abbot explained, "but their men came and escorted them away."

"Do you know where they went?" asked Hammad.

"Why do you ask?" the abbot inquired, "where have you come from?"

"I have come from Damascus," Hammad answered. "I waited until the battle had ended before beginning my journey."

"Do you know if the Muslims are coming this way?" asked the abbot. "The news of Damascus has terrified all our men, each of them fearing for himself. King Jabalah brought his family to this monastery to marry his only daughter to her cousin. Are they related to you?"

"No," Hammad replied, frustrated by the mention of Tha'labah, "but I have a close association with them."

"I could not help but notice that the maiden has no love for her cousin," the abbot said. "In fact, her father asked me to try and persuade her, but all was in vain."

"You are quite right," Hammad said. "She is being coerced into marrying someone she does not love."

"Oh, I know," said the abbot, recalling Hind's resistance, "but God has solved the problem."

"What do you mean?" asked Hammad.

"Her cousin was killed in the war with the Muslims very recently," the abbot explained.

"Are you sure of that?" said Hammad, a little too excitedly.

"I am very sure of it," said the abbot.

"Do you know this cousin's name?" asked Hammad.

"Yes," the abbot answered, "his name was Tha'labah."

"What happened after that?" asked Hammad.

"The family of King Jabalah remained here," answered the abbot, "but when Damascus fell, King Jabalah returned and took them away. But to where, I do not know."

Hammad, completely bewildered, gave his thanks, bade the abbot good-bye, and left.

Salman

Hammad made his way through the monastery, his mind a cloud of anxiety, and arrived at his room without realizing he had even moved. He saw a man seated at the door of his room, who got to his feet and ran to meet Hammad the moment they were in sight of each other. Hammad was relieved to find that the visitor was Salman, as his old friend took hold of his master's hand to kiss it. Hammad welcomed him home and praised their friendship. They went into Hammad's room without a word, each expecting the other to start talking.

When they were comfortably seated, Hammad asked, "Where have you been, Salman? How did you know that I was here?"

"I have looked for you everywhere and finally learned that you had left for the Holy City," Salman explained, "but I have news! Tha'labah is dead!"

"I have just heard," said Hammad, "but his tragic death comes too late, the king has taken his family and fled."

A tear rolled down Salman's cheek as he asked. "Do you know where they have gone, Sir?"

"No," replied Hammad, "that would have been too easy."

"Do not despair," said Salman, "I will help you to find them."

"I am out of patience, Salman!" said Hammad, "I have become weary of all of these problems that continuously interfere with my love for Hind! I feel weary of this life with all its contradictions and strife! How unfortunate I am!"

"Do not despair, Sir," Salman repeated, "have patience and trust in God."

The next morning, Hammad and Salman got up early and walked up a steep hill that overlooked the suburbs of the city. They passed their day walking through the streets watching the people of the city prepare to defend themselves. They returned to the hilltop outside of the city and saw in the distance a cloud of dust that rose and filled the horizon. When the dust settled they could make out the flags of the Muslim tribes. At the front of the procession, a flag fluttered powerfully with the picture of an eagle embossed on it. The Muslim army had arrived with thirty-five thousand men divided into seven detachments, each with its own general. Several days later, another detachment arrived led by the great commander Abu Ubaidah.

The Conciliation of Jerusalem

The following day, Hammad and Salman changed their clothing and left to meet the governor of Jerusalem, who was visiting the Patriarch. They were granted permission to enter, kissed the hand of the Patriarch, and showed the same courtesy to the governor. The governor asked them to explain their visit.

"I am one of the Princes of Iraq, and I have seen the Muslim army during their invasion of Mecca. I also saw the fall of Busra, and I was there for the siege of Damascus. Now I would like to be of service to you and the Patriarch," said Hammad.

"Why would we concern ourselves with surrender when we haven't even taken up defence yet?" asked the governor.

"We only wish to avoid bloodshed," said Hammad, "and it is impossible to settle with the people of Hejaz without conflict."

"We will not buckle so easily as the men of Damascus did," said the Patriarch resolutely, "for this city is the grave of our savior, Jesus Christ."

"May I suggest that you ask to arrange the conciliation through the successor of the Prophet Muhammad, Caliph Umar ibn al-Khattab, in order for you to maintain your dignity and prestige," suggested Hammad.

"We do not want the Muslims to regard our surrender as a sign of the fear of fighting or our inability to fight," said the governor.

"They will suspect nothing of the sort," said Hammad appealingly. "I will tell them that we wish to bring a peaceful resolution before any fighting breaks out and not because of any fear we hold for them. From you, Sir, I will need to have someone give us safe conduct through the ramparts, we do not want your men to think us deserters."

"That can be arranged," said the governor, "but your attendant will remain here until your return."

"Very well," Hammad replied as he mounted his horse. Hammad was then accompanied by the governor's guards to the gates of the city. He went directly to the camp of Abu Ubaidah, who met him with a welcoming smile.

"What business brings you here, young prince?" Abu Ubaidah asked.

"I am trying to prevent bloodshed with all that is in me," replied Hammad.

"Are the people of the Holy City inclined to open their doors peacefully?" asked Abu Ubaidah.

"I believe they are," said Hammad, "although I understand that as an honor to the Holy City, the governor wishes to discuss the terms of peace only with the successor of the Prophet, the Caliph. Do you think he would agree to a meeting?" asked Hammad.

"I am sure he will," Abu Ubaidah answered, "and what after his acceptance?"

"If you could assure me of his acceptance, I will serve as the means of communication between these two great men."

Thanking him, Abu Ubaidah said, "I will never forget you and what you have done today. I will help you whenever you need me."

"I will always be glad to serve you," said Hammad, asking for his leave to return to the governor and relay the message.

"Stay here awhile," said Abu Ubaidah, "I must first consult with the other Emirs."

A short time elapsed before Abu Ubaidah returned, stating that all the Emirs were opposed to the request of the governor because the arrival of al-Khattab from Mecca would take too long, they wanted to move more quickly toward victory. When Hammad returned with this message, the governor responded rather irately that he would not bow to them. So after many hard-fought arguments and parleys over the following weeks, Abu Ubaidah was forced to write to Caliph Umar ibn al-Khattab in Mecca to come for peace talks in Jerusalem. One day while Hammad was attending Abu Ubaidah, a messenger entered the tent smiling.

"What news have you?" asked Abu Ubaidah.

"There is an apostle at the door sent by Caliph," replied the man.

"Let him in," said Abu Ubaidah.

As the man entered Abu Ubaidah asked him, "What news of our Caliph, Umar ibn al-Khattab?"

The apostle bowed and replied, "I ride ahead of the Caliph, who is preparing for his journey here to the Holy City."

The Caliph

All of the Muslim generals turned out to meet Caliph Umar ibn al-Khattab. They were dressed in ornate silk clothing, and their horses were outfitted with elaborate silver saddles that they had acquired through plunder. Abu Ubaidah, however, was riding a camel and sat upon a horsehair mat that covered the animal's back. Abu Ubaidah also saw it fitting to wear a simple cotton jacket. At his side rode Hammad and Salman.

Hammad looked about curiously to take in the spectacle and spotted a man leading a camel, and upon the camel's saddle sat another man, white of face with highly flushed cheeks. A turban encircled his head and he wore a jacket made of patches of leather and wool wrapped with a wide belt of leather. He carried a pitcher of water and a sack of food. Salman looked at Hammad and said, "That is the Caliph, Emir Umar ibn al-Khattab!"

Then Abu Ubaidah and the Caliph dismounted their camels and embraced each other. Hammad was awestruck by the Caliph's display of humility. Then from the front of the assembly, the Caliph rebuked all those who had worn ostentatious clothing, calling their display the vanity of the unwise. When he had finished, each of the tribes returned silently to their campsites. The Caliph joined Abu Ubaidah and his entourage. A tent made of camel hair had been erected without adornment for the Caliph, and he entered it and sat down on the bare earth. Everyone took notice of this remarkable man and his selfless demeanor. Abu Ubaidah took Hammad to the side and asked him to go and inform the governor of the city that their great Caliph had arrived.

Hammad and Salman swiftly rode to the Patriarch's residence to meet with the governor. The Patriarch expressed his desire to meet with the Caliph in person. Hammad returned to Abu Ubaidah accompanied by the Patriarch, and extended the invitation. The Patriarch was taken aback by the simplicity of the Caliph's garments compared to the ostentatious pageantry of the Roman rulers and their disregard for the expense of things.

After their meeting, the gates of the city were opened and all the citizens of the Holy City gathered to ask the Caliph for peace. The Prophet's successor vowed that none would be harmed. On the following day, an armistice celebration took place with the Christian clergy acting as an integral part of the proceedings, for the treaty had been affirmed on the condition that they pay tribute to the Muslims.

The Valley of Tigris

With the commotion in Jerusalem resolved, Hammad and Salman decided to go to Iraq to look for Abdullah, and then the three could begin the search for Hind together.

They said farewell to Abu Ubaidah and made their way home to prepare for their departure. Their first stop was in Busra to sell all the precious items they had, since there was a possibility that once they had returned to Iraq they would not be coming back to Syria again. They hired a guide whose duty it was as well to see to the care and feeding of the horses. Once they were ready, they began their journey and passed through the sandy wilderness of Syria and its broken, mountainous, and rocky terrain. They passed through Palmyra as they headed east and finally, after fifteen long days of travel, came upon the famed Valley of Tigris.

They were utterly amazed by the magnificent valley with all its farms, bountiful orchards, and fruit trees that were surrounded by clear lakes and irrigated springs. Since it was nearing sunset, the guide set up camp while Hammad took a thorough look at the fertile plain that stretched before him, dotted with farms, small villages, and cities. He saw castles and masses of palm trees, and irrigated farms, and the low light of the sun sparkled brilliantly across the various waterways, somehow reminding him of Abdullah.

Salman, in the meantime, had been helping the guide set camp by arranging the inside of Hammad's tent. When he was finished, he walked over to Hammad and asked him to dismount. Hammad jumped off his horse, and Salman asked the guide to care for it.

"Where is al-Hira from here?" asked Hammad.

"It is the next city we will arrive at," Salman explained, "We will see it once we get closer to the Euphrates."

The following day, they rode non-stop until they had arrived at al-Hira late in the evening.

The Search for Hind

Dawn spread over the land while Hammad and Salman disguised themselves as Muslims and planned their search. Salman went looking for a farm owned by Abdullah, hoping to track his master down, and Hammad made his way to the Der Hind al-Kubra monastery in search of his sweetheart. He stayed at an inn for the night and arrived the following afternoon.

Hammad walked up to the door of the monastery and rang the bell. The door opened moments later and he was admitted entrance because of his attire. The monks welcomed him and waited wordlessly for Hammad to indicate what he might need. The monastery was not unlike Bahira's, so Hammad went to look for the abbot since he was familiar with the layout. He was warmly received and hospitably welcomed, but the abbot saw through his disguise straight away and asked Hammad if he had news of the outcome of the war in Iraq.

"The Muslims have performed astonishing wonders," said Hammad, "and the Persian capital city, al-Mada'in, has fallen to their might."

"I am glad to hear it," said the abbot, "the Muslims believe in God and not in fire, as the oppressive Persians do."

"Have you heard any news of King Jabalah of Ghassan?" asked Hammad.

"No, but we have heard some news about his daughter," the abbot mentioned, surprised by the coincidence.

"What did you hear?" asked Hammad nervously.

"We heard news from some travelers that the princess of Ghassan was seen in al-Hira," the abbot replied, "but the young woman they spoke of appeared to be very unhealthy, so they were not entirely sure that it was her."

After hearing this alarming news, Hammad made up his mind to go back to al-Hira to find out for himself. Excusing himself, Hammad bid the abbot good-bye and left, but it was evening already, and as he rode for the inn total darkness enveloped him. He could not see the path in front of him but was sure that he must be only a mile away from al-Hira. He saw a double-light off in the distance and hoped it was a campsite near the river's shore. As he drew nearer, Hammad realized that it was indeed a campfire, its light reflected on the water and gave it the appearance of two. He slowly approached and heard an Iraqi voice calling out to ask, "Who are you?"

"Just a stranger who has lost his way," answered Hammad.

"Welcome guest," the voice responded. The man to whom the voice belonged appeared with a burning torch in his hand. Hammad saw that he was old, he had gray hair and a gray beard, but had the energy and eyes of youth. He was a shepherd who, in all probability, enjoyed the company of a guest now and then. The old man led Hammad to a cottage built entirely of palm tree branches. A big dog sat at the door and Hammad could hear the bleating of the shepherd's goats in the stillness of the night. As Hammad reached the cottage, he decided against going in, explaining to his host that he would rather sit out in the open air.

"You are welcome to sit wherever you like," said the shepherd.

He entered the cottage for a moment and brought out a goat skin fur for Hammad. He then led Hammad's horse behind the cottage and tied it to a pole and came back laughing with the reins in his hand.

"What is so funny, friend?" Hammad laughed with the man.

"I am laughing about these reins," the shepherd answered. "As I recall, a horseman came by every night last week," he continued, "and the reins of his horse are exactly like yours. I enjoyed his company, as I enjoy yours."

"Who was the horseman?" asked Hammad. "What is it about us that you like?"

"The thing I admire in both of you are your disguises!" the shepherd laughed. "The horseman wore a silk cloak on his back and a scarf wrapped around his head and face. He kept talking like a woman! And you, dressed like a Muslim and talking like an Iraqi."

Hammad remembered Hind had met him at Bahira disguised in a silk cloak of that description, so he wanted to hear more about it. The shepherd left for a few moments and came back with a wooden dish brimming with milk and offered it to Hammad. Then the shepherd sat down next to the dog and patted its head, regarding Hammad intently.

"You mentioned the horseman without coming to the end of your tale," said Hammad.

"That is all there is to it," said the shepherd, "the horseman came by and asked if I would go to Der Hind al-Kubra monastery and find out if any travelers from Syria had come to lodge there, but I did not go. I just told him that I had gone and found no one had stayed there. Eventually, he came no more."

"Do you know which direction the horseman headed when he left?" asked Hammad, handing the shepherd two dinars.

"Along the shore," he pointed, "headed for al-Hira."

"How long ago was this?" asked Hammad.

"A week now," said the old man. "Would you care to stay for the night?"

"No, thank you" said Hammad, "I haven't time for sleep."

Going inside and coming out again with a silk robe in his hands, the old man said, "Take this to keep you warm and to sleep on, you seem used to such finery."

Taking the robe from the shepherd, Hammad's insides trembled – it was Hind's. He asked, "Where did you find this robe, Uncle?"

The old man nodded toward his dog, "He brought it to me. He wandered away a while ago and came back from the shore with it."

The Investigation

It was midnight.

Hammad looked to the stars in the sky and decided to move along the river bed in the hopes of picking up Hind's trail. He had told the old man that he could not sleep and intended to walk in the moonlight along the shore.

Hammad left, ominous images of Hind having fallen prey to some ferocious beast played with his anxieties, perhaps she even drowned herself out of despair! These thoughts made Hammad shiver from head to toe. As he walked down the shore, Hammad realized that he was crying like a baby. He was too tired from his overburdened thoughts to care and almost fainted, so he finally fell asleep right where he stood.

Hammad was shaken awake by a terrible dream, his mind clouded by self-doubt and uncertainty regarding Hind's well-being. He stood up and wrapped himself in her robe to keep the chill of the night air from his bones, and paced back and forth along the shore until dawn. As the sun began to break over the horizon, Hammad could hear church bells begin pealing in the distance. He scoured the shoreline trying to uncover some trace of Hind, but there was nothing to be found.

However, as he turned to go back to the shepherd's farm, Hammad heard a horse approaching. The horse was approaching from the direction of al-Kubra and seemed to be heading to the lake not far down the river from Hammad. As the horse drew closer Hammad's body tensed at the sight of the animal, it was Hind's! The rider, who rode bareback, was a young boy.

"Whose horse is that?" Hammad shouted vehemently as he approached the rider.

"It belongs to a prince," replied the boy.

"And when did this prince buy this horse?" Hammad asked.

"The day before yesterday," the boy answered.

"And from whom did he buy it?" asked Hammad.

"From a monk," said the boy before he led the horse away, glaring suspiciously at Hammad.

Hammad's questions were unproductive, and he feared that Hind had died before her horse was sold. Scanning the shoreline again Hammad, saw a few people heading toward the water's edge. He noticed that they were women accompanied by a man with an axe. They were carrying vessels and baskets and one of the women rode a camel. He studied their manner and their attire and concluded that they were from the monastery for they were all wearing black dresses and had black scarves covering their heads. He watched one woman carrying a pitcher to the shore, but she turned hurriedly and walked back to the group as if someone or something had frightened her. She reminded Hammad of Hind but she was too thin of figure. Still, something kept gnawing at Hammad, urging him to take a closer look at her. His eyes followed her as she walked to the woodcutter and indicated Hammad's presence to the man with a tilt of her head. The woodcutter began to walk toward Hammad, the girl with the pitcher following him. The woodcutter approached Hammad with warm greetings and the girl turned to continue down to the water's edge to fill her pitcher.

The woodcutter said to Hammad, "May I ask you a question?"

"Yes, ask," replied Hammad.

"Where did you buy that robe?" he said, pointing to Hammad's shoulders.

"Is it of any concern to you?" answered Hammad.

Ignoring Hammad's caustic reply, the woodcutter explained, "It was stolen from its owner."

"How do you know it is the same one?" questioned Hammad.

"Because the owner saw it and can identify it by some marks," said the woodcutter.

"Who is the owner?" asked Hammad.

"That damsel that you just saw," he said, nodding in her direction. "As soon as she saw you, she came to tell me."

"Why does she not ask for it herself?" asked Hammad.

"Because she is a nun of the Der Hind al-Kubra monastery and nuns are not allowed to speak to men," the woodcutter explained, "I am the servant who is in charge of such matters."

"How long has the lady been a nun?" Hammad inquired.

"Not too long," the woodcutter replied. "She just began the elementary term, and after a few months she might become a nun. She has donated all she owns, her clothes, her jewelry, and her horse to the monastery. Hammad knew that the maiden must be Hind and if it were not for his turban and Muslim clothing, she would have known him at first sight. He would have recognized her right away as well had it had not been for the black dress that accentuated her frailness.

He thanked God for the blessing that brought this discovery and for the unusual turn of events that had brought him to the river that day. Hammad wanted desperately to run to Hind and reveal himself, but did not want the sudden surprise to stagger her composure or cause problems with the other nuns, so he accepted the sight of her patiently as he had so many years before. He also feared that if she had taken her vows, all his efforts to find her and keep her safe will have been for naught.

He restlessly put his weight on one foot and then on the other and finally asked, "Has she already taken her vows?"

"She will not take her vows until her elementary term has passed," answered the woodcutter.

Hammad was reassured by the man's words and looked over to the maidens. They were all busy with their chores and too far away to hear or see distinctly. Hind had set her pitcher on the ground and sat on a stone waiting for the others to finish and accompany her back to the monastery.

"Go back to the owner of the robe," Hammad said, "and tell her that I will gladly return it to her but only hand to hand."

"I told you, Sir," the woodcutter interjected, "she cannot do that!"

"Then take this," said Hammad, removing his father's lace gown. He handed it to the man and said, "Give this to her instead of her robe."

Taking the gown from Hammad with a shrug, the woodcutter saw that it was more valuable than the robe. He took long strides as he returned to the maiden who still sat alone. Hammad watched as the man handed the gown over to her.

The moment she saw the gown she cried, "Hammad! Hammad!" and without delay jumped up and ran over to him. Hammad only saw his love, his life coming back to him. He found himself running to her, and as they met Hammad tore the turban from his head and hurled it into the wind. Hind fainted as they came together. The woodcutter, who had been watching the two curiously, brought some water to sprinkle on her. As Hind lay in Hammad's arms, she kept repeating his name, and he was so overcome with relief and happiness that all he could utter himself was, "Hind! My sweet love!"

Shyness enveloped her and she covered her head with the veil and sat up primly still looking very pallid.

"Where is your father, Hind?" asked Hammad.

"The Muslims killed him and I think they killed my dear mother too," she stammered, with tears rolling down her face.

"It cannot be! Are you sure that he was killed?" asked Hammad, distressed and sympathetic.

"I was told that he was," Hind replied. "He was arrested with my mother. Soldiers brought the news, so after losing my parents and you, my sweet Hammad, I found refuge in this monastery and applied for nunship. I have given everything I own to the monastery but kept the bracelet that you gave me as a token of our love. I asked a shepherd to bring me news of you which he had none to give, and I was so heavy with grief and almost out of my mind that I lost my robe on my way back."

Hind's Little Monastery

"It is against the conditions of nunship to behave like this," said the woodcutter scornfully.

Hind stood up, gathered herself, and said, "Let us go to the monastery and see the Reverend Mother."

She and Hammad walked together until they arrived at the convent. The servant who accompanied the women to the river hurried to inform the Reverend Mother about the boldness of this young man who had come dressed like a Muslim. Looking out through the open door, the Reverend Mother saw Hind and Hammad and noted that Hammad's head was bare and his facial features were that of an Iraqi so she consented to see them and hear their story. Taking them into a private room the Reverend Mother greeted them. Hammad took her hand and kissed it. Through this magnanimous gesture she knew that he was a Christian, so she asked him to share his plight with her.

"If you will permit me, I will tell you that this woman is my betrothed and has been for more than two years now," said Hammad. "The wars and strife in Syria separated us, but now God has permitted us to find each other again and meet through your grace."

After carefully studying Hammad's manner and speech, the Reverend Mother saw that he was worthy of esteem and deep respect. She asked him, "Are you not Iraqi?"

"Yes, I am from the tribe of Lakhum," he said.

"But Hind is a Syrian from the tribe of Ghassan," the Reverend Mother commented. "How did you meet her?"

"God made it so," he replied.

Hind's eyes became moist with tears as she remembered her parents and the years that had brought her to this point.

"Why are you weeping, my child?" asked the Reverend Mother benevolently.

"She is weeping for the loss of her parents during the war," Hammad replied on her behalf. The Reverend Mother began to console Hind, and Hammad's thoughts turned to Abdullah and Salman. Patience is a virtue, Hammad reminded himself, and he would just have to wait to see what tomorrow would bring.

Addressing the Reverend Mother, he asked, "Do you have any objection if Hind were to give up her nunship?"

"I can see no objection since she has not yet offered her vows," the Reverend Mother answered and then added, "Please go to the guest house of the monastery and stay the night with us."

"I am grateful," he answered, and he left after saying good-bye to Hind. As he passed the stable, he thought he saw Salman's horse and reeled from the coincidence. Hammad hurried to the guest house and was greeted with the smiling face of Salman, who greeted Hammad with a salute.

"Did my master see Hind?" Salman asked happily.

"Yes, I did, she is a postulant in this monastery," answered Hammad.

"Has she vowed her chastity?" asked Salman with alarm.

"No, Salman," said Hammad, laughing. "Have you had any luck finding my father?"

"Yes, I have!" said Salman, "I have located King Jabalah and Queen Saada as well!"

"What?! Where are they?" asked Hammad, excitedly. "The last Hind had heard, they had been executed by the Muslims!"

"They have been in hiding at your father's farm and they will come in disguise to meet us all here. They may arrive here tonight, but definitely tomorrow," Salman explained. "Were it not for Emir Abdullah, your father-in-law would have been dead a long time ago. My master implored those who had taken the king prisoner to spare his life and they did! So they released the king and queen into my master's care. He then hid them at his farm until Hind could be found. That is why I am here, Master! I was also looking for Hind."

The noble reader may only comprehend the force of Hammad's exuberance, boundlessly happy by the force of such fortuitous news. He thanked God for His divine mercy and vowed to go to Hind to tell her that her parents were alive.

Hammad turned to go back to the monastery, and he found Hind on the balcony overlooking the guest house, her mind would not rest easy unless he was constantly in her sight. When she saw him returning, she registered a look of surprise and teasingly said, "What is on your mind, Hammad?" She looked at him demurely and gave him an incredibly bewitching smile.

"My love," he answered, "I am about to give you good news but you must promise me to try to contain yourself!"

She looked at him with a mischievous grin not truly prepared for what he was about to say and nodded.

"Your mother and father are alive! They have been safely hidden at my father's farm not far from here," he said. "And they are coming here tomorrow!"

Without a care for the decorum of the monastery, Hind nearly flew down the stairs to him – she would have jumped for the wings she felt she had. Her face was radiant and he held out his hands for her to grasp. He pressed them gently and she responded by squeezing his.

"Hammad, are you sure that my mother and father are coming?" she cried in disbelief.

"Ask Salman, here," said Hammad, as the servant walked up to them, "he brought the good tidings."

Hind focused her eyes on Salman and looked at him in disbelief.

"Yes, Mistress, it is true," Salman confirmed with a laugh, "they will be coming in disguise with my master Abdullah. I must caution you not to tell a soul!"

"I do so promise," said Hind who turned and walked sedately to the monastery entrance.

A Happy Wedding

Hammad stared after Hind and then returned to the guest house. He decided that it would be a better show of good behavior if he went to meet Hind's parents and his own father first. He asked Salman to accompany him, and they decided to ride until they reached the traveler's oasis, a resting place through which King Jabalah and Abdullah would pass on their way to the monastery. They dismounted and sat down to relax, but they saw a figure dressed in black swiftly riding toward them. It was Hind!

"Hind!" Hammad exclaimed with a smile, "What are you doing here?"

"Why Hammad," she asked, "do you not know by now that I cannot tolerate being away from you, even for a moment?"

They sat down next to Salman to rest for a while, and all of a sudden they saw a cloud of dust filling the air from the direction of the Valley of Tigris. A group of riders emerged from the cloud who swiftly approached the oasis. Recognizing their parents, Hind and Hammad were charged with excitement, and they mounted their horses and rode as fast as the wind to receive their families. King Jabalah hugged and kissed Hammad, and Queen Saada embraced her daughter tightly. Hind kissed her mother with tears rolling down her cheeks. Queen Saada then embraced Hammad, and King Jabalah kissed his daughter. Meanwhile Abdullah stood with pride bursting in his chest, and watched the joyously tearful reunion. Abdullah then clasped Hammad to his chest and kissed him, his eyes brimming with tears and his voice choking in his throat. He was so happy to see Hammad that he found it difficult to speak and even harder to release the embrace. They were so completely lost in the emotion of the moment that the others had to separate them.

King Jabalah then addressed Hammad, "I ask, my son, that you pardon me, forgive me, for I am greatly ashamed for having caused you so much misery as a result of my indecision."

Hammad told the king as humbly as he could that this declaration was not necessary.

Abdullah worried about their surroundings and cautioned everyone, "We must not stay any longer in this hostile country for I fear the Persians may still cause us more trouble. They are still our bitter enemy. We can have the marriage ceremony performed at the monastery and then proceed back to Constantinople where we will be protected under the flag of Emperor Heraclius."

Hammad and Hind were married the very next day, brought together as husband and wife with glory and honor before God. After all their trials, after all their troubles, the happiness that Hind and Hammad had found shone upon their faces with boundless light. On the following morning, the happy couple and their family all departed for Constantinople, which is today known as Istanbul in Turkey.

THE END

About the Author

Jurji Zaidan is a Lebanese author who lived from 1861 to 1914. He is most famous for the journal *al-Hilal*, which he used to promote education and culture, particularly the preservation of Islamic history. His journal is also the means by which he serialized his 23 historical novels.

Zaidan's numerous historical fictions, including *Fatat Ghassan*, each take a particular historically significant event or subject and weave its historical details with a sweeping plot of mystery or romance. The stories themselves are purely fictional and serve as frameworks for the preservation and retelling of real world history. Many of the names of the characters in this story are based upon real people, but the timelines are often manipulated to facilitate a cohesive story.

We sincerely hope that this new translation will reach out to a larger and younger audience to share with them the popular Arabic fiction that is often so scarce in North America. While many of Zaidan's works have been translated across the globe, only five have been officially commissioned in English. *The Girl of Ghassan* will be the sixth.

We encourage you to explore both the real history of these people and the other works written by Zaidan because it was his hope, as it is ours at One Cent Press as well, that by sharing this history we can bridge the gaps between cultures, and find our shared heritage as human beings, regardless of race or religion.

You can learn more about Jurji Zaidan at the Zaidan Foundation:

http://www.zaidanfoundation.org

About the Translator

Basil Solounias is a Reverend Father of the Orthodox Church in Edmonton, Alberta, Canada, where he has run his ministry since becoming ordained in 1981. In addition to running his ministry, Basil works as a freelance interpreter for the Government of Alberta. He has spent his life promoting education, culture, and spirituality in both the Muslim and Christian communities alike.

Basil began work on translating *The Girl of Ghassan* shortly before completing his theological education and continued to work away at it over the years, serializing chapters of the manuscript for the Arab community of Edmonton through the *Canadian Edmonton Arab News* in much the same way that Zaidan serialized the original manuscript.

Basil was born in Ras Baalbeck in Lebanon, and educated at St. Vladimir's Seminary and the Adelphi University in New York, and at the University of Alberta in Edmonton. Father Basil has been a proud Canadian citizen for over thirty years.